The tenor of th[...] [...]
stroking. She was raw and eager with anticipation. His touch made her feel new, like she'd never been aroused before. It reduced her from a woman to a sixteen-year-old virgin, experiencing her first hot kiss that heated new and unmentionable places. His caress journeyed longer, swiveling around the inside of her thighs as it came back down. Veronica braced herself, expecting his fingers to brush over her shorts into uncharted territory with the next pass.

Edmond

Dear Reader,

Wow! It's been a long time coming, but *House Guest* is finally here. A lot of hard work and joy went into producing this book, and I hope you enjoy reading it as much as I loved writing it. In this story, Samantha Martinson is introduced as the main character's best friend. Samantha will have the opportunity to shine in her own novel, which will be published in the near future.

If you would like to get in touch with me, you can send me an e-mail at edwina@arnoldnetwork.com, or visit my Web site at www.edwinamartin-arnold.com.

Take care and God bless.

Edwina Martin-Arnold

EDWINA MARTIN-ARNOLD

House Guest

ARABESQUE®

HOUSE GUEST

An Arabesque novel

ISBN 1-58314-541-9

© 2006 by Edwina Martin-Arnold

www.kimanipress.com

Printed in U.S.A.

This book is dedicated to my sister, Paula Dennis, who passed on August 1, 2005, because when she read the manuscript, she told me this novel was destined to be her favorite.

ACKNOWLEDGMENTS

I would like to thank the following people:

John Arnold, Jeanette Arnold, Guillory Arnold,
Constance Arnold, Charlotte Foster,
Eddie Hill and Linda Gill.

Chapter 1

Dr. Veronica Howell approached The Total Health Women's Clinic she owned and operated with a growing sense of dread. She lifted her shoulder-length, black hair and rubbed the goose bumps she felt forming on her neck. "Not again," she whispered, mentally preparing herself to see the ugliness someone had taken the time to scribble across the exterior of her single-story building. The red paint seemed to lash out as she grabbed the handrail and walked up the three steps, getting close enough to read the words, *Witch doctor!* which were plastered across her door. Shifting her eyes to the window, she read, *Fertility Pervert!* It hit like a loudly yelled accusation, bringing bad memories to the forefront.

Pervert!

It was the same word her brother's attackers yelled as they beat him unmercifully. Intense anger replaced trepidation, and her wavy hair bounced as she hurriedly pushed through the heavy glass door almost knocking down her short, dumpy head nurse, Alice Tate.

"Whoa there, Dr. Roni." Alice said while her short arms wrapped around Veronica's waist as she balanced herself. The white uniform she wore was stretched to the limit by her efforts. Although Veronica was tall and thin, she was strong. She dug in the heels of her brown, suede pumps and neither woman fell. Alice stepped back and Veronica put down her briefcase, breathing heavily while straightening the bottom of the classic brown pantsuit she wore.

"I know, I know, Dr. Roni. That filth outside makes my blood boil, too." Alice placated her. "Why anyone would get upset because we help people get pregnant is beyond me. Besides, you'd think these kooks would notice the name of our clinic. Total Health. We help women with a variety of health issues, not just reproduction.

Veronica's arms folded in front of her chest before she said, "I agree, Alice, the graffiti doesn't make any sense, but this is the fifth time in three months." Veronica paused when the front door opened and Junior Ulu, the security guard, walked in. After greeting him, she turned back to the nurse, "We rarely have a chance to even help people with infertility issues. So why are we being harassed?"

Alice's head shook and Junior offered his opinion. "It's probably just some nut who lives near here and is too lazy to walk to the bigger hospitals and bug them. Some people are strange. Hey, remember that guy who sat crying in the lobby once you told him you couldn't help his wife get pregnant?"

"Yeah, I remember," Alice said. "The wife had left, and we almost had to call the police to get him to leave."

Veronica frowned and added, "Sure, people can be odd,

but that doesn't explain this. What about the crank phone calls, Junior? Those seem to be directly aimed at this clinic."

The big man shrugged, then asked, "Would you like me to call the police?"

"I already have," Alice stated.

"Good," Junior nodded, "I'll walk the building and make sure everything's all right then." He went out the door he'd just come in.

Veronica glanced at her watch. It was seven o' clock in the morning. From prior experience, she knew half the day would be gone before she saw an officer. Apparently, graffiti wasn't high on their priority list.

Picking up her briefcase, Veronica made her way through the small waiting room to her office. On the way, she said hello to Laura Williams, the receptionist, who was straightening the magazines on one of the two racks. Veronica stopped near the front desk to feed the goldfish swimming in a medium-size tank. In her office, she exchanged her fitted jacket for a white lab coat. She was just sitting at her desk when Alice poked her head in. She could hear loud coughing outside.

"Oh, I forgot," Alice explained, "when I checked the messages this morning, we had one from Mrs. Brown. She sounded so bad I called and told her to go to emergency. She refused and said her son was bringing her here."

"She's a stubborn woman," Veronica said as she got up and grabbed her stethoscope. "I suppose that's why she continues to smoke despite the fact that she's a severe asthmatic."

"Yes, she's pugnacious," Alice agreed. "Jeanie is putting her in room Two and she's taking her vitals." Alice handed her the file.

Within five minutes, Veronica had quickly reviewed the

stats on Mrs. Brown and had left her office. She found Alice in the supply room getting a breathing treatment ready, and she told her she would need a shot of prednisone, as well. Taking a deep breath, Veronica headed for the examination room, preparing for the overwhelming smell of cigarette smoke she knew would assault her the minute she opened the door.

An hour later, Veronica was back in her office extremely frustrated. That's how every visit with Mrs. Brown left her feeling. Veronica knew the poor woman's son, Charles, was equally annoyed, but he'd shrugged and told Veronica, "My mom is sixty-five years old and she's been smoking since she was twelve." With a sad chuckle he'd gone on to say, "My mother will be in heaven with a cigarette hanging from her mouth while she converses with St. Peter." Knowing the son was probably right hadn't stopped Veronica from trying to break through however. As she'd helped Mrs. Brown hold the tube, which carried the medicine to her mouth, she'd explained, "We could do this less often if you smoked fewer cigarettes, Mrs. Brown."

The crafty old lady's eyes had sparkled from her bronze face. She'd pulled the tube from her mouth and had said, "But doctor, I submit to these treatments so I can smoke more." All Veronica could do was shake her head while Mrs. Brown laughed, then coughed heavily. Fifty minutes later, Mrs. Brown's breathing was significantly better, and Veronica had been able to avoid insisting that she be admitted to the hospital. Instead, she released her with prescriptions after Charles promised to take her straight to emergency if her breathing worsened again.

Seven patients had come and gone when Veronica allowed herself to acknowledge she was tired. She stood in her empty office, and lifted her hands over her head, stretching until the lab coat bunched awkwardly. Next, she touched her fingers to her toes, stood and twisted from side to side working the sore muscles in her back. It had been a long day, but she was looking forward to the evening because she was meeting her good friend, Samantha Martinson, for dinner. She was just putting on her suit jacket when Alice came in and said, "Police are here." Dang, she'd forgotten all about the graffiti. Although, the encounter with the officer was brief, she was already twenty minutes late for dinner by the time she left the clinic.

Veronica practically ran the three blocks between The Total Health Clinic and Vito's Italian Restaurant. She was walking because her car was at the mechanic's until noon tomorrow. She'd gotten up an hour early that morning just to make the bus. When she entered Vito's, the host greeted her immediately. Standing behind a small counter, the older black man said, "You must be Veronica."

"Yes." She smiled. "I've never been to this restaurant. Do I know you?"

"No," the man answered. "Your friend told me she was waiting for a beautiful woman with dark, flawless skin, and shoulder-length hair flipped up at the ends just like yours. She described you perfectly."

If he wasn't old enough to be her grandfather, Veronica thought he might have been trying to pick her up. She took his arm when he came around the counter and offered it and let him escort her through the small, intimate restaurant full of old-world charm with large wooden furniture and red tablecloths tucked beneath paintings of rolling landscapes. "My, what a lovely pair you two make." The man flirted shamelessly when they reached the table where Samantha was sitting. "If your hair was longer, miss—" he pointed to Veronica "—you two could be twins."

Veronica laughed at that because she was thin where Samantha was voluptuous. Nevertheless, she said to the man, "Sir, my hair used to be down my back. I cut it off, put it in a bag and shoved it in a drawer. My hair will never be past my shoulders again, it's too much work."

"Well, all right then, miss," the man responded. "I bet you'd be beautiful even if you were bald-headed."

"Go on, you flirt," Veronica said before she bent to hug her friend. With a bow, the old man left.

"I see you've met Willie, the charmer," Samantha teased, her brown eyes sparkling. Veronica nodded, then sat down. "Hey, girl, I was just about to call you. I thought I was being stood up," Samantha said.

Veronica explained why she was late. Then she complained, "Samantha, the officer wasn't even interested in hearing everything. I tell you, the same man has been calling me now for about a month, yelling or whispering derogatory things about female doctors, and I couldn't even get the officer to listen. What kind of police work is that?" The question wasn't rhetorical. Veronica expected an answer from her best friend, because Samantha was one of the top defense attorneys in Washington State.

"Calm down, Roni. You have a legitimate point, but you know it's a question of resources. Sure, there have been some anonymous threats and scribbling, but no real violence." Samantha shrugged. "You're a victim of prioritizing."

"I know, I know. It's just so irritating. Although the San Diego police never solved my brother's murder, they were extremely thorough, and I keep comparing the Seattle police to them." Veronica laughed sarcastically and said, "But I suppose my comment proves your point, murder is much more important than graffiti."

"Yes," Samantha nodded sadly.

"Ugggghhhh, here I go, making myself depressed. I'm sorry, Sam. It's just been a tough week. Do you remember Yvonne, the young woman I told you about whose cancer was in remission?" she asked.

Samantha nodded, "Yes, don't tell me she's sick?"

"No." Veronica's head shook as she said, "her parents called me a few days ago and told me she was hit by a truck."

"Oh no! That's a shame," Samantha said.

Veronica nodded. "Yes, it is, and her poor parents didn't think to tell me until after the funeral so I've missed that, as well." Veronica sighed heavily.

"Life's weird," Samantha commented.

Veronica agreed. There was silence between the two women before Veronica said, "You know despite the karma I seem to be in right now, overall, I'm pretty happy with how my life is going. Sam, I'm living my dream. Look at me—" she pointed to herself "—I'm a doctor! I'm giving back to the community in the way I envisioned I would. What could be better than that?"

Samantha smiled and said, "You're right, girl. You've hit a few bumps in the road, but you're living the American dream, minus the man and kids. Anything new on that front?"

Veronica lifted the lemon off the side of her glass and squeezed the juice into her water before answering, "Heck, Samantha, you know nothing else is going on with me besides the clinic."

"No hot dates?" her friend asked.

Veronica laughed at that. "Not even a cold one, and don't you dare try to set me up with someone. I swear the last guy played with his nose too much."

"No, he didn't, Roni," Samantha protested. "I told you the man had allergies and rubbing his nose was just a habit." Samantha rubbed hers for emphasis, then said, "You should understand, being a doctor."

"I do understand allergies. I don't understand a finger near a nostril every five minutes. If the guy was so great, why were you pushing him off on me?" Veronica reasoned.

With a pout on her face, Samantha said, "Because I'm still recovering from my divorce."

"Dang, Sam, that's ancient history. You can't keep using it as an excuse."

"Yes, I can. You didn't suffer through my marriage," she retorted.

Veronica didn't have an answer for that, so it was a good thing the food arrived silencing both women until the server left. "How's work?" Veronica asked.

"Busy. Although, I did something that made me feel real good today. I helped my client get rid of his past."

"What? A not-guilty verdict?" Veronica questioned.

Samantha answered, "No, I got his criminal record expunged, all five of his felony convictions have been erased. See, my client was a bad boy when he was young, but the past ten years he's been a model citizen. He's a barber with a wife and kid."

"That's great, Sam. Hey, that means he can vote, right?" Veronica asked.

"Yes! He's never been to the polls before. The man had tears in his eyes when the judge granted our request. Made me feel like I'd just won one for the good guys, and as you know, in my line of work, I don't get that feeling often."

Veronica nodded and said, "Savor it while you can."

"I plan to," Samantha agreed, then said, "Hey, that lasagna

smells delicious. Mind if I try a piece?" Veronica was already putting some on a saucer. The topics flowed and Veronica was surprised when she looked at her watch and discovered two hours had passed. Samantha yawned into her hand. "You don't even have to tell me, Roni. I know it's getting late. Why don't you get the waitress's attention while I finish up your tiramisu."

Veronica was full to the bursting, so she gladly pushed the dessert plate to her friend and waved to their server. "Oh yeah, I need a ride home. My car's in the shop until tomorrow. Do you mind?" Veronica asked.

"No problem at all," Samantha said as she lifted the full fork to her mouth.

Thirty minutes later, Samantha stopped her convertible Mercedes in front of Veronica's small, brick house which sat on the shores of Lake Washington. "It's late, Sam," Veronica told her friend. "You don't have to wait until I'm inside."

Samantha answered, "Yes, I do. Girl, you forgot to turn on your porch light. I know this is a safe neighborhood, but the creeps come out at night."

Veronica chuckled. "You're paranoid. Do you know that?"

"Yes." Samantha leaned over and hugged her. "Turn on the light and wave when you're inside."

"Okay, Mom," Veronica said as she leaned back and lifted a hand to her forehead in mock salute. Then, she was out of the car and quickly moving across the small lawn to the steps that led to her front door. She opened the lock and slipped in, feeling for the porch light switch.

Something smelled funny.

She turned and glanced around her small living room. It was dark and all she could see were shapes, but nothing seemed out of the ordinary. Her fingers grazed the light panel, and she turned on the outside light as well as the room lights. Sniffing, she continued looking around. "It smells like paint?" she whispered to the empty room. It was odd, because she hadn't done any decorating. The coffee table as well as the two couches and chairs were spotless. As Veronica moved toward the kitchen, the smell became stronger. She passed through the swinging door with her nose and mind twitching. Whatever she'd left out had only been there since morning. What in the world smelled like paint as it rotted? She flipped the lights and her eyes grew wide as she stared in disbelief and growing horror. Thick, red liquid was smeared on the kitchen table. The substance dripped to the floor, creating little pools on the linoleum. If the paint smell wasn't so strong, she'd think it was blood.

Right hand over her mouth and nose, she turned to run, frantic with the knowledge someone had been in her home. "Oh God," she whispered, realizing the person might still be there. She didn't get far, though, because on the kitchen door, scribbled and dripping red, were the words *Satan's Helper! Family Killer! Fertility Fake!* Holding hard against panic, she hurried the way she'd come, trying to get out the front door. Dread won when she collided with someone, and they both began falling. She fought, grasping and scratching, until her head hit the floor hard, making her world go black.

Veronica's eyes flew open, her nose and throat on fire. Arms wrapped around her. "Shush, Roni, shush, it's okay." She recognized Samantha's voice and clung to the body holding her while struggling through an intense coughing fit. Leaning away, Veronica realized she was sitting on her living room floor, and she was clutching a white man, not her best friend. Her arms dropped. She looked beyond the man's shoulder to see Samantha standing close, looking very concerned.

"It's okay, ma'am," the man said. "I'm a paramedic, and I know smelling salts can be pretty rough. We needed to use them, though, because you've been unconscious for a while."

A vicious chill shook Veronica as memory came flooding back: blood red, her kitchen table. The medic placed a blanket around her and proceeded to asked questions while bandaging her forehead. Veronica answered to the best of her ability, but she was very distracted by the two male officers who were now standing beside Samantha. "Okay, ma'am. I'm going to let the police speak to you now, but you've had quite a bump on the head, and I'm taking you to emergency afterward."

Veronica's head shook as she said, "I'm a doctor. I'll be fine. I'm sure it's a mild concussion."

"Dr. Howell, may we ask you a few questions?" the short, stocky officer asked. Before Veronica could answer, Samantha was at her side, helping her to the couch where she sat beside her as the officers began peppering her with questions. Veronica told them what she knew, explaining that she had run into someone near the kitchen. Her hand touched the large bandage above her right eye.

"Sorry, Roni, that was just me," Samantha said. "You didn't wave or shut the front door, so I came in to check on you after getting my bat from the trunk, of course. We collided in the living room and you fell, hitting your head."

"Oh," was Veronica's only response. She was feeling dazed and slightly disoriented. Maybe she did need to go to the hospital. She listened while Samantha told the police about the problems at the clinic, and then she answered more questions. She was surprised when one officer told her that the back door to the garage was open. Veronica never used the door, so she couldn't imagine why it would be unlocked. She felt as if her mind was playing tricks on her.

Veronica supposed that's why she didn't complain too much when she was transported in the ambulance and treated at the hospital. Very mild concussion was the diagnosis and, although the treating physician wanted to keep her overnight for observation, she was able to get him to release her by promising she would spend the night at Samantha's. Truth was she was scared to go home by herself. She listened as the doctor lectured, advising her to take the next few days off. Veronica nodded even though she knew she would go to the clinic unless she was unable to get out of bed. Sitting around worrying about who had the nerve to invade her home didn't appeal in the least. She was thinking pretty clearly now; and the headache and slight nausea would probably be completely gone by morning.

As Veronica got into Samantha's car, she noticed her black pantsuit hanging in the backseat. Samantha said, "I figured you'd be staying with me, so I grabbed a few things."

Veronica smiled and thanked her friend, then asked, "Sam, why don't the police have more answers?"

"They're not magicians, Roni. It takes time to figure things out. But realistically, this has sped past what local law enforcement has the resources to do for you. You need private help," her friend said with a firm nod of her head.

"What do you mean?" Veronica asked.

"Roni, you need to hire a security firm for your house and the clinic."

"No," Veronica answered. "What I need is for the police to do what I pay taxes for. I need them to protect me and solve this."

"Wake up, Veronica," Samantha said loudly. "It was me you ran into in the hallway. You were hysterical, with good reason mind you, but it's time to stop trying to be super-woman and admit you need help. At a minimum, you need a bodyguard."

"No, I don't want to constantly be around a muscle head. It'd remind me too much of what happened to my brother, Mitchell."

"Veronica, what is Junior?" Samantha asked. "Have you forgotten your security guard at the clinic? He's one of the biggest men I've seen."

Veronica replied, "He's different, a gentle giant, and a rare exception to the rule. Besides, he's only at Total Health during working hours. He's not in my face all the time like a bodyguard would be."

"Girl, Junior is nice because you know him. Most people are cool when you get beyond the stereotypes," Samantha said.

Veronica sighed and rested the back of her head against the seat. Her left hand lifted to rub her temple. "Sam, I'm drained. Do we have to figure this out tonight?"

Samantha parked in front of her downtown condominium and asked, "If I drove you home right now, would you feel safe?"

A tear slid down Veronica's cheek. "Oh, honey," Samantha said before leaning across the console and hugging Veronica tightly. "I'm sorry, you know how I am when I get on a roll."

Veronica nodded into her shoulder.

"Okay, we don't have to answer all the questions right now, but I am going to call my friend, John Graham. Is that all right with you?" she asked.

Again, Veronica nodded.

* * *

The next morning, a very tired Veronica was pouring herself a cup of coffee in Samantha's kitchen when her friend came through the doorway and handed her a file folder. "Here you go, girl," she said. The cheery attitude surprised her because the two women had just finished battling about whether Veronica should go to work.

Veronica put the cup down and opened the folder. "Malik Cutler," she read from the top of the first sheet. "What is this?"

"Résumés and contact information for several security experts, however, John says the Cutler guy is the one we want. He's an ex-navy SEAL, and his client list is a veritable who's who in Seattle. We're lucky he's available, and that's why I put his information first. Read it because you have an appointment at four-fifteen with him today."

"Sam, I haven't checked my schedule! What if I have a patient? You had no right!" Veronica protested.

"I know you'll make it happen because this is important. You won the work argument, but I'm going to prevail on this one. It's time to face the fact that you're on someone's bad list."

"Uuuuuggghhh! Samantha, if I didn't need you to drive me to the mechanic so I can get my car, I swear I'd…I'd do something to you," Veronica threatened.

Her friend just laughed.

At four o' clock that same day, Malik Cutler approached The Total Health Women's Clinic with his square jaw lifted in the cautious awareness that his profession demanded. It was a hot August day, and he felt dampness as he ran a hand through his slightly wavy hair and down the front of his nut-brown face. He noted it was a single-story building, which

pleased him because the isolation of elevators was dangerous: a Russian roulette every time the doors opened. Also,
only one floor meant he wouldn't have to deal with securing
a stairwell if he accepted the job. Of course, the position
hadn't been offered yet. No matter. He was completely confident it would be, because he was very good at keeping
people safe. His entire adult life had been spent in service to
others; first, in the navy, and now as an executive protector.

The reality was he didn't want this specific assignment
because the clinic's reproductive services were distasteful to
him. It made him remember Thaddeus McCullough too
much. The neglected kid he'd protected who had been the
product of fertility treatments. When the boy died unexpect-
edly, the stoic parents' solution was to quickly schedule an
appointment with a doctor so they could manufacture another
heir. Geez, the world could be a cold, crazy place, and old
favors to even older friends could be exasperating, but one
thing his father had drilled into him was honoring commit-
ments.

Avoiding the front entrance, Malik moved his six-foot
frame with grace as he walked around to test the side doors,
staying in tune to who and what was around him. As he
surveyed the exterior, he adjusted the green canvas bag that
was strung across his body so it hung at his side. He noticed
there were no guards, no cameras, just ugly words spray-
painted on the walls. He stared at the graffiti, before shifting
the bag so he could pull out an eight by eleven photograph
that Graham had given him. It was a picture of the words
painted on Dr. Howell's kitchen door. He couldn't tell if the
writing matched. He put the photo away and continued
moving around the building. The sun beat down on him while
his hand rattled a knob and his shoulder pushed against steel.

It was locked. He quickly moved away from the hot metal penetrating his clothes. It was way too warm for a jacket, but he figured the tie against the crisp, white shirt made him look professional enough.

When he checked the other two doors, he met the same result. At the last one, he reached into his pants and withdrew something that looked like a business card holder. From it, he slid out two thin metal prongs, which he slipped into the keyhole. Ten seconds later, he opened the door. *Too easy.* It should have taken him twice as long to gain entry. *What good is steel when the lock is junk?* he thought. Malik cracked the door, peering inside, seeing no people or mechanical devices to spot intruders. His dismay continued even though his physical discomfort was eased by the cool breeze from the air-conditioning.

Slipping in, Malik gently closed the door behind him. Moving on soft-soled black shoes, he crept toward an intersecting corridor. He encountered no one, yet he could hear voices in the distance, and he detected the odor of coffee right before he heard a slurping noise. Glancing around the corner, he saw a heavyset guard to his right. The uniform made him easily recognizable. The big man's profile faced Malik as he leaned against a wall with one hand in his pocket and the other holding a steaming foam cup.

Useless, Malik thought. *His hands would be worthless if I was a bad guy and attacked him.* Malik walked toward the unsuspecting man. An older woman strolled by, and she began exchanging pleasantries with the guard until she saw Malik. At her startled gasp, the equally surprised guard looked to his side before coming to awkward attention. He was even larger than Malik expected, at least six feet six, and very broad. *Samoan*, Malik guessed, judging from the dark tan skin, wavy black hair and slightly almond eyes. The guard's large hand left his pocket, but the other still clutched the cup.

Malik immediately slackened his facial features, trying to make himself nonthreatening. He slightly hunched his frame, hoping he looked smaller.

"Hi, I'm Malik Cutler. I have an appointment with Dr. Howell," he said. For some reason, people interpreted his Southern accent as friendly. At eighteen, he'd left Texas to travel the world with the navy. The accent was faint now, but he intentionally thickened it, trying to put the big guard at ease.

"Oh yeah?" The guard said, handing the cup to the lady. He puffed up his already enormous chest. "Why are you coming from the back? Front's that way."

"I got lost," Malik replied, smiling wide. "Can you show me where?"

His manner seemed to give the guard confidence. Without questioning Malik's story, he said, "Follow me. I'll show you the way. It's all right, Alice. Dr. Roni said to expect this guy. I'll take care of it." The guard turned his back on Malik. The woman continued to eye him suspiciously.

As a former navy SEAL, Malik knew numerous ways to dispose of foes. He could have dealt with the guard in less time than it took to pick the lock. Instead, he stayed close as the man led him to the front desk, noting that the guard was acting solo. Incompetence was the thin line between this clinic and danger. Any maniac could do severe damage in a blink of an eye.

Malik talked to the receptionist while taking in the homey feel of the small lobby. It might have been a parlor except for the front desk and computer. It contained a sofa that matched the half-dozen chairs and coffee table. The guard stood to the side with spread legs and hands clasped behind his back, once again rendering them worthless. No one asked for identification, or checked him or his bag for weapons before the receptionist left him alone in an empty office.

The room was sizable, tastefully furnished, and light jazz played from hidden speakers. Still, Malik frowned. Directly across from him, behind the desk was a large window. The open blinds gave anyone in the parking lot, the surrounding businesses or the apartments a lovely view inside. It would be child's play for a sniper to quickly dispose of someone sitting in the chair. Malik stood to the side and looked at the numerous plaques adorning the walls. He expected the diplomas touting the doctor's educational accomplishments. However, the expressions of gratitude from civic leaders, community groups and her patients surprised him. Apparently, quite a few people thought highly of Dr. Howell.

The door swung open and in walked the older woman who had glared at him before. She was still frowning.

Good, Malik thought, *at least someone around here is wary.*

"Who are you, and what business do you have in this office?" she asked.

Malik looked into the hard, blue eyes of the rather dumpy woman and delivered his most engaging smile before saying, "I have a meeting with Dr. Howell."

The short, overweight woman put a hand to her hip and stood up straight as if her five feet two inches would intimidate him and said, "Are you here about that filth painted on the building outside?" When he didn't answer, her tone switched to slightly gossipy. "Can you believe it? Those nuts are complaining because we help people have babies. You can't win for losing. So, you don't have to be silent around me. I'm Alice Tate, the head nurse here."

Malik's smile broadened because he knew there were only three nurses in the specialty clinic. They stared at each other and Malik appraised her. She looked as if she should be somewhere baking cookies for a bunch of screaming kids, instead of confronting him. As the seconds ticked away with no answer from Malik, Alice nodded, shifting the brown hair that hadn't seen a stylist in ages and said, "I must be right because if you were a pharmaceutical salesman, you would've talked my ear off by now and offered me a thousand samples. You can be tight-lipped if you want to, but I, for one, am glad you're here. Don't let Dr. Roni scare you off. If I know her, she'll think she doesn't need you."

Alice hadn't been gone long when the door swung open a second time, and in walked the doctor, judging from the white lab coat and chart she was reading. A bandage graced her forehead, and she hummed the lively tune playing from the speakers until she turned to see him standing in the corner. Reaching up, she removed her black, wire-framed glasses and flashed a polite smile that dazzled despite its lack of warmth.

Seeing beautiful women was nothing new to Malik, so the thumping of his heart was completely unexpected. Although her face would have been comfortable on any magazine cover, beautiful wasn't quite the label for her because the allure wasn't classical. A much better description was jolting. She was tall, thin and angular, wearing no makeup to mar the skin that was as dark as ripe, black raspberries. But it was her eyes that had Malik's heart beating erratically. The intense ebony orbs that were beginning to look at him inquisitively.

He knew those eyes. It had been a number of years since

he'd seen them, but he was dead certain because only her gaze had the power to reach in and make something inside him tilt. Especially when she combined it with the full force of her smile, which was like pure sunshine, spreading out brightening all in its path. He never thought he'd see her again, and here she was, a doctor of all things. The last time he'd had the pleasure, he'd been a SEAL, and she'd been moving gracefully in very high heels and an evening dress, while belting out a soulful jazz tune.

He saw no recognition in her face. Clearly, she didn't know him from Adam. But why should she? Making eye contact was just a trick of the trade, he supposed, that was memorable to the lucky audience member, but meaningless to the entertainer. Lights and flashy personalities were what he bet performers remembered, and he wasn't so insecure that he had to constantly try and make himself stand out. He was sure that he was one in an endless throng of people that had held her eyes for a moment in time. *Roni!* He remembered that was the name of the show, *An Evening with Roni.*

"You are the security guard?" Long, thin fingers toyed with the stethoscope that hung from her neck. Veronica had read the information carefully that Samantha had given her, and she knew the question had to insult one with his expertise, but she recognized the lustful look on his face. Although he swiftly covered it with a blank expression, Veronica wasn't fooled. His eyes had pranced up and down her form, then he'd gawked as if he were seeing his first woman. The look was nothing new, yet on him, it disturbed her. Maybe because if her defenses were down, she'd be looking at him the same way. He was trim, but not slight. There was more than a suggestion of muscle beneath the loose tie, Dockers and white shirt. Her gaze took it all in. Skin the color of polished bronze; strong, square jaw; full lips and high cheekbones made for a very rectangular face. His hair was interesting. It was caught somewhere between straight and curly, and it was just long enough to try and do both. The resulting look was springy and kind of unruly.

Despite all this, she refused to let herself be attracted because she'd already placed him in a category: testosterone-filled meathead with antiquated ideals and values. Okay, so perhaps she needed one of those *types* to protect her, especially after her fright night, but she didn't have to like it or him.

To her surprise, he laughed instead of being angered by her question. "I suppose that's one way of putting it," he said and Veronica noticed that his voice was arrestingly deep. "I prefer to think of myself as an executive protector, ma'am."

Ma'am? The term was so polite, and his speech patterns hinted at a Southern accent. She stepped closer and shook his hand; a social necessity that she quickly regretted. The large palm and rough fingers engulfed hers, and she felt his energy, even though the contact only lasted seconds. Her eyes centered on his chest. Dark skin shimmered through the white shirt, making her quickly look away, but not before she sensed the same power that had vibrated from his hand. The man was like caged heat, or fire under a blanket.

Stepping back, she rubbed her palm against her lab coat, trying to rid herself of the sensation that she'd been branded by the handshake. "Well, I'm sorry for keeping you waiting," she said. He smiled the big, solid smile of a playful, college athlete. She noticed that his nose was slightly crooked, a sure sign that it'd been broken before. The imperfection only added to his pull. The man looked a little rough and a lot handsome.

"No apology necessary, ma'am. The name's Malik Cutler. You can call me Malik," he said.

"I'm Dr. Veronica Howell and I appreciate the respect, but you don't have to call me ma'am, Dr. Howell will do."

"Dr. Howell, huh?" he questioned.

"Yes. Won't you please have a seat?" she said, pointing to the chair in front of her desk.

"I would love to after I close the blinds, if you don't mind, Dr. Howell?"

"Why?" she questioned. "I cherish every bit of sunshine we get in Seattle."

He answered, "It leaves you vulnerable, an easy target, Doctor."

She looked from him to the window. "Ah, now I see. You do realize this is the interview process? I haven't hired you yet." She said the words although she knew she was between a rock and a hard place. Her home had been violated, and she was scared to be there alone. She was too busy for time-consuming interviews, and this man was supposed to be the best. At the twenty-four thousand dollars a month base price she'd seen in the file, he'd better be.

"Call it a force of habit, Dr. Howell," he said, placatingly.

Veronica watched as he removed his bag and put it on the floor, then walked around her desk and lifted his arms to close the blinds. His triceps were partially visible, and they rolled like iron pipes beneath his skin. His movements were controlled and economical, kind of like watching Bruce Lee or some other karate master move. Then he sat in the chair opposite the desk and looked at her. The pause was long enough to make her feel silly.

She hurriedly sat down, fighting the flush she felt heating her blood, and began speaking quickly. "Your services come highly recommended. According to Samantha, you're the best in the Northwest at what you do. I understand that your clients are a hundred percent satisfied."

The engaging grin was Malik's only response.

"And, are you humble, as well?"

He shrugged, "I suppose that's a matter of opinion. I must commend you, though. Your sources are excellent."

"One of the advantages of having a friend who is also a superb lawyer," she answered.

"I see."

"You know, you're not what I expected," she said.

"Oh yeah? How so?"

Veronica paused slightly, leaning back in her chair. "I can tell you're athletic, but you're no bodybuilder. I expected someone bigger than Junior with a bald head. Like that man in *The Green Mile*."

Malik laughed outright, then said, "Sorry to disappoint you. I'll go back and tell Graham you want a freak of nature to scare all the bad guys away."

She crossed her arms and said, "Are you saying Junior's a freak?"

"Is that the Samoan guard?" he asked.

She nodded.

"No, but he is inexperienced." He told her how easily he got into the building.

"I really think this entire cloak-and-dagger stuff is premature—you sneaking into the clinic, closing blinds, et cetera," she said.

He held up the canvas bag at his side and responded, "Dr. Howell, if the information given me is correct, someone has been in your kitchen." He put the bag down.

A chill jerked her. "I know. I don't need to be reminded." She immediately regretted her tone, but she felt as if this man was trying to play on her fears. Subconsciously, she touched her bandaged forehead, a reminder of her collision with Samantha. She felt a slight headache forming.

Veronica looked at Malik, who was waiting patiently, and then her eyes lowered. "I hate this," she whispered. Again her hand lifted to her forehead briefly before she ran her fingers down the front of her face. Then she put the hand in her lap. In a slightly louder voice, she continued, "However, I detest it more that some nut has figured out where I live, so she or he can leave me nasty presents." Her eyes met his. "So, what would you do if I hired you?"

In a very professional tone, he went through the procedures he would execute: installing cameras at the clinic and her residence, competent guards at both places, alarms and a personal protector.

Bodyguard. For the life of her, she didn't want anyone shadowing her every move. "Oh come on now!" she protested. "I don't want or need someone with me 24-7. I think better locks and a few cameras are all that's necessary." Veronica ignored the part of herself that reminded her she was scared to be home alone.

"That brings up an interesting point." Malik paused and crossed his legs before continuing to speak. "If I take this position, it will mean a delicate balance between you and me, or I won't be effective."

"The position has to be offered for you to accept it," she countered.

"Touché. Should I continue explaining my philosophy, so you can decide if I'm your man, or should I wait for you to offer to hire me first?" he asked.

Her man! Is he flirting with me? This business arrangement would never work if she had to fight *that* as well as the man's magnetism. However, she had to admit that the game developing between them was exciting. Lately, the only thing that remotely stirred her was deep, intellectual conversations about topics like medical ethics or cutting-edge procedures. She wasn't even sure if this discussion would qualify as thought provoking, but it was sure as hell stimulating in a way she hadn't been aroused in a long time.

"Go ahead, explain," she said.

"We will have a very symbiotic relationship."

"Symbiotic?" her voice rose. "You mean like a tapeworm or a tick? You must be referring to your fees."

Malik laughed, then in a slightly tense voice he said, "Far be it for me to drain anything from you, ma'am."

What the hell does he mean by that? One minute he's borderline flirting and the next, he acts like I'm an ogre.

Her face must have shown her feelings because he immediately softened his tone and the Southern drawl was back. "What I mean is that I am going to serve you by protecting you, but I can't do that if you don't listen to me. In certain matters, I have to have strict obedience to ensure your safety."

The effect wasn't lost on her. The man's voice could melt butter when he wanted it to. However, what he said caused her grave concern. Control was the most precious thing she possessed, and she hated to surrender any part of it to him. When she spoke, she aimed for a joking tone, but her voice was too strained to pull it off. "Oh, so you mean that you're the master and I'm the servant?"

Malik smiled, full lips flattened out against strong, white teeth. "Don't worry. You get to be the boss, too, sometimes. You tell me what you want to do, and I tell you how we do it."

Veronica coughed into her hand after that one. It wasn't

so much what he said, but the way she was interpreting it. She was so used to one-way attraction: men quickly desiring her for whatever reasons, and she being unresponsive because she wasn't feeling the same. However, there was something about this man. He was…interesting for lack of a better word. Considering all this, she thought it prudent to perhaps interview others. Guilt wouldn't allow her to be enthralled with someone who was trained for violence. It would feel too much like an affront to her brother's memory.

She told him, "I have no further questions, and frankly, I'm not sure if you're the person for me. My life would be altered too much."

Malik nodded and stood. He reached into his back pocket and pulled out a wallet. From it, he withdrew a card and scribbled on it before handing it to her. Then, he said, "That's fair because I'm not sure if I want to work for you. We can both think about it." He picked up his bag and slung it across his body.

Her eyes widened. The last thing she expected was hesitancy on his part.

"Call me when you're ready to talk about it," he said. "You can always reach me at the number on the back." He wasn't obvious, yet she still noticed that he watched when she put the card in the breast pocket of her shirt.

The man was almost to the door when she shouted, "Is working for a woman offensive to you?"

He turned back. She still sat at her desk. "Not at all," he responded.

Veronica crossed her arms and leaned back in the chair. "So, it's something about me, personally."

It wasn't a question, but he seemed to take it as such. "It's not you, doctor. It's what you do."

She uncrossed her arms, putting her hands on the desk as she leaned forward and said, "Providing women at all economic levels with quality medical care in a nonjudgmental, supportive environment causes you problems?"

"No," he answered.

"Well, that's what I do here," she said, chin jutted forward.

"No, doctor, you do more than that. You fiddle with the building blocks of life."

She was confused for a minute, then the lightbulb flickered on. She said, "Are we talking about fertility, by chance?"

Malik nodded.

"Forgive me, but let me get this right. You object because we help women get pregnant?"

He nodded.

"For goodness' sake, why are you here when you obviously agree with the garbage spray-painted on the building?" Veronica asked.

"I don't necessarily agree with the graffiti, and I most definitely disagree with the way this person expresses him or herself, but you are tinkering with a system that has worked just fine for about two million years," he accused.

She responded, "That long ago we were living in caves. Do you have the same objections to toilets, running water and penicillin?"

"That's not what I'm talking about." Malik's legs spread, bracing him firmly.

"Why not?" she questioned. "All are advances we enjoy in the modern world."

"Not all progress is good, especially when the motives are questionable," Malik reasoned.

"What do you mean?" she asked.

Malik answered, "Why do these people want children?

Will they be properly cared for, or just another asset to be put aside?"

Veronica said, "Those same questions are present during the natural process, as well."

"Yes, but there are inherent limits to that process. Who restricts science?"

Her mouth slammed shut. She'd thought of this, even argued with colleagues about it, playing devil's advocate and taking each side. And still, the heart of the issue lay unresolved deep in her chest. When do the potential risks to the child outweigh the parents' desire to procreate?

She locked eyes with Malik and answered his question the best she could. "Society dispenses limits, just as it does in many other areas."

He actually laughed before saying, "Well heck, that sure explains why so many children are messed over." Hands on hips, he presented a tightly packed, impenetrable force despite the cynical smile on his face. Suddenly, his expression became serious. "I'm curious, Doctor, did you see the recent news story where a couple had treatment that resulted in sextuplets? The pair divorced, pops split and mom ends up abandoning the poor kids. Are you aware of that case?"

Veronica nodded. She had read the story and it sickened her. However, who did he think he was coming into her office and challenging her in such a way? Anger seethed through her. "Mr. Cutler," she said in a cold, tight tone, "how do you feel about the opposite side of the issue? People who can conceive naturally, but are not in a position to care for an infant. For example, there may be substance abuse issues, or they suffer from a mental or physical handicap. Should these people be prevented from conceiving for the well-being of the child?"

Suddenly, his face resembled a frustrated bull. Veronica instinctively knew she'd hit on something deeply troubling to him. He took a deep breath through his nose, put his hands out imploringly and said, "This is useless and going nowhere. Let's agree to disagree and leave it at that." Before Veronica could react, he stood ramrod straight, clicked his heels and said, "It's been a pleasure." With an about-face turn that left his bag swinging, he was gone.

Veronica sat there, eyes blinking, more than slightly stunned. The receptionist came in as soon as the door closed and said, "Dr. Roni, you have fifteen until your next patient. Here's a ham sandwich."

"Thanks, Laura," Veronica said, putting the food on her desk as anger began to burn away the shock. She picked up the phone to call Samantha, planning to give her an earful for recommending such an arrogant, opinionated muscle head. She was out, so Veronica left a message, asking her to call as soon as possible. She pulled the wrapper off the sandwich and began munching angrily on the wheat bread. How dare he judge her! Her private line rang, distracting her; and assuming it was Samantha, she grabbed the receiver.

"Witch, did you like the present I left in the kitchen? You will be stopped, one way or another!"

The sneering, male voice made her jump out of her seat and slam the phone down. She immediately picked the receiver back up and pressed *69.

"This is your last call return service," the recorded voice informed her. "The number called cannot be reached. Please hang up now."

She uttered an expletive.

Veronica slammed the receiver down again and put her head on her desk. It was the same voice! The knowledge made her tremble. Her crank caller was the one who had invaded her home! She lifted her head, feeling as if she had to do something or panic would consume her. With shaky fingers, she grabbed her purse from the desk drawer and dug until she found her wallet. From it, she pulled out the card from the officer that had come to her house. She left a message, telling him about the crank call.

She stood, not knowing exactly what to do, but following the urge that told her to keep moving. The phone intercom beeped, startling her so much, she bumped her thigh against the desk. Laura's distended voice let her know that the last patient of the day was in room one. Smoothing out her lab coat and putting a tight rein on her composure, Veronica left the office.

Chapter 2

As Malik got into his car and left the clinic, a heavily muscled man clutched binoculars and watched with obsessive intensity from his vantage point, the apartment complex across the street from the clinic. This man referred to himself as Shadow because in his line of business, it was best to use nicknames. A shadow was hard for the Drug Enforcement Agents to see or find, so it was an excellent choice for him because he was good at staying hidden. Keeping in theme, Shadow was dressed in his usual attire, black jeans and T-shirt that did nothing to enhance his light brown skin. But Shadow didn't care if his clothing choice made him look pallid. Right now, what he cared about was unfinished business. He'd taken a vacation from his colleagues in San Francisco to come to Seattle and fulfill his dream of capturing the Jazz Singer, turned doctor. However, others were trying to get in between him and his desire.

First, he'd had to contend with Shawn Hailey. A person

he considered to be incredibly stupid and very weak. It amused Shadow to refer to the man as Weasel, an appropriate moniker for that waste of flesh. When Shadow had first discovered someone else was interested in the good doctor, he'd followed Weasel for two days. He was confident that he knew him well. All the man seemed to do was work at his dead-end job, drink and devise little plots to annoy Dr. Howell. Shadow was certain that Weasel was too self-absorbed to understand the true significance of the security man's presence, the new person that had popped up between Shadow and Dr. Howell. Shadow had understood as soon as he saw the man snooping around the building.

Initially, Shadow had cursed, but now he was happy. Dr. Howell was a special woman, not like the others. He prized her, and she would learn to appreciate him. So it made sense that he'd have to work a little harder to get her. She was so exceptional; he'd spent the last two weeks just watching when he could have swooped in and made her realize she was his on numerous occasions. He was still savoring the fact that he'd found her again; getting to know her real good. It was kind of like dating. Yes, indeed. The thrill was in the hunt, the stalking. The muscle between his legs twitched a little. He ignored it, and the blood eventually reversed. Shadow prided himself on incredible restraint. Every activity had a time, a place, and theirs was coming real soon.

Shadow adjusted his binoculars when he saw Weasel was on the move. He watched the middle-aged, pudgy, white man leave his car, which was parked in front of the apartment complex, and hurry as he tried to sprint across the street in gray slacks that were too tight. The strain from the exertion was clear on his red face when he looked backward, towards Shadow, before entering the phone booth. Shadow chuckled;

his competition tickled him. The man was an angry, out-of-shape amateur, a dummy with a grudge.

However, Shadow didn't think the little trick at her house was funny. He wanted his girl to feel safe at home, and then he'd take her from there. Plucking her from the place where she felt securest was a delicious thought. Weasel had chased his goal to her friend's house, and now Mr. Security had showed up. But no matter, all that did was add a new twist to the hunt, a slight bend in the dating ritual. He still had the advantage because he'd reached the playing field weeks before his strongest opponent.

Weasel was out of the phone booth and walking as fast as he could. Through the binoculars, Shadow could see sweat dripping from his short brown hair into his face. In less than a minute, he was in his car, where he rested for a second before driving away. Shadow didn't even consider following him. He was completely confident he could find Weasel if he needed to.

Shifting his binoculars to the closed blinds of Dr. Howell's office, he wondered how long it would take for Weasel to be sniffed out and eliminated. If it wasn't done fast enough, he just might have to take matters into his own deadly hands because there was no way he could allow his *prize* to be hurt, accidentally or otherwise, by anyone other than him. Only he had that right, and that wasn't what he wanted to do with her. He wanted to love and cherish her, on his terms, of course.

Malik left Total Health Clinic, intending to visit John Graham, the man who had asked him to take this job because he felt obligated to let his good friend know what had happened. He called the office and was told Graham had gone home. As he drove to his friend's house, Malik looked up to see Mt. Rainier as clear as day. It seemed to be just down the street, instead of eighty-seven miles away. Usually, he enjoyed the awesome sight, but today it seemed as if the ominous mountain was glaring at him, mocking him because of his stupidity with Dr. Howell.

How could he let the memory of her crooning across stage overshadow his professionalism, his principles? Steaming, Malik began to analyze his behavior. He was very unhappy with himself for two specific reasons. First, he never ever discussed the ethics of a client's business with the client! It wasn't his place. Shaking his head, he realized he'd never openly shared his feelings on fertility, and somehow, he'd ended up in a heated debate.

Second, he'd flirted with her. The woman was taboo on so many levels: potential client, and most of all, what she did at her clinic! Working with the rich and influential, he'd seen children neglected time and time again. Single or married people manufacturing babies for every reason but the right one, and then abandoning them to nannies, maids, boarding schools or executive protectors. They were quick to give a dollar, but never around to offer a hug.

The real problem was the situation reminded him of a part of his childhood he'd rather forget. A time he thought of as the Dark Ages when he'd lived with his birth mother, a woman who was too worried about scoring her next hit to care for him. The stench of garbage still filled his nostrils when he remembered crawling into the Dumpster containers behind restaurants looking for something to eat. It was pitiful, and he was pitiful, until his father found out he existed and rescued him when he was seven. He later found out that his parents had never been married, and his father had been in Vietnam when he was born. His mother didn't even protest when his father took him from her filthy apartment. Her last words still rang in Malik's ears, "Take the brat, Mark Cutler, but you could at least lay a twenty on me."

Bitterness still smoldered in Malik and those words had been uttered years ago. They were the last words he'd heard his mother say. The next time he saw her, she was in a casket.

Casket. The word alone was enough to bring up unpleasant memories of another person passing. This time it had been a kid, Thad. The boy he'd befriended when he provided services to Thad's father for over two years. The family had been receiving death threats because the stock had dropped in the Internet company that the father had founded. Malik was one of a team of executive protectors, and he'd been assigned to Thad. "Keep my high-tech baby safe, Malik," Mr. McCullough would say to him, referring to the fact that his only child was a product of fertility treatments. However, Mr. and Mrs. McCullough were too busy living the high life to say much to their son.

In the beginning, Malik didn't have much to say to the kid, either. Not until he watched him playing chess by himself, pretending to be two different people. So used to being ignored, the boy actually jumped when Malik sat across from him and began moving the black pieces. To his surprise, he lost that first of many games to the lonely boy who reminded him so much of himself. Malik ended up spending many hours with the shy ten-year-old, discovering that he was bright, witty and charming when he came out of his shell.

By the time the job came to an end, Malik really liked the child, more than he cared to admit back then. He still remembered how Thad clung to him when he heard that he was being sent East to boarding school. Two months later, Thad died while swimming in a river close to his prep school. Malik was told he panicked when his legs were caught in weeds, and he drowned before help could reach him. Every time Malik thought about how the child had hugged him that last time they were together, it tore him up.

Malik took a deep breath, easing the ache in his chest. Their surrounds may have been different, but the result was the same: he and Thad had been neglected and ignored. His father had saved him, and he felt as if he'd kind of done the same thing for Thad. At least that's what he thought until he attended the kid's funeral. There, Thad's mother pulled him aside and shared what her son had written in his diary a week before the accident, "If I were to leave this earth, nobody would care, not even Mr. Malik." The words filled him with shame as Thad's mother just looked at him with a blank expression. How could he be so arrogant, thinking his little time with the boy would be the major difference in Thad's life? He should have done more, written the kid letters or something to let him know he wasn't forgotten. What else he could have done, he wasn't sure.

Malik's mind was jolted from his thoughts as he slammed on the brakes to avoid running a red light. "Enough of the past," he told himself harshly as the light changed to green and he moved the car forward. Still, he slapped the steering wheel as he neared Graham's house in the elegant neighborhood of Queen Anne. Telling himself to get a grip, he took deep, calming breaths and focused on the beauty of his surroundings. Located on a hill north of downtown, Queen Anne supported oak-lined streets and hillside homes with majestic views of Puget Sound as well as a busy shopping region. The neighborhood tended to draw the upper middle class who wanted to be within walking distance of downtown Seattle.

Not that Graham did a lot of walking. He'd gained a bit

of weight since his days as a tough Chicago cop and then a DEA agent. He blamed it on his love of steak, potatoes and good red wine. He'd left the agency because he claimed they wanted to shelve him behind a desk. In other words, they tried to get him to leave the field and become a supervisor. Instead, he took early retirement and started his own business.

When Malik left the navy, Graham heard about it and told him to come to Seattle. With nothing better on the horizon, Malik agreed. That was almost five years ago when he knew very little about executive protection. Oh, he knew about weapons and some surveillance techniques, but he didn't know how to detect a bug or engage in evasive driving. Since he was eighteen, the navy had trained him to be a combat swimmer, and he could maneuver anything that traveled by water; however, driving was something he did for fun on shore leave. Graham made him practice so much he began wondering how he could have ever considered the activity enjoyable.

Malik pulled up to Graham's three-story colonial. He knew all the guards, and the suited man nodded as he passed through the gate. The front lawn itself looked to be an acre and the house and grounds took up more than a city block. The beauty of the house hid its monitored, state-of-the-art security system. A servant led Malik to his friend, who was sitting in the parklike backyard, sipping iced tea and reading the paper under the shade of a large tree.

At sixty-five, Graham still looked like the clever, go-getter, brainy white boys that Malik saw often in the navy. He was a thick man with thinning blond hair and he tended to be intense, but that didn't stop him from possessing a quirky sense of humor. In deference to the weather, he was dressed in linen shorts and a short-sleeved shirt. Malik knew that his old friend would realize what it meant when he saw him so soon after his meeting with Dr. Howell, but Graham still gave his standard greeting, "How's the Pontiac?"

The man knew Malik hated the car. Even so, Malik answered, "It's boring as ever." Malik had permanently parked his prized Porsche in the garage at his house due to Graham's insistence, and he invested in an ordinary-looking, late-model Pontiac that had been outfitted with a reinforced suspension, armor paneling, bulletproof glass, and a powerful V-12 engine. Malik understood the necessity, yet the plain-looking car was far from his dream come true, and his friend liked to tease him about it often. A small price to pay to the man who had helped him develop his own niche in the field of personal protection. Although Malik wasn't Graham's employee, Graham often referred cases to him, or sometimes brought him on as an independent contractor.

Now that Graham had confirmed his feelings for the car, he switched topics. "It didn't go well, I assume?" He continued before Malik could answer. "Darn," he said shaking his head, "I know how worried Samantha is about this friend of hers. What was the problem?"

Malik shrugged and said, "I'm not sure, but we discussed that I don't like everything she does in her women's clinic." Almost every protector had cases she or he wouldn't take, and Graham was well aware of the clients Malik would not accept: Drug dealers, militant groups and terrorists. Philosophically, fertility or abortion were pretty close to Malik's red line, and Graham knew this. However, the ex-cop had explained he couldn't resist Samantha's pleas, and that's why he'd asked Malik to take the job. Malik had agreed because he owed the man more than a few favors. When a joint operation between the navy and the DEA had gone awry,

Graham had stood up for Malik and saved him from disciplinary action.

At Malik's words, Graham's eyes widened, and he dropped the paper in his lap. "You discussed artificial insemination."

Malik could hear the "I schooled you better than that" in Graham's voice. He was still surprised himself that he'd been so honest with her. He didn't bother trying to explain himself to Graham.

When his friend got tired of staring at him, he sighed and said, "I know I trained you well, and you have always been the consummate professional. This woman must be unique, to say the least, to get you to avoid the basics."

Still no response.

Graham chuckled and put the paper on the side table. He stretched in his seat, arms above his head before saying, "Oh well. I guess I need to call Samantha and suggest someone else from the list who won't protect the woman nearly as well as you. You know, Malik, you never told me why you feel so strongly about this issue."

"No, I suppose I haven't," Malik answered.

Again Graham laughed and replied, "I presume by that answer you don't intend to enlighten me now. It's very polite of you not to say mind your own business."

Malik sat in the lawn chair next to him and commented, "If you're going to recommend someone else, you should know that wasn't the only issue. I sensed that the doctor doesn't like to give up control."

"Oh, really?" Graham asked.

Malik nodded and said, "I don't think she was fond of the idea of having to follow rules other than her own."

"Great. I can't find anyone to protect her if she won't listen to reason," Graham grumbled.

Malik nodded, "It does make it hard, but it's not my problem now. I did as you asked, offered my services to the lady. This is just a courtesy call to let you know what happened. By the way, I know her, or at least I know of her."

Graham's look was questioning.

"She was a singer in a jazz club when I was in the navy."

The look changed to surprise, then Graham said, "You know, I received additional information on her this morning, but I haven't looked at it." Graham picked up the manila folder that lay on a small, nearby table. "Yes, it does say she sang with a group called Rhythm Street, but how did your paths cross?"

"A few guys in my unit were out on the town, drinking too much. They stumbled into the club and were mesmerized. They talked it up so much I went to see what all the fuss was about. She sang every Thursday night, and the men in my unit were quite infatuated, especially one guy we called C.C. One of the *C*s was for Crazy. Anyway, I never saw so many hard heads ready to listen to classical jazz. Then, poof. She disappeared." As Malik talked, frame after frame flickered through his mind like a music video playing in staccato. Legs strutting, bottom swaying. "It was amazing. I'd never really listened to jazz before and I suppose her voice was better than average, but she had so much stage presence. Charisma oozed from her and made each audience member feel special."

"Special, huh?" Graham's tone was teasing.

It annoyed Malik, so he didn't tell him about the images toying with his mind. How Dr. Howell's hair was longer then, and sometimes she'd bend forward as she sang, causing the hair to drape her features and her chest. Then she'd belt out a note and thrust through the veil, dazzling the audience with her penetrating stare and style. Her hair barely touched the top of her shoulders now. Malik wondered when she'd cut it.

"Well, it sounds like the lady made quite an impression." Graham's words interrupted his thoughts.

Malik answered, "She really did and that's another thing. Everyone could tell that she was a real lady, not just faking it. She was quite a performer."

"And now, she's a doctor," Graham commented. "Incredible how careers change! Do you think her current problems could have something to do with the past?"

"I suppose anything is possible," Malik shrugged. "I doubt it, though. She was singing in San Diego and that was a number of years ago."

"I know the environment may have been unique, but you navy guys are no strangers to pretty women. I'm still amazed you remember her," Graham said, shaking his head.

Malik didn't bother denying his friend's words. He went into the navy straight from the country, and he was like an eager puppy, frenzied to test the delights of every aspect of nightlife in each place he was stationed. But, by the time he saw Dr. Howell, he'd seen it all and done it twice. It took much more than a pretty face to excite him. He'd discovered long ago that a whole lot of ugliness could hide behind a beautiful exterior. Despite his world-weary attitude, Dr. Howell had touched him the first time he saw her grace the stage. Heck, the spectators had been silent while she sang, and the applause was thunderous after each song. She had the audience captivated with her style and grace, and his buddies paid homage by going to see her performances often.

"You know…" Malik's tone was reflective. "I've experienced women from here to Europe and Asia in a variety of settings, and I can honestly say she's the only entertainer that stands out."

"Wow! How long were you in? Fifteen years? The lady must have been performing magic on that stage," Graham said.

Malik nodded and patted his friend on the back before saying, "Good luck finding someone. She's not only one heck of a performer, she's feisty. You may have to come out of retirement and go protect the doctor yourself." Malik turned to leave.

Graham's laughter and teasing voice followed him to the door. "Humph. Fat chance of that happening! Although I may be tempted if the lady were willing to give me a private concert and only sing love songs."

Malik's back was to Graham, so the man didn't see him frown. The knowledge that his friend was joking didn't stop the *no* from shouting in his mind. He dismissed his reaction. Dr. Howell wasn't his concern. *The lady could work that voice on whoever she wanted to.* His caustic thinking did nothing to make the scowl leave his face.

Veronica tried to forget the phone call as she cruised by her cottage that sat on the shores of Lake Washington at around nine o'clock that evening. Leaving the small Toyota running, she parked across the street from her house, and clutched her can of mace while waiting for Samantha. After much pleading, her friend had agreed to spend the night. Veronica had yet to tell her that she didn't hire Malik, and she predicted that a lecture was in her immediate future.

Veronica turned this way and that, looking around her quiet neighborhood. Everything seemed as it should be. She pulled her car forward a bit, so she could catch a glimpse of the lake that lay beyond the houses. The first time she'd come to Seattle, its beauty had struck her. The serrated peaks of the Olympic Mountains to the west, and the massive Mt. Rainier to the east dominated the landscape. The Emerald City itself was squeezed between two bodies of water: the Puget Sound, an inlet of the Pacific Ocean; and Lake Washington, a freshwater lake that spread fifteen miles long and three miles wide. Veronica's cottage was perched about four hundred yards off Lake Washington, which she struggled to see. It was too dark.

Veronica began whispering over and over, "This is my home, and I will not be chased out of it."

Trying to bolster her courage, she reminded herself what the responding officer had told her the night of the incident. "Most of these guys are chickens, ma'am. They usually wait until the home owner is gone before they strike."

Samantha's Lexus came around the corner, and Veronica interrupted her mantra to say, "Finally." She used the remote control to open the garage door, and then drove inside. After parking in the driveway, Samantha had to run in high heels and a skirt to avoid being hit by the closing garage door. The curls on top of her head bounced defiantly along with the rest of her well-endowed figure.

"Dang, you trying to kill me!" Samantha said, her brown skin glowing in indignation.

"Sorry, I just wanted to get the door closed," Veronica explained. The two women hugged. At five foot nine, they were the same height. "Thanks for agreeing to babysit."

"That's okay, besides this is a temporary gig, right? When does the security guy start?" Samantha said eagerly.

"Well…" Veronica stalled.

Her friend yelled, "Ahhh, Roni, don't tell me you didn't hire him!"

"Look, Sam, I'm beat. My last patient, Mrs. Gans, ran real

long. She's having a problem with cysts, and I'll probably have to operate. Let me take a shower, and then you can fuss at me, okay?" Veronica soothed.

The light's soft glow was welcoming to Veronica as they made their way through the kitchen and into the living room. The fact that it was spotless, bearing no evidence of the previous evening gave her immeasurable comfort.

Samantha put her purse and small suitcase down before saying, "The cleaning service did a great job."

Veronica nodded and said, "Thanks for recommending them. Why don't you put your things in the guest room?"

"I will. Let me just stretch my back for a minute." Samantha's hands rested on her hips as she leaned backward. Next, she reached for the ceiling and said, "I know I've told you this before, but it's worth repeating. I really love what you've done here. Cedar-planked walls, hardwood floors, and that wood-burning stove is the perfect touch. I feel like I'm in a log cabin on the top of Mt. Rainer."

"Thanks, Sam," Veronica said around a huge yawn.

Her friend laughed. "I hear ya, girl. I'm beat, too."

Veronica picked up the suitcase, and Samantha followed as she carried it into the guest room, where Samantha promptly plopped down on the bed. Shaking her head, Veronica went to her bedroom. In the bathroom connected to her room, Veronica's shower beckoned like a siren's song. She knew it was what she needed to ease the anxiety still tightening her shoulders.

Her skin had started to wrinkle by the time she stepped out of the shower and ripped off the plastic cap. A loud noise immobilized her, and the towel she held slipped from her fingers. Her hands instinctively flew to her breasts and groin when Samantha came crashing in wearing the sneakers and sweats she'd changed into.

"Tell me you made that noise, Roni," her friend demanded. Roni's head moved from side to side, and her muscles congealed with adrenaline. There was another crashing sound.

"Roni, I think someone's inside. Good Lord, they must have been watching the house." Samantha's Reeboks gripped the floor as she tried to muscle the big dresser in front of the door. She stopped long enough to toss her cell phone to Veronica. "Call 911." With the phone to her ear, Veronica helped push. The dresser wouldn't budge. She grabbed the mace she'd put on the top of the dresser while the operator assured her help was on the way. Then the line went dead.

"Your phone's out. The police are coming, but what do we do?" Veronica asked.

Samantha retorted, "Get the hell out the house."

Samantha tossed Veronica the silk shirt and slacks she'd worn to work. Something bumped Veronica's hip. Reaching down, she realized her mobile phone was still attached to her pants. Not bothering with shoes, Veronica followed Samantha out her bedroom window. Something fell out of her shirt pocket when her feet hit the ground. Picking it up, she realized it was Malik's card. Indecision flew out of her head when she heard another noise. The officer's comments were obviously wrong. She needed additional help. Using the soft glow of her cell phone, Veronica dialed the number as her toes anxiously gripped the soft grass of the backyard.

"What are you doing?" Samantha's voice was so low Veronica strained to hear her.

"Calling the cavalry," she responded. "Hello, Mr. Cutler." As she spoke, she kept glancing toward the small deck off her living room. There were no bushes or trees, and she reasoned that it was the only area a creep could hide.

The deep, gentlemanly, "Hello," sent shivers down her spine despite the danger.

"There are noises, and I think someone's in the house!" she whispered, frantically.

"Tell me your address and get outside, Dr. Howell," Malik yelled.

"I'm already out and I called 911." She whispered her address to him.

He ordered, "Find a safe place and stay put."

Samantha leaned toward her ear and softly asked, "Is he coming?"

Veronica nodded before saying, "He knew who I was."

"What?"

Veronica's lips almost touched her friend's ear. "I didn't say my name, and he knew it was me."

"Great. We're about to die, and you're trippin' because the man knows your voice. Where can we hide?" Samantha asked, head moving from side to side.

Looking around her dark backyard, Veronica decided there really wasn't anywhere to take cover, unless they crawled beneath the deck, an unpleasant idea since she'd once seen a mouse scurrying from there. The situation was a blessing and a curse because there were limited places for her, or the maniac to take cover. Veronica supposed they could go sit in the freezing lake water that lapped gently just beyond her property. Slip underwater until all was well.

Samantha's lips were at her ear again. "Let's stay put. The next noise we hear, we'll go the other way, and you mace anything that comes near us."

It made perfect sense to Veronica. Besides normal night

sounds, all was silent. It occurred to her that she should call the police again when she detected a smell. She sniffed the air; the scent was acrid. She turned to the left and saw light flickering around the corner of the house where she stored firewood.

Veronica tapped Samantha's shoulder and said, "Fire!" They both ran and recoiled at the corner when a blinding light flashed in their eyes. The heel of Veronica's bare foot got caught on the house. She cried out and resisted the urge to bend down and check the damage. The small hole of a gun barrel centered between her eyes kept her up.

"Stop—police!" a male voice yelled.

Samantha's often-repeated words kept her immobile, "Nothing is more deadly than a scared officer." Any sudden moves would probably mean a bullet somewhere in her body. Veronica kept her hands at her sides, hoping the mace she clutched wouldn't get her shot. The gun shifted to Samantha who must have been equally stunned because she wasn't talking their way out of this.

A second female officer had a fire extinguisher and was spraying the flames that were just about out.

"My hands are up, and I'm behind you." A calm, deep voice came out of the darkness. Still everyone was startled. The woman dropped the extinguisher and drew her gun.

The sound of Malik's voice was so welcoming to Veronica that she went limp against the side of the house and put the mace in her pocket. The gun was away from them and aimed at Malik.

"Dr. Veronica Howell is the home owner, sir," he said to the male officer. Malik stood absolutely still with his arms raised. "She lives here, and I'm a friend."

Gun still drawn, the male officer escorted all three of them to the front of the house while the female officer made sure the fire was out. He asked for identification. Samantha explained why they didn't have any while the man thoroughly inspected Malik's license. Finally, the officer holstered the gun. By that time, his female counterpart was walking up to join them.

Malik was listening to the officers when Samantha scooted real close to Veronica. She whispered, "Now I understand why you got excited when he recognized your voice. I'd be pretty happy if that bodyguard noticed anything about me."

Veronica elbowed her.

The two women straightened up when the female officer turned to Veronica and told her she was very lucky. The fire had been contained to the woodpile, leaving the house untouched. One officer left to go through Veronica's window to secure the house while the other began asking the two women questions.

Although Malik wondered who the other lady was, his eyes stayed glued on Dr. Howell while she focused on the police. Not hours before, he'd told himself he'd never see this woman again and now he'd rushed to her aid. Nothing mattered but reaching her, as he hopped into the Pontiac and used its powerful engine to rush the fifteen or so miles to Dr. Howell's house. Thank God he was familiar with the area she lived in. Malik had seen man's inhumanity to man up close and personal. Violent images of injuries he'd witnessed ran through his mind, compelling him to mash the gas pedal to the floor. Seeing her safe was the salve he'd needed to clear the ugliness from his head.

He supposed that's why he couldn't look away from her now. Poised and professional, she conversed with the officer, but her body was responding to the anxiety and the warm evening. The skin above her sheer blouse was moist, and the material was beginning to clasp and cling to interesting parts of her anatomy, which made it clear she wasn't wearing a bra. The issue wasn't size because she wasn't big in that area, but she was visible. His eyes were transfixed, waiting for her to move so the flesh would wiggle slightly until he noticed the male officer's eyes darting below her face, and he wanted to kill the man.

The jealousy surprised him a little, nonetheless, he still chastised himself. This wasn't his woman. Sure, the phone call had shaken him, but he reasoned that he was a man and the urge to protect was natural. Maybe that's why he'd given her the number to the cell phone that was always with him. He usually waited until he was hired before he gave out that information, but not so with Dr. Howell.

Hell, who am I trying to kid?

His body wouldn't allow him to feel the indifference he craved now or back at her office. Perhaps it was because they had history, even though she was unaware of it. Also, he had to admit that he was proud of her. He imagined not many women shifted from the entertainment industry to doctoring. Even if he didn't approve of everything she did as a physician, it didn't stop him from appreciating the fact that she'd done it. No one had the right to hurt, or threaten her.

They were both logical, well-adjusted adults, and they could put their differences aside until she was no longer in danger. Malik realized his brain was rationalizing what his gut insisted he do from the moment he received the phone call. He was going to keep Dr. Howell safe whether she consented or not. The woman raised his protective instincts more than anyone who had come before.

The last time he'd felt so protective was when he was on

the mission where Graham had stepped up to save his butt. He was working on an operation with the DEA when he stumbled across a kidnapping ring. Malik interrupted the men while they were abusing their female captives, and the navy didn't like how he dealt with the whole affair. His superiors ignored his argument that there had been a justified use of force. Anyway, he hoped this situation ended better than that one. They would just have to agree to disagree and not talk about it. As he looked at Dr. Howell, he assured himself that his reasoning made perfect sense.

A Ford Explorer drove up and captivated everyone's attention. Both of the officers smiled and yelled greetings when they saw who got out of the car. Veronica watched as the black woman walked over, shook Malik's hand and apologized for not getting there sooner. Then she shifted to Samantha and said, "Counselor Martinson, I must say I'm surprised to see you here."

"The feeling is mutual," Samantha answered. The handshake between the two was brief. "I'm here for my friend, Dr. Veronica Howell." Samantha opened her hand in Veronica's direction. "Roni, this is Sergeant Ross." Veronica shook the woman's hand, as well. The tension between the sergeant and Samantha was palpable.

"I'm here for the same reason, counselor. To support Malik." With that said, Sergeant Ross excused herself and walked to the officers.

Veronica's eyes followed the woman who was at least six feet. The purple slacks and tailored, lavender shirt she wore accented her athletic build. She was very pretty and her manner exuded confidence. Veronica heard the male officer say, "You know him, Sergeant?" He pointed to Malik.

Sergeant Ross nodded.

"Good thing I didn't shoot him then." The officer began explaining how Malik had come on the scene.

Samantha started speaking, and Veronica's attention shifted. "Let me formally introduce myself to you, as well, Malik. I'm Samantha Martinson."

Malik's hand covered hers. "So you're Graham's friend, the defense attorney extraordinaire. Is that how you know Sergeant Ross?"

"Yes," Samantha answered, "we've been on opposite sides of tough cases too many times for me to count. She's a hard nut to crack on cross-examination."

"I see. I'd hate to be caught in that cross fire," Malik said.

"You're a smart man," Samantha retorted, then asked, "How do you know Sergeant Ross?"

Veronica listened. The easy banter between the two grated a nerve.

Malik answered, "I helped her with a case about a year back. I called her on my way over here to make sure this situation gets the proper attention."

Samantha tapped his shoulder before saying, "Oh, so we have a cop on the inside?"

Veronica swore Samantha's eyes batted. She crossed her arms, refusing to analyze why she was becoming so irritated.

"Sorta." Malik shifted to Veronica and said, "Dr. Howell, your feet are bare. Why don't we wait inside?"

Veronica shrugged and moved to the front door.

"Wait," Malik's hand touched her shoulder. "I know the officer has been in there, but I would like to check it out before you go in."

"Oh, well, if you think it's necessary," Veronica responded.

"I do. I heard you tell the officer you went out the bedroom window. I would like to go in that way. Where is it?"

Veronica pointed as she gave directions.

Once inside, Malik absorbed every detail. Cozy came to mind when he first entered her bedroom. It sheltered a queen-size bed, tucked across from an alcove with a window overlooking the water. Malik imagined Dr. Howell watching the fiery sunrise over the tips of her toes as he rechecked the lock on her escape route.

The damp towel lying on the floor had him visualizing other things, like a very naked Dr. Howell in the shower. He quickly left to inspect the rest of the house. As he did so, he couldn't help noticing how the wood of the walls and floor mixed with the antiques and large comfortable furniture to give the place a very rustic feel. It didn't take him long to find the source of the noise that had scared the women from the house. The kitchen and living room windows were broken and large rocks rested on the floors of each room.

Malik opened the front door and noticed Dr. Howell limping as she walked. "Are you hurt?" he asked.

"I just nicked my heel. It'll be all right," she replied.

At the porch, Dr. Howell and Samantha hesitated. Malik looked down and saw the red stain. "Was that left over from the other night?" he asked as he closed the door after the women entered. "I thought the vandalism occurred in the kitchen?"

"It did," Dr. Howell answered.

"I recommended a cleaner that specializes in crime scenes. I guess they missed this spot. I'm going to call them and demand a partial refund," Samantha said.

"You do that." Malik's voice was full of laughter.

All the laughter was gone when he spoke next. "There's the source of the noise."

Both women turned and looked at the melon-size rock lying on the hardwood of the living room floor.

"That's a good-size rock," Samantha said. "I'm surprised so much of the window is still there. Although looking at those cracks, I guess it could go at any minute."

Malik touched the window. "It'll hold till morning. Its twin is in the kitchen." Malik noticed that Dr. Howell's eyes were wide and blank. She looked as if she felt numb. "I'm going to go tell Sergeant Ross about that spot on your porch."

As he left, Veronica felt Samantha's eyes on her. "Hey, are you all right?" her friend asked.

"I don't know. I just feel surreal, like this is happening to someone else," Veronica answered.

Samantha put a loving arm around her friend's shoulders. "Girl, it's going to be okay. You're not alone in this." Samantha was quiet for a minute, and then she said, "I know what will help. Food. I have Chinese in the car. I forgot to get it earlier with all the confusion. Have a seat." She led Veronica to the couch. "I'll be right back."

The others were coming in when her friend opened the door. Veronica noticed that the three officers immediately went to the rock, but Malik didn't join them until Samantha was safely in the house. After she put the food in the kitchen, Samantha joined her on the couch. They watched as the others talked and looked around the house. Samantha grabbed her hand and the two sat silently.

Soon the two uniformed officers left, taking the rocks with them, and Malik stood in the living room with Sergeant Ross. Watching the two of them together made the inside of Veronica's belly itch, like a ball of scratchy wool was rolling around in her stomach. She ignored it, pressed her hand against her middle and suppressed the feeling into nothingness. Then she convinced herself that the now-controlled emotion had been some sort of delayed reaction to stress, because there was nothing in their manner to indicate anything other than a professional relationship. Even if the two had a thing going, it made no difference to her. She didn't need him for *that*. She just needed his skills to keep the bad people away.

Veronica reared when Sergeant Ross stuck out her hand. The grip was extra firm. "Dr. Howell, I'll leave you in Malik's capable hands—however, I will be outside for just a minute. We believe the red mark left on your porch is a partial shoe print. I want to photograph it, get an impression, et cetera before I leave. After I'm gone, the spot can be cleaned."

"Thank you," Veronica whispered.

Sergeant Ross turned to Samantha, and said, "Ms. Martinson, it's always a pleasure."

Samantha nodded.

Malik followed the sergeant to the door, where she shook his hand. "Malik, I'll be in touch."

The prickle flared again in Veronica. It reminded her of the throb in her heel. Samantha vanished into the kitchen, and Veronica lifted her foot and looked at the cut. Nothing serious, but it did need to be cleaned and bandaged. She glanced up to see Malik watching her.

"Where's the stuff? I'll get it," he said.

Her chin jutted a little before she said, "It's minor. I can take care of it."

"I insist, Dr. Howell. You've had quite a shock, and I think you should sit still for a while. Let someone else do the doctoring." Veronica wasn't sure if she liked the firm tone of his voice.

Samantha suddenly appeared in the kitchen doorway. "It's in the bathroom cabinet, Malik," she said.

"Thanks." Malik smiled. Soon, he stood in front of her with cotton balls, hydrogen peroxide and a bandage. He knelt to the floor, then lifted Veronica's foot.

Good Lord, Veronica thought. Her feet had never been a hot spot, but the feel of his rough, warm hand was treacherous. An electric sensation began circling her navel. Her hand pressed against her stomach, and she ordered her body to behave. It ignored her, and, as she watched him, she became more and more enthralled. She studied his fingers as he wiped the nickel-size wound with a soaked cotton ball. There was nothing feminine about them. They were long, thick and as flat at the end as the coffee table he leaned against. His nail beds were large, smooth and incredibly clean. Not all of his fingers were straight, and a few of his knuckles were slightly bigger than they should have been. Telltale signs that he'd broken or seriously jammed a few digits in his day, but the effect only enhanced the attractiveness. He was definitely a man's man, and despite what her brain wanted, she was attracted. The wound was tender, yet she remained absolutely still, lost in the way he ministered with those hands.

Veronica breathed deeply when he finally put on the bandage, fighting the fact that she was quite flustered. He looked up as he gently put her foot on the floor, and she focused straight down, avoiding his eyes. Hard brown nipples poking against white silk made her realize how transparent her situation was. Mortified, she managed to utter, "Thank you," before she bolted up from the couch.

Malik rose, as well. Veronica shifted too quickly, trying to avoid contact and stumbled. His arms surrounded her and a delicious warmth engulfed her. Her face was quite near his neck and he smelled of talcum powder, a pure, comforting smell. Against her will, she felt herself relaxing slightly into his hold. The sheer maleness of him was magnetic. Her mouth touched his throat and she felt more than heard his soft moan. His large hand began branding her back as it moved up and down, and she felt his lips in her hair.

A loud bang from the kitchen caused them to jump apart. They both looked at the closed door as Samantha yelled from somewhere within, "Sorry, I knocked a pot off of the counter." Veronica shifted her wide eyes to Malik's unreadable gaze.

The urge to bolt was strong, but Malik began speaking. "Look, Dr. Howell. It's been one heck of a stressful day for you. Let's chalk what just happened up to that, a little human contact at the end of long day, nothing more and nothing less."

Veronica nodded and took a deep breath in an effort to gather her composure. Being a doctor, she knew that stress could make people do odd things and that's all the contact had been, a brief respite from the anxiety. In a voice that only shook slightly, she told Malik, "I'm sure you're right. Thanks for being so understanding." She turned from him and quickly went to her room.

Chapter 3

Malik noticed that it took Dr. Howell exactly twenty minutes to come out of her room. When she emerged, she had changed into light cotton pants and a matching high-necked, green top. Malik and Samantha had cleaned the broken glass, and they stood making small talk when she walked past them and sat on the couch. Malik noticed that Samantha's eyes frequently strayed to Dr. Howell. He wasn't surprised when she lightly touched his arm and said, "Excuse me, Malik. I think girlfriend needs a little something, something. Come with me, please."

Malik followed Samantha to the kitchen. She stopped in front of the stove. "Up there, Malik." He stretched and opened the cabinet where there were about five different bottles of alcohol. "Hand me the Rémy Martin," Samantha ordered. He did, then watched as Samantha got a glass from another cabinet, and without speaking, went back into the living room. Malik stood just inside the swing door, watching Samantha pour the drink before handing it to Dr. Howell.

Dr. Howell looked surprised, and then the two women started whispering furiously. Malik couldn't hear every word, but he caught enough to understand that Dr. Howell had a low tolerance for alcohol, and she didn't want to be tipsy while he was in the house. He smiled at that.

Samantha won the argument and she grinned broadly when Dr. Howell took a healthy sip, and squeezed her eyes against the burn. Then, her face smoothed out and her shoulders gradually slumped.

Samantha turned to Malik and said, "Now, if I could get her to eat, I'd really rejoice."

Dr. Howell took another sip and opened her eyes. "Did you say something to me, Sam?"

"I said it's time for you to eat," her friend responded.

She shook her head and stuck her hand out. "Since you've got me started, I may need more."

Samantha laughed and handed her the bottle.

"Come on. I know you love shrimp fried rice. Let me fix you some," Samantha said before she disappeared into the kitchen as if her friend had said yes.

"Sam's a nice woman who cares about you," Malik commented, then moved to sit in the armchair across from the couch. "You're lucky to have her as a buddy."

Veronica answered, "Yeah, we met in the library at the University of Washington. I was just beginning med school, and she was in her last year of law school."

Malik asked, "So, you two brainiacs just hooked up."

Dr. Howell chuckled and said, "Something like that. More like misery loves company. We were the only two sisters constantly in that section of the graduate library, so we finally said hi to each other. I forget who spoke first."

Samantha yelled from the kitchen. "I'm sorry, Malik. Do you want me to fix you a plate, too?"

"No, ma'am. I had a huge dinner about an hour and a half ago."

"Ma'am? My mother's not here! Just call me Sam," she shouted.

"Yes, ma'am."

Samantha appeared in the doorway with a plate and said, "You did that to bug me, didn't you?"

Malik retorted, "I couldn't resist. If you ladies don't mind, I'm going to excuse myself while Dr. Howell eats."

"And a sense of humor, too." Samantha muttered as Malik left.

As soon as he was gone, Veronica said, "Where in the world did you find this guy?"

Samantha handed her the plate, then sat beside her on the couch, and said, "I already told you. Do I really need to repeat it? Eat, Roni, and stop harassing me."

Samantha glared until the fork lifted. Then she kept talking. "Look, I want to stop whoever is behind this. Graffiti, hate mail, even crank calls at the clinic is one thing, but this *arsonist* has taken the time to figure out where you live and that scares me. Believe me, after years in the underbelly of society, I know the limitations of the police. You need extra help. You are doing too much good down there at the clinic to let some wackos stop you."

"I got another call today. Right after Malik left," Veronica said. Samantha looked at her. "He called me a five-letter word that implies I ride on broomsticks and I...I hung up."

Samantha lectured, "I'm telling you, Roni, I get that you

see this as an encroachment on your independence, but you need security. Did you tell Malik?"

She shook her head.

"Well, I think he should know. Let me see what he's up to," Samantha said, getting up. Within minutes, she was back. "Girl, put that food down and come see this."

Veronica did as told and followed her friend to the front door. Samantha commanded, "Look in the peephole." Veronica did and saw a distorted view of Malik on his hands and knees, scraping the paint off the porch.

She stepped back and looked at Samantha. She was at a loss for words. Samantha seemed to realize she was mute and just started talking as she led her back to the living room. "I was going to do that myself. The Warrior Prince beat me to it."

That made Veronica laugh and say, "Now you know you're exaggerating. Maybe it's included in his ridiculous fee."

"Now I doubt that. He doesn't seem like the sort of man that'd get on his hands and knees for just anybody," Samantha quipped.

Veronica didn't comment. They'd reached the couch and she gingerly sat down, wondering at Malik's unsolicited act of kindness. Maybe Samantha sensed her mood because she was quiet, as well. Saying nothing, she lifted Veronica's plate and put it back in her lap. The silence didn't last long because soon Malik returned. Samantha left the couch and began telling him about the crank call.

Veronica watched the two and found herself concentrating on Malik. Without even trying, his presence filled the room. Not for the first time, she appreciated the sight of him in a pair of snug jeans and black T-shirt. Then she realized it was the man, not the clothes: Malik would have presence whether he was wearing rags or a tuxedo. She wondered if it was just her, or did Samantha feel the electricity that he seemed to carry around in his hip pocket, or maybe it was his front pocket right next to that natural bulge that looked as if it could grow to sizable proportions.

Her thoughts made her feel flushed. She looked up to see Samantha peering at her strangely. Avoiding her eyes, she reasoned that anything was better than feeling fear. She hated being afraid and detested that some nut or nuts had brought out that emotion in her. However, she warned herself that thinking about Malik's body was dangerous. The circumstances of her brother's death were enough to convince her that muscle and outdated ideas were a lethal combination. And Malik's view on fertility certainly didn't cast him in the liberal category.

"Veronica?" Samantha said, giving her a puzzled look.

"What?" Veronica snapped.

"Are you all right, honey?" her friend asked.

Malik looked at her, too, but his blank expression was harder to interpret.

Veronica took a deep breath and answered, "Yes, I'm fine. Did you say something?"

"No. Malik asked you a question," Samantha explained.

"Sorry," Veronica said and focused on Malik.

Malik asked, "Dr. Howell, do you have anything I can use to cover the windows—preferably wood, but cardboard will do and some duct tape or nails?"

"Ummm, in the garage, I think there are some boxes and in the cabinet is the tape. That stuff on the side of the house was the only wood I had," Veronica answered.

Malik nodded and said, "I'm sure the cardboard will do for the night." He headed toward the garage.

Samantha sat down again and looked at her. "Am I mistaken, or were you checking him out?" she asked.

"Girl, please!" Veronica retorted.

Samantha said, "I've known you quite a while now, and I've never seen you look at a man like that. You almost looked…hungry."

"Sam!" Veronica shouted. Then she put her plate on the coffee table and rubbed her face while saying, "No matter how I may have looked at him, in the end I'd never go for his type. He's a Neanderthal, just like the guys who hurt Mitchell."

"Oh, Roni. Don't condemn everyone who has muscles and a Southern accent just because of what those hatemongers did. Don't let that stop your hormones. Find out what the man's about," she advised.

Veronica laughed harshly before saying, "Listen to you, Sam. We don't even know if he's married."

"Humph, I doubt it!" Samantha said. "The man came running way too fast when you called to have a woman in his house."

Veronica shook her head. "Sam, put the bows away. Even if he's single, the cupid act won't work here. The man and I have already argued."

"Good, opposites attract." Samantha accented her words with a head nod.

"Not when the argument is fertility," Veronica answered.

"What does that have to do with anything?" Samantha asked.

Veronica replied, "Nothing, except for the fact that he shared with me that he doesn't approve of it occurring any other way but the natural way."

Samantha said, "Heck, he looks like quite the lover. I'm

sure you'll have no problem with that if you two ever get to the point where you want kids."

Veronica laughed loud and hard before saying, "You know you're incorrigible, and you're oversimplifying this."

Samantha shrugged.

Veronica tried another tactic. "Sam, if you have your way, I'm about to hire this guy. A relationship would be inappropriate when the man's in my employ."

Samantha responded, "Well, I'm confident it won't take Malik long to figure this one out. He won't be your employee forever. But let me say, he has quite an air about him. And that hair. I want to pat it down and watch it spring up again. I was about to ask him to grab a brush and follow me to my house until I caught him looking at you."

Veronica was aware that her curiosity made her dreadfully transparent, but she couldn't help but ask, "Looking at me how?"

Samantha chuckled. "Let's just say I don't believe he was thinking about you being his boss, or the fact that you two had argued earlier." Samantha grabbed Veronica's plate from the coffee table and put it back on her lap.

"Sam, how am I supposed to pay for this?" Veronica asked.

"That's easy. The same way you paid for the clinic. Ask your parents for the money."

Veronica said, "That's not an option."

"Why not?"

Veronica lifted the full fork, sighed, and put it back down without eating the food or answering her friend.

Samantha continued to question her. "Aside from mentioning they helped you with the clinic, you never talk about your parents."

"Sam, you're like a bull in a china shop! My parents aren't important."

"Yes, they are if they're the key to you getting protection. I'm your best friend in Seattle, so I have certain rights. Stop shutting me out and let me know what's up with your mom and dad."

Veronica chuckled, a short abrupt sound, and said, "It's not a pretty story."

"I can handle it," Samantha assured her.

"I don't like to think about it, much less talk about it," Veronica said.

"Roni. Stop stalling and get on with it before Malik gets back."

Veronica's hand ran down the front of her face, then she started talking. "After my first year of college, I told my parents I wanted to go to medical school. Do you know what my mother said?" She didn't wait for an answer. "'I told you to marry a doctor, not be one.'"

Samantha laughed.

"It's not funny, Sam. Her comment made me so angry that I became laser focused. Every time I faced a hard class or a condescending professor, all I had to do was think of my mother. Boys and hanging out with friends became less important. Everything was secondary to being a doctor."

"It still is," Sam commented, continuing to chuckle softly.

Veronica ignored her. Now that she'd started, she had the need to get the whole story out. Besides, she didn't feel like arguing about her social life, or lack thereof, so she simply kept talking. "My mother is quite a woman. She had my and my brother's life choreographed years before we were born. We were supposed to be friends with the right people, go to the right schools, adopt the right charities and marry the right people. I went along with the program until I was about sixteen. She saw me kissing the wrong boy behind church after choir practice. 'Nice, but too poor' is how I think she put it. The woman went ballistic."

Surprise killed Samantha's amusement. She sat up straight and stared at Veronica, who continued speaking.

"If I wasn't so humiliated, I probably would have kept my mouth shut. Instead, I defended myself for the first time. You see, no one talked back to my mother. Every once in a while, my dad put his foot down, but he did this behind the closed doors of their bedroom, and when they emerged, my mother would pretend like she had changed her mind. Anyway, my mother didn't like it when I challenged her."

"You go, girl!" Samantha cheered. "What'd she do?"

Veronica answered, "Slapped me once so hard that the boy ran away. I guess he thought he was next. This was the first time she'd hit me. There was no need to before, because I was a perfect child. I had excellent grades, took all the dance lessons my mother insisted on and played piano for the church choir. I still did all those things, but I gradually stopped looking to her for approval. I figured if I satisfied my own expectations, then that was good enough. This monumental move toward independence prepared me for what happened with Mitchell when I was in college."

"How so?" Samantha asked. Veronica had told Samantha that her brother had been murdered, but not how it affected her relationship with her parents. She sighed, stood up and stretched her arms before crossing them and turning to Samantha. "It was the summer after my junior year in college. I'd tried to get as far away from my parents as possible, so I had left Boston and followed my brother to San Diego State. He'd graduated and was working as an accountant."

Veronica moved to the middle of the living room and began pacing as she talked. "I'll never forget that night. My brother picked me up for dinner and we met his partner, Jim, at the restaurant. While we were eating dessert, Mitchell told me he was going to come out to my parents. I was so happy he was finally going to do it that I shouted and hugged him. The news was a surprise to Jim, too, and he hugged and kissed my brother. The two were usually more discreet in public, but we were all so excited."

Veronica stopped moving, arms tight across her stomach. "Mitchell never got the chance to tell my parents face-to-face. We waved bye to Jim, and I dashed into the bathroom, while Mitchell went to get the car. When I came out of the restaurant, Mitchell wasn't there so I started walking to where we had left the car and…and he was being attacked." Veronica took a deep breath. "After his death, his sexual preference became public knowledge, mostly because I told anyone who would listen. I thought the news coverage would help find the attackers. My parents were just as devastated as me. First, that their son was dead, and second, that he had died in a gay bashing. My dear mother ordered me to be quiet about the gay part. She said that was private family business. When I refused and kept talking to the media, she cut off the money. I felt like I'd lost my brother and my parents."

Samantha stood, walked to Veronica, and pulled her into a hug, while saying, "I'm so sorry, girl. I know all of that must have been very difficult."

Veronica nodded into her shoulder, but her arms remained wrapped around her own waist. "I got through it." She gently removed herself from Samantha's arms. "Whoever said, if adversity doesn't kill you, it makes you stronger, was right. It was hell, but I suppose I'm a better person for it. Back then, singing became my salvation. Of course, Mother didn't approve of that, either. She never was specific about why."

Veronica moved to the couch and Samantha followed. They both sat, and then Samantha said, "I thought you sang for kicks. Did you do it to spite Momma and pay for school?"

"Well, not quite," Veronica answered. "The little bit of money I made with the jazz group didn't even cover my gas to get to the gigs. In fact, I had to sell the car to make ends meet. I greatly lowered my standard of living, relied on friends and got by on loans to pay for school. I sang because it made me forget and most of all made me happy."

Veronica grabbed the brandy she'd placed on the coffee table, sipped and continued the story. "Anyway, graduation day came and I had surprise guests, my parents. When my dad asked, I told him how I slept on my friend's couch and managed to get by. A small frown appeared on his face, and I distinctly remember how he whispered, 'I'd hoped the reports about your living conditions were exaggerated.'

"A month later, the checks started coming. I guess daddy took mother in the bedroom and had a talk with her. But by that time, I'd been accepted to UW's med school and offered a free ride here in Washington. I refused to use the money and mailed it back. Undeterred, my dad started wiring it directly into my account every four weeks, like clockwork. I don't know how the man got the account number. I don't like to think about it.

"The funny thing is, my parents showed up at my medical school graduation. My mother had adjusted her thinking and laid out her new plan for my life. She informed me it was okay to be a doctor until I found a suitable husband, and then it would be time for me to bear fruit. The woman just doesn't get it. She thinks her ability to financially cut me off has some leverage. She doesn't understand that I emotionally cut off from her a long time ago."

"So, the cash represents control after you've achieved complete independence," Samantha stated.

Veronica answered, "Yes. You got it. I don't want the yoke reattached, literally. That's what using their money means to me."

"So, let me get this right," Samantha said. "This money has just been sitting in the bank, gaining interest?"

"Yes. The bank kept hounding me, so I do let them manage it. The clinic was the first time I used the money. I rationalized by telling myself that I was laundering it clean. I erase what it represents by using it for the greater good. It helps me provide holistic medical care for women, including some services they may not be able to afford otherwise, like fertility treatments. In a way, it's bittersweet for me to be able to help give life when I couldn't stop it from being taken before."

Samantha shook her head and said, "I hear you, girl, and now I even understand where you're coming from, but you need protection possibly to defend your own life. If your parents' money is the only way to pay, then so be it."

"Oh no." Veronica smiled wearily and said, "Your lawyer side is coming on. I suddenly feel like I'm about to be badgered."

Like the good friend she was, Samantha immediately picked up on the vibe that Veronica needed the mood lightened. "Darn right," she said, "how tough do I have to get before you're convinced?"

Veronica didn't get a chance to answer because Malik came through the doorway. She wondered if he'd heard anything. His facial expression didn't give her a clue. He carried a large piece of cardboard and duct tape. Both women watched as he worked to cover the window. His shirt shifted as he moved, giving tantalizing glimpses of washboards abs and a rippling back. Veronica didn't even blink, not wanting to miss seeing the toned, firm-looking flesh.

He was putting the last piece in place when Samantha asked, "Are you married, Malik?"

Veronica elbowed her friend's side hard right before Malik turned around.

He looked at them both, his head tilted to the right and he answered, "No, why do you ask?"

"You will soon learn, Malik, that I am incredibly nosey. The secret to my success as a lawyer. Don't tell anyone."

"Oh, yeah? I'll have to watch you, Sam," Malik commented.

Veronica found the crooked smile on his face endearing. It melted into a serious expression when he sat in a chair near them. He addressed Veronica, "Tomorrow will be a busy day. I've spoken with Graham, and the technicians will be here at seven in the morning to secure this place, and then the clinic. We need to discuss your options."

Protest was a temporary notion in her mind. Before she could form the words, he had her making decisions about safety. Maybe her conversation with Samantha had prepared her for what was becoming a reality. The alcohol had her feeling loose, and she didn't want to analyze why she was acquiescing so easily. Besides, she had called him in her moment of need. She reasoned that hiring him was just a technicality after that, even if the payment and fertility questions were still up in the air. She kept a blank face and made rational decisions about her safety. The alcohol dulled the razor-sharp pang that went with admitting she needed this man.

She supposed that's why she didn't flinch when Malik looked in her eyes and said, "I'm staying the night because you have two broken windows that can't be replaced until daylight."

He must have taken her silence as an objection because he asked, "Do I need to speculate on what can happen if this person returns?" His tone held all the warmth of a stone barricade.

She glared at him, sitting there as handsome as he was arrogant: elbows on knees, hands clasped, square chin jutting forward slightly. An odd twinge resonated from deep inside. It didn't take her long to identify it as comfort. Having such an immovable force present in her recently volatile world was…soothing.

"No, you don't need to tell me horror stories," she answered in a matter-of-fact tone. "Are you sure you want to do this knowing the full gamut of services I provide at the clinic?"

He continued to look right in her eyes when he said, "Breaking and entering a physician's home isn't nearly the right way to get a doctor to change her political views about what happens in her clinic."

Veronica was surprised, given that he was a man trained for violence.

Malik shrugged and admitted, "I may share some similar beliefs with who's doing this, but no one has the right to threaten you."

She was stunned.

Her face must have shown this because he smiled. Then he stood up while saying, "I'm going to get my gym bag out of the car. I've got clothes and a toothbrush in there."

Veronica lifted the bottle she'd placed at her side and

poured. Samantha excused herself to go take a shower. The world seemed bizarre and surreal. Muscle heads conquered differences with their fists. Wasn't that what war was all about? Yet Malik's words seemed sincere. They were so different than the phrases that were yelled while she held a limp Mitchell all those years ago. She shuddered, remembering the spit that rained down with every ugly word. Veronica stared at the amber liquid she'd just poured, comparing the color to the deep red that had flowed from Mitchell's face.

Muscled arms, revealed by T-shirts, and combat boots made the three men seem as if they were military, but their hair was too long, and they were filled with too much hatred. Paramilitary, Veronica remembered thinking. She shivered, reliving the white men's twisted faces and jerky movements as she bent over Mitchell, trying to stop the kicks from reaching his battered body. But their words weren't only for him. They yelled with Southern accents that America wasn't for "queer-loving sissies."

"He's my brother!" she'd shouted.

The one who had a tattoo on his shoulder yelled, "Then we've done you a favor." He spat on Mitchell. Veronica would never forget that tattoo, an anchor with a corded rope circling around it. As she wiped the spittle from Mitchell's brow she glared at them, trying to figure out if she knew these animals. She had noticed how the men had stared when Jim had kissed Mitchell, but she'd thought nothing of it because they soon turned and began talking amongst themselves.

Shaking her head, Veronica tried to lose the memories, push them aside with a sip of alcohol, but they followed like a heavy shadow, trying to blanket her. By the time Malik got back, she was sitting on the couch, warring between feeling tipsy or facing the images playing in her brain like a bad B movie.

Dr. Howell looked tired and a little intoxicated to Malik, as if the day's events had wrenched the vitality out of her. The hollow dark patches forming under her eyes made her look wan. She wasn't the tiger he'd argued with earlier, or at least he thought that was the case.

He tried to put her at ease by saying, "I'm glad the couch is long. I don't have to worry about my feet hanging off the end, going numb."

Dr. Howell smiled absentmindedly, more out of courtesy than humor it seemed to Malik. Then she said, "Yes, I imagine that would make it hard to chase a bad guy, but you know, I do have a spare bedroom. Sam would probably switch with you."

"I prefer to sleep on the sofa and let her have the bed. Once I secure the window in your room tomorrow, they'll have to get through me to get to you," he explained.

Dr. Howell tiredly shrugged her shoulders, then said, "Let me get you a pillow and blankets." Malik noticed she swayed as she walked, especially when she returned, balancing the linens in her arms. She looked relieved when he took the bundle and began transforming the couch into a bed.

She sat down gingerly and he said, "My parents trained me well."

He realized his attempt at levity failed again when she replied, "I didn't mean to imply otherwise."

He sighed. "It's okay, Dr. Howell. I know today's been less than perfect, and I guess my silly sense of humor isn't helping."

She looked at him and said, "It's not only you. The last few days have been awful. This weirdo is just icing on the cake. A few days ago, a patient died. A young woman with cancer whom I'd grown quite fond of. It wasn't even the disease that killed her—it had gone into remission. She was crossing the street when a truck hit her. It wasn't the driver's fault. The brakes had failed. She died instantly."

Malik shook his head before saying, "Believe it or not, I do understand. In my life, I've decided that death doesn't make any sense most of the time. The innocent get slaughtered while the evil just keep on ticking."

Dr. Howell nodded and said, "That's a realistic view, but what happened? Weren't you just trying to perk me up with corny jokes a minute ago?" Now, she smiled, but it still wasn't the type of grin Malik had been aiming for. It drooped around the edges too much. He watched the glass go to her mouth. After she sipped, she said, "I can't claim to be exactly innocent, so hopefully I can avoid an untimely demise."

"Don't worry, Dr. Howell. No one will harm a hair on your head while I'm on watch," Malik said and pushed up the long sleeves of his T-shirt.

Veronica gasped and looked as if someone had just poured cold water on her head. "Dr. Howell, what's wrong?" Malik asked, moving toward her.

She recoiled, saying, "No, don't touch me. I'm…I'm okay. Your tattoo. It just surprised me."

"My anchor?" Malik asked, as he ran his fingers along the rope intertwined around the anchor. "Lots of sailors and merchant marines get this one. Does it bother you?"

Dr. Howell nodded. Malik pushed his shirtsleeve down.

"No," she protested, "you don't have to do that. You're going to be around a lot so it's probably better if I get used to it."

"For security purposes, do I need to know why it bothers you?"

Her head shook, and she gulped more brandy. Next, she

said, "I bet you were a nice little boy. I bet all of you start out as nice little boys. Tell me, how does a kid grow up into a...killer?"

"You're assuming a lot, aren't you?" he countered.

"Are you saying that you've never ended a life?" she asked.

"I've done a lot of things in defense of my country and others," he stated.

She questioned, "I'm sure you have. The ends justify the means, huh?"

"Now, I thought that was your line of reasoning with man-ufacturing kids?" he retorted.

He could tell the comment almost stunned her into sobriety. He knew she was still reeling when he moved on. "My father used to say that every death should count for something. I've tried to hold true to that."

He watched her blink and settle herself before saying, "Tried?"

"No one's perfect," he admitted.

Dr. Howell nodded into her cup, then lifted her eyes and said, "Ain't that the truth, but think how boring it would be if we were." She chuckled, probably as amazed as him at the ebb and flow of their conversation. She drank the last of the golden liquid in the crystal tumbler, which was a sizable amount.

Malik said, "Maybe you've had enough of that." He was happy when she didn't deny it. He was becoming tired himself and not in the mood for thought-provoking conver-sation. He strongly suspected that further examination of his conscience or hers would only produce answers that were gray, instead of the preferred black-and-white.

Dr. Howell looked at the empty glass and whispered, "Am

I drinking because of the immediate past, or the fast-approaching future?" She laughed and sniffed the glass before putting it on the coffee table. She looked at Malik, and he wondered if she knew that she was talking out loud. Apparently not because her lips kept moving. "I guess you calling the shots is less threatening than the psycho who's trying to manipulate me, even if you have that disgusting tattoo."

Malik's eyebrows rose. Alcohol appeared to be a truth serum for Dr. Howell. He decided to press the advantage when he said, "Well, since you seem to be amenable to my suggestions at the moment, let's get the big issue out of the way." He paused briefly. "I think I should stay with you until I get a handle on this. That means I need to live here even after the windows get fixed."

"No way," she whispered, mostly to herself it seemed. He had to strain to hear her as she continued talking without looking at him. "Veronica, it was no fun being dripping wet and wondering if some nut was going to try and put your blood on the kitchen table. To Mommy and Daddy's money we go. I suppose this is using it for the greater good." She blinked, looked up and focused on him. "So, you will be my houseguest. Should I write you a check now?"

"No," he answered, "I'll bill you once a month."

Veronica threw her head back and closed her blurring eyes, saying, "Okay, do what you must with my life." She waved her hand dismissively.

If only that were open to liberal interpretation. Her words and his thoughts caused his blood to rush below his waist. He watched her neck as she breathed and swallowed. A leg, a thigh, a breast all were obviously erotic, but Malik questioned his reaction to seeing her ebony throat work. Man, he had to control himself before his desire became a liability. Besides, even if his body liked Dr. Howell, his brain was vehemently opposed. Despite how good it felt when her face was against his neck, he and Dr. Howell were morally incompatible.

Chapter 4

Veronica woke with a start when her alarm clock buzzed at 5:30 a.m. She'd set it yesterday, forgetting that it was Friday and she could sleep in the next morning. Feeling slightly disoriented, she wondered if last night's events had been an extremely bad dream. Shaking her head, she knew it hadn't been, as she wiped her damp chest. Seattle was in the grip of an unusual heat wave, and from the condition of her skin, it hadn't cooled off. "I should get air-conditioning," she muttered. Right now she didn't care that it didn't make economic sense because it rarely got hot enough to use air in Seattle's mild climate.

Yawning, Veronica's body urged her to hurry up. She was a creature of habit, no matter what the day, so she usually stumbled into the kitchen to start the coffeepot before she took a shower. She liked to brush her teeth after she drank the strong brew to avoid offending her patients when she moved in close to examine them. So, after throwing on a robe that ended midthigh, Veronica cat-stretched and made her way to the door. She opened it slowly because she didn't want it to creak and wake Malik. Then, she crept to the couch and peeked at his prone form. Confident he still slept, she moved silently to the kitchen.

Malik woke the moment he heard her moving around. For some perverse reason, he lay absolutely still when he felt her peering at him. As she walked away, he opened one eye and then the other. Malik stared wide-eyed. *Good Lord,* he thought as he watched her legs move her away from him. They were like a dancer's limbs: slim, toned, incredibly long and feminine.

By the time she disappeared into the kitchen, he was very aroused. When she reappeared, she was humming a low tune to herself. Malik strained to hear, and it sparked memories of how sultry she could be holding the microphone, singing a slow song that made the whole audience fall in love with her.

Malik decided it was time to let her know he was awake. "Good morning," he said in a strong, clear voice as he sat up.

Unfortunately, he startled her and she gasped while backpedaling. "Ouch!" she yelped, and he guessed that she must have stubbed her injured heel. She yelled an expletive, dropped to the floor, and her robe opened enough to reveal more than a glimpse of her silky breast.

Malik was up and moving to help her despite a raging hard-on. Before he could reach her, she practically shouted, "No, I'm fine." Her embarrassment was clear as her right hand pulled the robe closed.

Next, they were both startled as Samantha threw open the door of the spare room.

"It's all right," Malik told her, "I just surprised Dr. Howell."

Samantha took in the situation. A mischievous grin appeared and she said, "I guess you two can handle this on your own." She shut the door.

Malik looked at Dr. Howell's bowed head and did as she requested. He turned around and walked back to the couch, wondering at her awkwardness. This assignment was going to be pretty tough if she couldn't get used to him being in the house.

Veronica picked herself up off the floor and walked into her room. There, she struggled for composure, taking deep breaths, hoping it would stop the shaking. Her palms were wet when she tried to manipulate the shower knob, but she managed to turn it on, and step into the spray. The water's pulsating massage was stone-cold when Veronica felt calmness easing in and overshadowing the silly embarrassment. Yet, the water needling her skin did nothing to wash away what she'd seen. She'd only looked at his body for seconds as he walked back to the couch. No matter because the images were burned into her brain: wild hair; bare back rippling as he walked and spanning into what were really nice forearms; lean hips; sturdy, hairy legs that ended in long, slim feet. His clothes disguised just how muscular he was. But that's not all she saw. The man's life hadn't left him unscathed. Scars peppered his back.

Later, when she came out fully dressed, Malik was nowhere to be found. The covers he'd used were neatly folded and placed at the end of the couch. She went in the kitchen to be greeted by a smirking Samantha who was sitting at the dinette drinking coffee.

"What was that all about?" her friend asked.

Veronica answered, "I thought he was asleep. He scared me when he sat up and said hello. Then, my robe popped open when I fell. This whole thing is making me way too jumpy, although I did sleep like the dead last night."

"You'll be all right, girl. Your nerves will settle down," Samantha said, patting her shoulder. "And the sleep thing doesn't surprise me. You didn't sleep well at my house, you drank that wonderful brandy, and you had your protector on the couch. You were supposed to be out like a rock." Sam chuckled. "Speaking of rocks, I suppose some parts of him were hard as one after your show."

"Sam! I just told you it was an accident."

Her friend's lips said sorry while her eyes were twinkling far too much for her to be sincere.

Veronica sat down and put her head in her hands while saying, "I know I need help, but having *him* may be a mistake. There's too much…stuff floating between us."

"Stuff!" Samantha shouted. "You mean he liked the peep you unintentionally gave him? The man would have to have sugar in his tank not to react to that. Just wear your clothes tight, and you'll be all right."

"Stop, Sam! The situation is embarrassing enough without you making jokes about it!" Veronica stood up and looked around the corner into the hallway.

Samantha said, "Don't worry, he can't hear us. He's outside doing the bodyguard thing, looking at bushes or something. Besides, I don't see why you're so upset? All he saw was a flash, right? You've probably shown more skin at the beach."

The comment made Veronica pause, and she leaned against the kitchen counter and looked at her friend. "This is my home and being on display to a virtual stranger is not what I want." she finally stated.

"Come on, Veronica," Samantha countered, "it wasn't a big deal."

"No, hear me out. It's all about expectations. I'm in my home, where I'm not expecting to be on display unless I want to be. The thing with Malik was… just wasn't supposed to happen. It was outside the boundary."

After a moment, Samantha said, "Okay, okay, I can see where you're coming from."

Veronica's fingers worried her temples. "Geez, Sam, I can see where you think I'm being a bit silly, and maybe I am. I have to admit that I haven't felt this way…well, since I was in high school."

Samantha quickly said, "That's because you've gone too long without."

Veronica protested, "It hasn't been that long." A smile spread across Samantha's face, and Veronica spoke fast, not giving her a chance to comment. "But that's not important. It's more than attraction. There's some kind of weirdness between us."

"Weirdness? It's called chemistry."

Veronica didn't deny it, instead she said, "My misguided hormones are confused. He isn't the man these emotions should be aimed at."

"Why not?" Samantha questioned. "And don't start with that stereotyping again. I agree that you two shouldn't start anything until this threat is over, but hey, see what happens after that. Maybe you can compromise on the fertility issue. If the Berlin wall can come down, it seems like you two can compromise."

Veronica interrupted the lecture, "Sam, he has a tattoo just like one of the animals who hurt my brother."

"Oh." Samantha was silent for a moment, then she said, "But those guys were white, right?"

Veronica nodded before saying, "I know he wasn't one of them, but seeing that *thing* is painful."

"I hear ya, girl, however, you know tattoos can be changed," her friend suggested in a small voice.

Veronica put her hand out, palm up and said, "Samantha stop! I know you must have stuff to do today."

"Okay, okay, I can take a hint," Samantha said as she stood up. "Well, it's a beautiful Saturday morning, and I'm going to enjoy it by being a mole in my office. I have a heavy trial calendar the next couple of weeks, so I don't know how much I'll see you." She came over and gave Veronica a hug before grabbing her bag and slipping out the kitchen door. Veronica heard her speak to Malik, but he didn't come into the kitchen. So, after going to the coffeepot and pouring herself a fortifying cup, she went to see what he was doing.

She sipped as she looked, enjoying the strong, vibrant taste that jolted her already keyed-up senses. She found him standing just inside the window to the deck at the back of the house. Immediately, she noticed that a large Band-Aid covered his tattoo. Although she told herself the gesture wasn't necessary, she appreciated his respect for her feelings. He held his own steaming cup of coffee as he looked out at the water in his Seattle Supersonics T-shirt, jean shorts, with his long bare feet. After the briefest of glimpses, she consciously avoided his muscular legs. Looking at his hair, she assumed he'd had a shower or at least washed up because the wet strands lay flat in most places.

Without looking at her, he said, "You sure know how to make it." He held the cup higher. "I haven't had coffee this good outside of Texas."

So, that's where the accent comes from. A real cowboy's protecting me. "Texas, huh? What part?" she questioned.

He answered, "Galveston, by the water."

"Oh." Veronica logged the information away.

"How's the foot?" he asked.

"Fine."

Silence. He continued scanning the area, and then he stopped and stared at her before shaking his head.

"What?" Veronica said.

"Aren't you burning up with all those clothes on? It's already eighty degrees out there and you're drinking hot coffee."

Veronica wore jeans, a long-sleeved cotton blouse and thick blue socks. She answered, while ignoring the sweat tickling her scalp, "No, I'm quite comfortable."

"Uh-huh." He didn't sound convinced. "Look, I'm sorry about this morning. Soon we'll be in a routine and that type of thing won't happen."

Suddenly she felt shy. Goodness, the feeling was unfamiliar to Veronica. It usually took a lot to unsettle her, and the moments quickly passed. She had assumed she was over the morning incident. This man had her off-kilter, uncomfortable, and he was going to be in her home for an indefinite amount of time. All of that equaled to…to what? She wasn't sure. She didn't like being unsure, so her defenses shot up, and the coldness was evident in her voice. "It's nothing but an interesting anecdote now."

Malik looked at her with a slight smile in his eyes, on his lips. Without responding, he turned back to the water. A moment or two later, he spoke in a serious tone. "This concerns me."

"What?" she questioned. "The beautiful view of Lake Washington? Aren't you a dolphin? A combat swimmer according to the information I received. You're supposed to love the water."

He chuckled and said, "A SEAL, not a dolphin, and you're right, your view is spectacular. It's the accessibility that bugs me. Combine that with the limited lighting at night, and we have a problem. A small craft or swimmer could easily land, and boom, the bad guys are on your back porch. Of course, a nice high fence would help the situation."

Veronica looked from him to the water beyond the deck before saying, "Malik, people don't live on waterfront property to block the view with wood or wire."

"You do know that your bedroom window faces the lake?" he asked.

Her arms crossed while she said, "If you're next suggestion is bars, forget it."

"Are you opposed to dogs, as well?"

"Not against, just severely allergic," she countered.

Malik shook his head, saying, "Lady, you are a challenge."

The cold tone just might have been rude, but Veronica lost all perception when his warm eyes lingered on her for a moment. The man had the uncanny ability to make her feel offended and giddy at the same time. He was confusing the hell out of her. A small, possibly erotic tickle scurried through her even as he turned back to the water.

"Okay," he continued, "the opposite shore is miles away, there's only a few skinny trees near the house, and the surrounding homes aren't close. That's good because it means that a sniper would have to be on a boat."

Veronica was happy to see nothing on the water.

"I could put sensors out there, but the effectiveness would be limited. At normal sensitivity, a strong wind or small animal would set it off. The constant beeping would drive us, and the alarm company, crazy. On the other hand, the less sensitive setting could leave us susceptible."

She found herself focusing on the word *us*. She wasn't facing this threat alone, and this brought immeasurable comfort. She asked, "Do you really think someone is going to go through the water to get here? I know the last few days have been incredibly warm, but the lake is still freezing!"

Malik turned and met her gaze. "It's the way I'd come if I wanted to get you," he answered.

"Come on, Malik. What're the chances that a navy SEAL is after me? Last I heard, Special Forces guys didn't target women's clinics. I appreciate your thoroughness, however, I believe that the sensors will be sufficient."

"All right, Dr. Howell. No bars, fences or dogs." His cool tone matched hers.

Veronica became suspicious. "Malik, why do I feel like a huge *BUT* is about to come out of your mouth?" she asked.

A slight smile passed his lips before he said, "Because you're very perceptive, Doctor. Outside security shutters. They are very attractive and virtually impenetrable. The type I'm suggesting have no exterior locks that can be picked, and they can be operated electronically. Think about it, Dr. Howell, no more rocks or anything else through your windows."

"Are you talking about those things that cover some of the downtown businesses after hours?"

He nodded and said, "I know a wholesaler who can get you a variety of colors and styles at cost. It'll only enhance the beauty of your home."

"Dang, Malik. You sound like you get a kickback on each sell."

He laughed from deep in his belly. It was a full robust sound that had Veronica staring. She was sorry when his merriment ended. She realized that she could listen to this man express his enjoyment for a very long time.

Seemingly unaware of his effect on her, Malik said, "I

don't get any money, just the satisfaction of knowing I'm doing my job very well."

"Not just good, but very well, huh?"

"Yep," he answered, while rolling up and down on his toes.

"Well, okay. I'll get the shutters, provided that I can find some that'll match my house. Now that that issue's resolved, why don't you tell me what else is going to happen to my house today."

They went to sit on the living room couch, and Malik did tell her in nauseating detail. "The crew will be here any minute now, Dr. Howell. I imagine it'll take most of today to secure this place, and then tomorrow, we can hit the clinic. Everything should be done by Monday, so we won't interfere with your patients." He went on and on, and still, she wasn't prepared for the invasion of armed technicians. They came with a variety of weapons: screwdrivers, wire cutters, miles of cable, wrenches. They were like locusts—swarming through her house, crawling in her attic, eating away at her with annoying questions.

Veronica sat on the couch slightly shocked as she watched her home being transformed into a jail. As promised, they didn't put bars on her windows, but they did put on some type of coating. The technician explained how this would protect her even when the shutters were up because, when struck, the glass would capture the object, making it virtually bullet-proof. Another benefit, the technician told her, was that the glass shards wouldn't shatter and fall out. The most it would do is fracture and the coating would hold it intact.

Veronica laughed at his description, and from the look on his face, she could tell he thought she was strange. But heck, the man could have been describing her. Seeing all of these people in her house had her cracking inside, and only her skin was holding her together. As she sat on the sofa, her eyes were drawn to Malik who was examining a small security camera. *A first-class prison, and I have to live with the warden.*

Veronica almost went into convulsions when she saw a man with a camera headed toward her bathroom. She shot off the couch ready to defend her privacy and tackle the technician. Malik must have seen her expression because he intercepted her with an arm around her waist. "Relax, Dr. Howell," he said. "The man just has to use the facility. We're not going to put anything but coating and a sensor on the window in there. I promise."

"A sensor?" she questioned.

"Yes. If anyone tampers with the window, the alarm will be triggered."

It was too much. Her house was being filled with tapeworms, infested with parasites in the form of cameras, sensors, receivers and phone lines. The security devices were intimidating and endless.

Striving for physical comfort if not serenity, she changed out of her sweaty clothes. She glared at Malik and dared him to react when she came from her room wearing a short-sleeved blouse and khaki shorts.

He walked up, and she prepared herself to be teased. He surprised her by saying, "Why don't we go sit on the back porch?" Before they went outside, Malik looked around. He explained that he was making sure there were no crafts on the water or anything else suspicious. He had Veronica sit in the crook created by the house and deck while he sat in front of her at an angle never quite looking at her, always focused on the surroundings. "You looked like you could use some air, Dr. Howell. Don't worry, it just seems bad now. By the time they're done and have put everything back together, you'll notice very few changes."

Veronica nodded and tried to look around Malik to see the water, hoping it would calm her.

Malik slid a catalog in front of her and she jumped slightly. "Pick a shade," he ordered. "I can get the shutters installed today if I call the distributor within an hour."

Veronica flipped through the pages, trying to concentrate. She eventually picked a tan color that she hoped matched the trim on her house. Sitting back, she breathed deeply and focused on the little piece of green she could see just beyond Malik's shoulder. His next question jerked her upright.

"Do you have a lover?"

She shouted, "I beg your pardon!"

"Look, Dr. Howell, I'm not asking because I'm interested in the position. I want to know so I can be efficient at my job."

"Oh, you don't want to kill the wrong guy?" she questioned.

"Something like that if the person doing this is a guy."

"Oh, it's a man," she assured him.

He asked, "How do you know? Do you think women are incapable of violence?"

"Women are capable, but you know what the odds are," she responded. "Most serial killers and stalkers are men. Besides, my mystery caller has a male voice."

"The caller may be disguising his or her voice," he countered. "Also, you're a very unique person, Dr. Howell. It wouldn't surprise me one bit if anything about you defied the odds."

His words caused Veronica's mouth to close. There was a compliment hidden in there somewhere. She was sure of it.

Malik pressed his advantage by saying, "Regardless of the gender of your harasser, I need to know all the people who are close to you."

Veronica looked at him hard. After a moment, she began to comply. Her words came out slowly at first. "I've had relationships that fizzled once the men got tired of me rescheduling them so I could meet my obligations at the clinic. They all demanded time I couldn't give them."

"I'll need the names," Malik said.

Veronica laughed and said, "You're assuming I remember them. Anyway, my last real boyfriend was Neil Prosser, and he was a medical resident with me. Our relationship ended with the residency."

"How long ago was that?" Malik asked.

"About three years."

"How was it?" he questioned further.

"What?"

"The breakup, Dr. Howell. Were either of you angry when it ended?"

"Oh." Veronica looked down before saying, "No, being a resident was like being on a never-ending treadmill. Once the wheel stopped turning, we realized we had nothing in common." Veronica decided to tell the whole truth. "We occasionally call each other for...dates, but that's about it."

"Dates?" His voice rose slightly.

"Yes. Companionship and friendship."

His eyebrows lifted and a hint of a frown passed over his features.

Is he judging me? Veronica thought. *Does he think a male and female can't just have a platonic relationship?* Veronica sat a little straighter. *This man is starting to remind me of Mother.*

His tone was a bit harsh when he said, "I see. I'll need his contact information. When was the last...date?"

Something about his manner, the stiff way he held himself made her rethink her earlier assessment. *Is he jealous?* The idea was preposterous, and so was the jolt of pleasure that shot through her at the thought. She answered, "About three months ago." She told him the rest of Neil's information.

Malik pulled a small pad out of his back pocket and wrote until she was done. Then he looked at her, all business. "Anybody else I should know about? Any close friends besides Samantha, any groups that you meet with routinely?"

Veronica was about to shake her head, then she said, "There are some girlfriends I meet with the third Saturday of every month. Their names are Belinda Morris, Shane Smith, and you already know Sam."

He looked up and said, "Change it."

"Excuse me?"

"I said change it. The date. Any routine you have needs to be shaken up," he advised.

"But we've been doing this in the same place on the same day for years," Veronica protested. "Even my residency didn't stop it."

"Look. I'm not saying don't meet."

"Malik, it would be a huge inconvenience to my friends. All of us work. Shane is a social worker, Belinda is an executive at Microsoft, and you know Sam's a lawyer. We all have other important responsibilities, and we'd never find another time when we're all available."

He sighed and said in a very calm voice, "Dr. Howell, it is extremely important that we be unpredictable. That's why I have to insist that your group meet on a different day, at a different time."

"No," Veronica said, arms crossing, "I just don't see how I can ask my friends to rearrange their schedules."

Malik cut her off and said, "Okay. It's been a pleasure." He closed his notebook, stood and began walking away. She followed a few steps behind him as he moved through the house and outside the front door. He was in his car about to turn the key when she banged on the window. His eyes constantly scanned the neighborhood as he finished starting the car before rolling down the glass.

"What're you doing?" she asked.

He answered, "Leaving. I'll call Graham and he can take over."

Her perplexed look turned to anger. She said, "That's why you wouldn't take a check. You wanted to have the power to just leave."

Still focused on the surroundings, Malik shook his head. "That's not it at all, Dr. Howell. I told you up front this wouldn't work if you didn't listen to me."

"I listened very well. I just don't want to obey."

He reached to put the car in drive. A number of curse words went through her mind. She knew she couldn't let him leave so she yelled, "All right, all right! I'll change the date! I promise to play by your rules." She threw her arms up, turned and headed back to the house. After a few steps, she looked over her shoulder to make sure he followed. A growl of frustration bubbled in her throat, because she could have sworn she saw a ghost of a smile on his lips as he got out of the car.

Chapter 5

By Sunday afternoon, Veronica was questioning her pledge. She was mad and searching for the source of her anger, Malik. The tan, loose, linen shirt she wore over matching shorts ballooned as she rushed through the clinic. She was upset because Junior, her trusted guard since the clinic opened, had called her to say goodbye. Malik had fired his security firm, and Junior had been reassigned to another location. Veronica waded through the army of security technicians that had been crowding the clinic since early that morning.

She finally found him outside, talking to a guy on a ladder who was installing the same security shutters she now had at her house. Malik nodded in her direction, and then his gaze was away from her, sweeping rapidly around the perimeter. "I'll be just a minute," he said without looking at her. "Why don't you wait inside?" Then he continued his conversation with the technician. His command and easygoing attitude galled her, and the unmerciful sun, searing her forehead as she looked up at him didn't help. *Dang*. The back of her hand swept her face. Malik wasn't even sweating in his blue polo shirt and cargo-style shorts and here she was beginning to feel faint. Ignoring his request, she leaned against the brick building, trying to take advantage of the shade from the eaves and tapped her sandal-clad foot. Despite the cover, moisture continued pouring from her scalp and underarms. She noticed a man scrubbing away the graffiti and when she glanced back at Malik, her eyes were drawn to the bandage that still covered the tattoo. A wave of appreciation breezed through her, but it did nothing to alleviate her irritation.

Finally, Malik turned to her. She hissed, "May I speak to you for a moment, please?"

"Sure, but why don't we go inside," he suggested.

"I don't feel like it. Malik, it's safe! I'm surrounded by men because there are only two women in this work crew you have out here. I've watched you check the area countless times, and besides, I refuse to be a mole cooped up all day!" She stomped to the side of the building, and spun to see Malik following, his eyes scanning the area. "How dare you let Junior go!"

Malik stood at an angle in front of her, the brick at her back. He didn't look directly at her, but out and beyond. "He's too green," he said, shifting and gazing the other way.

"Stop moving around and look at me!" she ordered. He gave her a millisecond. He seemed impervious to her anger and that infuriated her even more.

Very calmly, he said, "We're outside. I have to be alert to the surroundings. We'd be much safer in your office. Shall we go there? My eyes would be only for you then."

That response threw her off balance. She decided the man would do just about anything to have his way. She countered,

"Why? So the tool-belted army crawling around in there can be entertained by our argument?"

A small grin appeared, then he said, "I'm really sorry about all this, but you know why I brought in the large crew."

"I know, I know," she answered. "You don't have to tell me this is for my benefit again." It was still disconcerting that his eyes fell everywhere but on her. She was determined not to let it faze her as she said, "Back to Junior. He has been here since I first opened the doors. Granted, I haven't been in business that long, but all of us have been here since the beginning. We are a family. Can't you train him or something?"

"That's not my function here," he said.

She expelled air that shot around the block and came back by the time she did a 360 on one foot. The move was elegant, and she noticed that Malik's eyes stopped roving until they met hers. He immediately returned to his routine.

She questioned him, "Are you a robot, Malik? Can't your precious rules be bent a little, not broken just bowed?"

His head shook and he said, "Absolutely not. My training and my gut have saved my life too many times."

She crossed her arms and glared at him before asking, "Tell me, what happens when the two conflict?"

He answered without hesitation, "The gut always wins, and neither of the two are telling me to waste precious time and resources on Junior."

She wanted to slap him. She did another pirouette, reminiscent of her stage days and stormed off.

Malik watched and followed until she was inside. Suddenly, he looked over his shoulder. He scanned the area. Nothing seemed out of the ordinary, yet something didn't feel right. He'd had that feeling most of the day. Malik walked the perimeter of the clinic, stepping over tools and around workers. Even though he saw nothing to cause alarm, something had his insides on full alert. He took a deep breath as if he could smell where the danger was coming from. All he got was a noseful of city air: car exhaust, dry dust, and burgers from the nearby McDonald's.

At the front doors, he stood and gazed around. His eyes stopped on a bum who was lying down near a closed car wash about fifty feet away. The man had been sprawled there when they arrived. Earlier, Malik had walked by him and said hi. He had breathed through his mouth to avoid the putrid smell. The man grunted and burrowed into his armpit. Not a threat, Malik had determined. The clinic was in the center of an economically depressed area and street people were a common sight. He came to the same conclusion again as he stood in front of the clinic. The bum probably wasn't the cause of his raised neck hairs. The man didn't look as if he'd moved since Malik had last approached him. Remaining on extreme alert, Malik backed into the clinic.

Shadow was quite impressed with himself, and he wasn't easily awed. Here he was, practically under Mr. Security's nose, and the fool didn't suspect him. Sure, his competition had sensed something was wrong, but he hadn't figured it out. It was exhilarating! Almost as much fun as courting Dr. Howell, but he wasn't surprised, because he was good. The best when he put his mind to it, and even though he'd had only a short amount of time, he'd put together one hell of a disguise.

Saturday night, he'd gone to a shabby secondhand store on Broadway and bought the worst clothes and shoes available. Then he'd lived on the street last night, pouring Mad Dog on himself, wallowing in garbage and eating breakfast bars he'd stashed in his pockets. He rolled around in filth, letting it fill his pores and scalp until he could barely stand to smell himself. He'd worried that the time hadn't been long enough to let the stench set in, but it'd worked.

He loved reconnaissance. That's what he'd told his associates in California: that he was going on a six-week recon mission to take care of old business. He remembered a former teacher saying that once you stop learning, you stop living. Well, he was crackling with life, burning up with the knowledge he was gaining about his prize and feeling like a king because he'd deceived his foe.

Thinking back, Shadow wished he had stopped Weasel Friday night. It truly surprised him that the nut had enough guts to strike while she was at home. Shadow had been watching from the kitchen window across the street. Dr. Howell's neighbors were nice enough to go on vacation, taking the family dog with them. When the mail began backing up in the mailbox, Shadow knew for sure that the people were gone. Being his clever self, he'd quickly picked the lock and slipped in the door of the nonsecure house. It was a perfect place to keep an eye on his honey and all those around her.

So he'd seen Weasel park down the street, and he'd watched the man case the home for a few minutes before throwing the large rock through the window. When nothing happened, the man came out from the car he'd hidden behind and tossed another rock into a different window. Again, he'd dashed behind the car. Shadow remembered being amused. *What did the nut expect? Dr. Howell to come out with guns blazing?* The man then left the car and disappeared around the side of the house. Shadow had been about to go and see what he was doing when he came back running and took off in his car. A moment later, Shadow had seen flames coming from the side of the house. He'd slapped the kitchen counter. Weasel would suffer a long, painful death if Dr. Howell were hurt. For the first time in his life, Shadow had been tempted to call the police. Dr. Howell's safety was paramount. He'd been so happy to see the officers arrive that he'd had a tiny urge to run out and thank them.

Shadow had anticipated that Mr. Security would try to secure the house, then the clinic. He'd watched until Saturday afternoon, and then he'd left to prepare himself. His hunch paid off when he'd seen the cars arrive from his vantage point on the ground early that morning. However, Shadow hadn't expected the man to try and build Fort Knox. *But hell*, he consoled himself, *an impenetrable system was a contradiction in terms*. He used a small pair of binoculars that he'd tucked into his waistband to watch the workers. He looked for anything that would give him an advantage like the one he'd discovered yesterday while watching the house being secured.

Whenever his mark poked her head out, his concentration wavered. She looked pretty upset a minute ago, storming back into the building after talking to Mr. Security. He must have made her angry, and Shadow whispered, "I'll take care of him for you, wife."

Wife? He chuckled at himself. He'd never had anything official, much less long-term, with any of his women. Why did that word slip out? "Maybe because it makes sense," he told himself. She wasn't like the others where his attention was temporary. "I have real feelings for her," he whispered. "Besides, she needs to be protected from the likes of Mr. Security." *Oh, yes. It felt right.* Dr. Howell was so special because she was meant to be with him. At least for the rest of her life.

* * *

Veronica was so irritated she called Samantha to vent. Her friend wasn't there, so she left a message, telling her to call the clinic. A couple of hours later, Samantha showed up. She breezed in wearing a tank top and light cotton pants, talking a mile a minute. "I heard your message on my way home from shopping and decided to stop by. Hey, did you ask Malik's guys to clean the graffiti?"

Veronica's head shook.

"Well, they are. Malik is quite a…" The sentence sputtered and died as Samantha looked hard at her friend. "Uh-oh, hon, what's wrong?"

"That…Neanderthal out there fired Junior," Veronica said. "His company reassigned him."

"Why?" Samantha asked.

Veronica repeated Malik's cryptic reasons.

Samantha said, "Roni, the man is the expert. Your safety is paramount here, and Junior's still working. It's not like he's out of a job." Samantha sat down in one of the two office chairs. "Stop glaring at me, Roni. You know I'm right. Girl, you are getting too frustrated. You need a good workout. Why don't you go home and dance or something?"

Geez, Veronica realized she hadn't danced since this mess started. She did it routinely all through medical school and her residency. Until two years ago, Veronica had lived in a small studio apartment. She would move the furniture aside, put in a compact disc to suit her mood, and dance until she was limp. During her residency, that took about fifteen minutes, considering how exhausted she was before she started.

"I can see you're thinking about it," Samantha said as she got up and turned on the radio. Soon an upbeat melody filled the room. Samantha and music didn't get along, and she knew it. She chased the elusive beat enthusiastically until Veronica held her side in laughter. Then her friend sprawled out in the chair, fatigued. Veronica wiped the tears from her eyes and lowered her head to her forearms that rested on the desk.

"Feel better?" her friend asked.

"Yes," Veronica admitted.

"I've done my good deed for the day then."

Malik found them that way when he entered the office after a brief knock. The first thing he noticed was the closed curtain, and then he took in the women. Samantha slouched in a chair and Dr. Howell lifted her head off the desk, a silly smile on her face. He found himself enjoying the expression. Dr. Howell looked relaxed, yet he knew his next request would bring the tension back. A part of him wanted to go, but duty wouldn't let him. He would leave no stone unturned, even if that same rock was eventually thrown at him.

He greeted them. "Hi, ladies."

Only Samantha responded.

"I hate to interrupt," he said, "but I've been mulling something over. You said you couldn't think of anyone who has a grudge against you, right?"

Dr. Howell nodded.

"About how many patients ask for help having a baby?" he asked.

Veronica answered, "Actually, not many. Most of the people who can afford the services go to bigger, more well-known clinics. My goal here isn't just to offer fertility treatments. It's to offer women who may not always get it the full gamut of quality medical services. I don't necessarily highlight any particular one of those services."

"Well, that supports the theory that I've been kicking around," Malik said. "I think someone is targeting you for specific reasons. I need to see your patient files."

Dr. Howell sat up straight, all laughter gone. She said, "No. Sam, will you please tell this man about doctor-patient confidentiality."

"She's got a point, Malik," Samantha said, turning her chair, so she was sitting between them.

Malik explained, "I'm not doing this to be nosy. The thought of reading all that medical jargon doesn't exactly thrill me. I'm looking for any clue that might lead to who's behind this." Malik's back rested against the closed door, and he crossed his arms. "Look, the person who is doing this is obviously ticked off about fertility." The word came out too harsh, and Malik saw the women exchange looks. "If you don't do enough treatments to be a blip on the radar, then it's logical that you've been singled out for personal reasons. Those files might hold the key or, at a minimum, some kind of lead."

Dr. Howell nodded and said, "Okay, your reasoning makes sense. I'll dig up and look at all the charts where I've done or recommended…the treatment."

Her avoidance of the word wasn't lost on Malik. Rather than focus on that, he said, "No offense, doctor, but I'm concerned that you may miss something important."

"Don't worry. I won't," she countered.

"Oh yeah. How much investigative training have you had?" he asked.

"Plenty. I can spot a disease from twenty paces away."

Malik sighed and stood away from the door while saying, "Doctor, we're not trying to diagnose an illness. You're going to fight me every step of the way, aren't you? Remember how we agreed that you would obey me?"

Malik saw Samantha's eyebrows rise. Her head swiveled to Dr. Howell, who said, "Well, excuse me, Malik. I draw the line at you being master when you ask me to break the law!"

"Oh, come now, Dr. Howell. I'm sure you've broken a rule or two in your day," he responded.

Samantha shot up as if she was making an objection in court. Dr. Howell's open mouth closed. With a raised hand, Samantha said, "I have a solution to this impasse. As your attorney, Roni, I'll do an in camera review of the records in questions. Malik, I've been a criminal attorney for many years, and you can rest assured that the records will be reviewed as if they contained exculpatory evidence in the trial of the century."

Malik nodded and said, "Okay, okay. You know Graham said you were one of the best. I can live with that compromise."

"Roni?" she said.

Veronica replied, "Oh, all right. Although I don't want anyone going through my charts, I suppose I can put up with you, Sam."

Malik reached behind him and opened the door before saying, "The sooner the better, ladies. Oh yeah. I just got a call from Sergeant Ross. She twisted some technician's arm and got him to analyze the material from your porch. It was definitely a shoe print, and the paint was mixed with other substances on the bottom of the shoe. There were traces of animal matter, things like feces, tissue and blood. Ross suggested the guy might be a farmer, work in a meat house, something like that. Think about it as you go through the files, ma'am."

Samantha rolled her eyes at him and said, "Get out of here before I hurt you, Malik. You better stop using that old-lady address with me."

After the door shut, the still-sitting Veronica said, "How come he jokes with you? I always get the serious bodyguard persona." Veronica knew that wasn't necessarily true, but she was feeling catty.

"Do I detect a hint of jealousy?" Samantha questioned. "Don't worry, Roni. He only has eyes for you. I just bring out the silly side of men. That's why I always end up with jokers like Nate. Sorry, did I bring that dreaded name up? Forget I said that."

Veronica didn't say anything at first. Samantha's ex-husband, Nathaniel, was one area where her friend couldn't be rational. Veronica decided to change the subject by saying, "See why we argued about fertility. The man doesn't even like to say the word."

"I saw," Samantha acknowledged. "You weren't exaggerating. However, I don't think it lessens his effectiveness. I'm sure the navy trained him to separate his feelings from the job."

The phone rang.

Both women looked at it, sitting in the middle of the desk. Veronica said, "That's strange. Everyone knows we're closed on Sunday." She lifted the cordless receiver on the third ring. "Hello, Total Health Women's Clinic."

"You should be stoned to death for breaking up families."

Veronica's hand tightened on the receiver. She immediately recognized the voice as her harasser. Glancing up, she saw Samantha and Malik come through the doorway. *When had Sam left?*

"Next time the rocks I throw through your windows will pummel your body. I'll use them to crush you and then you will be stopped."

Fury charged into Veronica so quick and hard that she felt

dizzy. Striving for balance, her free hand gripped the edge of her desk and in a trembling voice, she said, "You coward. You don't have the guts to throw anything at me, face-to-face. You're a snake who won't be able to hide much longer. I have security, and they're going to find out who…" Veronica's head reared back, and she pulled the phone from her ear. She focused on Malik and Samantha. "He hung up." The two looked at each other, and Veronica saw something pass between them. "What?"

Samantha responded, "Roni, honey, you're shaking. Let me have the phone."

Her friend reached across the desk and pulled the receiver from her hand. Malik took it, pressed some buttons and listened.

"Honey, you told him about Malik. He probably hung up because he thinks the phones are bugged," Samantha told her.

Irritation and shame shot through Veronica. She barely noticed Malik putting the phone down. Her chin sank to her chest and she whispered a few choice words. Then she centered on Malik. "Tell me the line's tapped and we got him."

Malik shrugged, saying, "Sorry, Dr. Howell. They will be by the end of the day. If it's any consolation, I don't think the conversation was long enough to trace anyway. I tried *69, but the number's unlisted." His tone was a unique mix of professionalism and sympathy. For some reason, it only made Veronica feel worse. Head lowered to her desk, she groaned.

Chapter 6

That evening, Veronica met Carl Rourke, a handsome, red-headed giant with muscles like the Incredible Hulk. Malik explained that Carl would be with her whenever he couldn't be there. Veronica couldn't help wondering about his motivation. Did Malik choose Carl because of her initial comments about Malik's size and the guy in *The Green Mile*? Fearing he'd laugh at her, she wasn't brave enough to ask. Malik disappeared and came back with a suitcase he stowed in the guest room.

The next morning, Veronica discovered that Carl also doubled as the chauffeur, which sparked a terse argument. It ended when Malik reminded her that he had already explained that a driver would be necessary on Friday night. The night she'd enjoyed the brandy too much. One of the details that apparently had slipped her mind. So Malik told her again that they needed to be as unpredictable as possible. Arrive and leave at different times, out of different exits, varied routes to and from work. Veronica's irritation shifted to herself when she remembered her actions on the phone yesterday. She resorted to praying that this would soon end because someone else running her life was making her crazy, and it had barely been three days.

As soon as they reached the clinic, Malik disappeared again. Plain stubbornness prevented Veronica from asking his whereabouts. A busy Monday morning helped keep the questions at bay.

Veronica balanced on a rolling stool, smoothing out the blue slacks she wore beneath her lab coat, and looked at the girl perched on the examination table. She was proud of Deirdra. The young woman's drug rehabilitation counselor had first introduced them a year ago. Back then, she'd been Olive Oyl thin, and the crooks of her legs and bends of her elbows had been swollen and full of needle tracks. Now, the only reminder of her addiction was dark marks in those areas. Her body was fit and sculpted with muscles. The tight nylon pants she wore into the clinic had something to cling to that had nothing to do with skin and bones. And her hair was beautiful. Small braids all over her head created a wonderful cascading halo that ended in the middle of her back. It was nothing like the ruins of a perm that she'd come in with a year ago: hair different lengths, clinging sloppily to her head.

The young woman was doing well. She was working at a local grocery store and had recently moved from the rehabilitation center into her own apartment. From Deirdra's latest question, she was apparently ready to reactivate other areas of her life, as well.

"Look, Doc. Stop looking so shocked. I'm sure I'm not the first one who's asked for the pill, and *pow*—" the woman shoved a card in her face "—full medical coverage and benefits. I'm past probation with Safeway."

"Congratulations," Veronica said, hugging her. "No, you're not the first to request birth control. You just caught me off guard." She'd just completed Deirdra's yearly physical, and the young woman was still sitting on the examination table putting on her shirt. Deirdra was smart. Even at her worst, she'd never shared needles and had avoided diseases like AIDS and hepatitis that had killed the majority of her friends. She was strong willed and that went well with her now-healed strong body. Deirdra had beaten the odds, and Veronica held the young woman in high esteem.

"Caught me off guard, too, Doc," Deirdra admitted. "There was a time when brothers like Roy wouldn't of given me the time of day. I'd beat myself up too much." The shy smile was endearing on the young woman. She looked at Veronica, "But I still made him work his butt off before I gave up the digits, and now that he's shown me the paper, proving that he's disease free, well, let's just say I'm ready to give him something else. So how about a prescription 'cause I'm trying to be a wife, not somebody's baby's momma."

Veronica couldn't hold back the laughter. Deirdra joined her and stumbled as she got up to retrieve her pants. She accidentally pushed over the chair her jeans were sitting on. There was a very loud bang that had both women giggling harder. After a brief knock, Malik entered the room. Veronica gasped, surprised he was back; and Deirdra yelped, holding her pants in front of her partially nude body.

"Sorry, ladies," he apologized. "I'm just making sure that everything is okay." He left as quickly as he appeared.

"Who was that, Doc?" Deirdra said, lowering her pants.

"Malik. He's helping us out with security," Veronica answered.

"Well, he scared the crap out of me, but that didn't stop a sista from noticing he's a hunk, and that Southern accent is kinda tight, ya know?"

Veronica did. The man could pour it on when he wanted to. Thank goodness he didn't use that voice too often.

Deirdra kept talking. "His plain pants and long-sleeved shirt are beyond boring, but he still looks like he should come with a health warning and one of those belts."

Veronica's head tipped sideways.

"Ya know, Doc, one of those medieval things they used to lock the girls' goodies up," she explained.

Biting her lip didn't hold back Veronica's laughter. Still, she managed to say, "A chastity belt?"

"Yeah, that's it. He looks like he could have a few babies' mommas out there somewhere."

That thought stopped the laughter. Veronica's head jerked to her patient. The young woman put a leg in her pants and didn't see Veronica's reaction. She continued chatting. "I saw him in the lobby and just assumed he was waiting for somebody." She finished snapping her pants and looked at Veronica before saying, "You said he's here for security—what happened to Junior? He was nice."

"I know. I miss him, too," Veronica said.

"Hey, Doc, you're not in trouble, are you?" the young woman asked.

"No, everything's fine, Deirdra. Here's your scrip. Watch yourself and call me if there are any problems."

"All right, but you take care of yourself, Doc. Stay next to the hunk and I predict you'll be okay. Just don't let him make you a baby's momma," her patient teased.

"Deirdra! Get out of here before I grab a tongue depressor or something and hurt you."

With a look that contained more smirk than concern, Deirdre waved bye and left the room.

The door barely closed before Malik opened it, saying, "I wanted to apologize again. I heard lots of noise coming from in here, and then, the bang. I thought I should check it out. I hope I didn't offend anyone."

"Do you have any children?" After seeing the look on his face, Veronica wished she could rewind the question back into her mouth.

His expression went from surprise to blank. Then in a neutral voice he said, "No, why do you ask?"

Alice came in the room and said, "Hi, Malik."

"Hi, head nurse," he responded.

Alice's giggle was so girlish that Veronica just stared. *Did every woman turn to mush around this man?*

"Dr. Roni, your next appointment is here. I put her in room Two. Here's the chart. Bye, Malik." Alice actually wiggled her fingers at him.

That evening, Veronica and Malik were the last to leave the building. Nothing was said as he watched her set the alarm. The process was still new to her, and it took a couple of tries to get it right. Carl pulled up just as they opened the back door. Malik must have summoned him with the cell phone.

"Um, excellent timing," Veronica murmured. At first, she felt offended when Malik didn't offer to open her car door until she remembered that he liked to keep his hands free at all times. With her protector standing directly behind her, she got in the car. Malik quickly followed, and they rode home in silence.

Once inside the house, Veronica turned off the alarm, and

Malik did a perimeter check. She fixed herself a cup of tea, and Malik leaned into the doorway. She looked at him and instinctively knew her reprieve was about to end.

He confirmed her suspicions by saying, "Why'd you ask if I had kids, Dr. Howell?"

She shrugged in what she hoped was a nonchalant gesture and said, "No reason. I was just curious." Before he could ask another question, Veronica said, "Where do you keep disappearing to?"

Malik didn't answer until she looked at him. Veronica supposed that was his way of letting her know he was very aware of the subject change. Finally, he spoke. "I've been pounding the pavement. Why didn't you tell me you had a block watch?"

Veronica responded, "It never occurred to me to mention it. I went to a meeting, and I was the only one there besides the poor person hosting it."

"That doesn't surprise me," he commented. "Your neighbors weren't very supportive when I went knocking door to door."

Veronica paused, somewhere between horrified and happy. She didn't relish the idea of everyone knowing her business, but then again, the more alert eyes the better. "Isn't that what police are for?" she still asked.

"Yes. Sergeant Ross actually had a uniformed officer knock on the doors of a few of the houses around you, and she came up with zero. I just thought I'd double-check. A kid on a bike saw a white guy running from your house right before the fire started. He watched the man get into a tan car. A police artist is going to do a sketch."

Veronica was elated. She said, "Geez, maybe this is going to end."

Malik said, "Don't worry, Dr. Howell. I'll definitely end this one way or another."

* * *

Malik woke before sunrise on Friday morning. Looking at his watch, he knew it would be about a half hour before Dr. Howell's clock would buzz, vibrating the whole house. The woman must sleep like the dead because her alarm was loud enough to stir an entire graveyard. As time went by, they'd settled into some sort of routine. They would both get up with her loud alarm, and he would immediately check the house, then head for the guest bathroom while she put on a robe and headed to the kitchen. They usually met in the hallway and exchanged mumbled greetings. Malik would quickly shower, eat something light, and then wait for her to get ready.

While he waited or had idle time during the day, he couldn't help noticing things about her that he thought he didn't necessarily want to know. Like her knack for misplacing things, especially in the morning when she was in a rush. She'd search frantically for a shoe, an earring, a key, until inevitably, he was drawn into the hunt. Maybe due to the chaos of his early years, he was an incurable neat freak. He should have been annoyed by her behavior, totally exasperated by the same routine almost every morning, but instead, he found it endearing.

The same way he found it appealing to watch her work. He'd be at the computer or doing a security check at the house or the clinic, and he'd see her concentrating: eyes wide and focused behind the glasses, mouth slightly parted, and occasionally a forefinger would lift to tap those lips. He even knew when she was fatigued or stressed because her right hand would run down the front of her face. Living with her provided an intimacy that was hard not to respond to. Malik began to doubt if he was up to the task of being an impersonal bodyguard.

He didn't ponder the issue long because right on time, Dr. Howell's alarm screeched. She came stumbling out of her room and was startled by the fully dressed Malik standing by the coffeepot. "I'm sorry," Malik said as he reached out to steady her. He'd already checked the house and taken his shower. Now, he stood before Dr. Howell dressed in his standard uniform, pressed Dockers and a white shirt.

Still sleepy, Veronica stared at the forearms bracing her and had the strangest urge to caress them. That thought jerked her awake.

Malik misunderstood. "Oh, I'm sorry," he said, as he withdrew his arms and rolled his sleeves down.

Veronica hadn't been thinking about, or looking at the tattoo.

Malik continued talking. "I was up earlier, so I took the liberty of making your coffee. No sugar with a drop of milk, right?"

Another shock to Veronica's morning brain: Malik had watched closely enough to notice how she preferred her morning beverage. She managed to say, "Thanks, Malik. I'm sure it's perfect." Veronica took the cup from his outstretched hand and was touched by the fact that he'd put it in her favorite mug that displayed a large, yellow smiley face. Veronica drifted back to her bathroom, and thoroughly enjoyed drinking coffee in the shower while the spray pelted her back, killing the last vestiges of sleep.

On the drive to the clinic, the heat wave broke and rain thundered against the car. "It's raining," announced the radio disc jockey, as if they didn't know. "Gray clouds are coming by the thousands to be trapped in the teeth of the Olympic and Cascade Mountains. It might be time to move to Phoenix, folks, or at least take a vacation because we're in for a wet one."

Veronica sat behind Carl, and she tapped his seat. "My God, could you change the station?"

"Sure thing, Dr. Howell, but I thought you liked talk radio," he responded. Soon smooth jazz filled the car, competing with the sound of the hammering rain. Veronica heard Carl yell, "Dang, hold on," right before her body was flung forward. The seat belt tightened, and she was inches from slamming into the back of the driver's seat when she was jerked backward just as quickly. She tried to catch her breath, but Malik, who sat next to her, put his hand on her nylon-covered thigh. It made her spasm more. Veronica breathed deeply, suffering her body's reaction to the intense pleasure that the warm pressure of his hand brought.

"Sorry, folks," Carl said, twisting to them before turning back to the road. "It looks like we have traffic."

Veronica was so lost in the hand moving ever so slightly against her leg, she wasn't sure what Carl was talking about.

"Are you all right?" Malik asked and took his hand away. *How dare he,* her heart protested. She was reaching out to put it back against her quivering flesh when common sense intervened. Wide-eyed, she stared into Malik's puzzled face. "Dr. Howell, are you okay?"

"Yes, yes, I'm fine. I was just…caught off guard," Veronica answered, looking away from his concerned eyes, attempting to regain her equilibrium. She noticed that her navy-colored skirt was bunched around her thighs. She wiggled while she straightened it. Glancing up, her face burned when she saw that Malik was still watching her, his face blank. The moment was very awkward, and Veronica's frazzled brain tried to cover it with conversation. "I don't get it. Seattle has got to be the wettest city in the world, and people always act like they can't drive when the first rain hits."

Malik's eyes lifted to her face. "It's the oil," he finally said.

"What?" she said.

He explained, "Cars leak, the rain comes, and the roads are slick until the oil gets washed away."

"Malik…" She tried sarcasm to alleviate the arousal. "I really didn't expect an explanation."

"Oh?" he responded. "I thought that's why you asked." His crooked smile returned the flame to Veronica's overheated senses. Without answering, she turned to the traffic and breathed deeply. No one spoke until they reached the clinic.

At the office, Veronica tried not to let the weather affect her mood, but she kept thinking that she'd missed Seattle's two weeks of sunshine, and it was probably gone until next year. Also, if she were truly honest with herself, she was upset over her reaction to Malik's touch. Afraid of thinking about that too much, she forced herself to be happy and upbeat at the clinic. Still, she spent what little free time she had at her desk behind closed doors.

Around noon, Veronica had just completed a routine physical on a middle-aged woman and was walking to her office when she saw Malik move his head oddly. She realized he was listening intently to his earpiece, the connection between him and the others watching the building. He moved to the front door, and Veronica hung back, glancing around the corner. She sighed in frustration when she saw who was causing all the ruckus. It was Mr. Tigrai, a man trying to hold on to his little girl, even though she was twenty-two years old. He demanded to see the woman in charge, and since that would be her, Veronica slid in front of Malik.

"It's okay, Malik," she said. "Mr. Tigrai's daughter is a patient. I'll talk to him in my office."

Malik stepped around Veronica, putting himself between her and Mr. Tigrai. "Not until he goes through the metal detector," he demanded. With a huff, the tall, thin man walked through the device Veronica hated seeing at the clinic's entrance.

Inside her office, Veronica sat behind her desk and rested her palms on the polished wood. Mr. Tigrai ignored her offer of a seat. She looked beyond his scowl to see Malik standing quietly by the closed door. Swallowing her irritation, she focused on the angry man in front of her.

Veronica interrupted the tirade by saying, "Your daughter is an adult, Mr. Tigrai."

He yelled, "Who says so? I provide her support, woman!"

The man refused to address her as doctor. She told him, "She can receive services without your consent."

"You have no right. I am her father!" His voice rose even higher.

Veronica informed him, "The law says I can do this, Mr. Tigrai. I have explained this to you more than once."

Veronica sat straighter as Mr. Tigrai leaned over her desk. The next thing she knew, Malik was standing next to Mr. Tigrai saying, "Excuse me." The angry man didn't even glance in his direction. If Veronica weren't so upset, she would have been amused. She doubted that Malik had ever been ignored so blatantly. He tried again, "Excuse me, sir, but this can be dealt with in a better way."

Mr. Tigrai continued fussing, getting louder and louder. Veronica kept her face wooden, letting the irate man have his say. She still sat straight and tall despite the finger waving inches from her face.

Malik snatched the offensive digit out of the air and

twisted Mr. Tigrai's arm behind his back. His hand tightly gripped his victim's elbow, and Veronica knew that a small move up would break Mr. Tigrai's arm. "Malik—" she jumped from her chair "—I can handle this!"

"I'll sue you," the angry man hissed.

"You're assuming a lot, aren't you?" Malik questioned. "It may be your family suing on your behalf. Dr. Howell, the human body has two hundred and six bones, right?"

She answered, "Yes. Malik, let the man go."

He ignored her order and said, "That's a heck of a lot, mister, but I'll take the time to break each and every one if you don't apologize." He squeezed the elbow. "Another inch and we'll only have two hundred and five to go. Ever had anything broken before?"

"I'm sorry," the man grunted out.

Malik released him and smoothed out Mr. Tigrai's suit. "Now, if there's a misunderstanding, I know you two can discuss it amicably."

The man refused to look in Veronica's direction as he said. "I have nothing to say to that woman. I will talk to my daughter." Malik escorted the man out of the clinic.

Veronica glared at Malik from her office door. She moved aside when he came back so he could enter. Then she closed the door behind him before leaning against it. "I was handling it, Malik," she said.

"Yes, you told me. What was that all about?" he asked.

"His daughter's twenty-two and likes the ways of America better than Ethiopia. He can't control her so he tries to manage those around her. He usually fusses for a little while and then he leaves. I had it handled."

"All right. Next time, I'll let him poke your eye out with his bony finger."

Veronica's grimace became more severe. Deep down, part of her was happy he'd been there. Although she wouldn't admit it to Malik, Mr. Tigrai had been more animated than usual. But, darn it, she felt cheated somehow because she hadn't faced the man by herself. "I doubt that would have happened. In the future, please wait until I ask for your help," she instructed.

"Yes, ma'am," he answered.

Although he didn't smile, Veronica felt as though he was humoring her. His next question confirmed her suspicions. "Do I have your permission to let Graham investigate Mr. Tigrai?"

Head held high, she replied, "Do what you must. For the record, I think it's a waste of time."

She moved from the door so he could leave. As he left, she remembered how he'd looked holding Mr. Tigrai's arm. She'd expected to see rage, not a blank face. He maintained no expression even when the man was humiliated. She expected mockery at the very least. He was in complete control and it was a little frightening.

Half of Alice's body entered the office, and she said, "I saw Malik showing Mr. Tigrai the door. Are you all right?"

Veronica answered, "Yes. It was the same old routine."

"Good. Malik said something to him right before he left, and from the look on his face, I don't think he'll be back. The man looked terrified." Alice started to close the door and suddenly stopped, saying, "Hey, you know, the song is right."

"What?"

Alice sang the classic that played softly over the office system. "The morning showers have stopped, and the sun is making a strong comeback," a smiling Alice said as she shut the door.

"Fickle Seattle weather," Veronica uttered, really cursing the tingle she felt as she remembered the morning ride to the clinic. She went to the window to feel the sun. She expected to hear Malik shouting "No" when she lifted the blinds slightly. The bright sunlight slipped through, causing her to blink furiously.

The sliver of light wasn't enough.

She wanted to be outside, without boundaries. Releasing the blind, she glanced at her watch and realized that she had about a half hour before her next patient. Starbucks sat just across the street, and a caffeine jolt sounded really good to her right now. Besides, nothing had happened since Malik had shown up. Probably, whoever was bothering her had seen that she was well protected and given up. Her hand was running down her face when she heard a soft knock.

Malik opened the door and said, "Alice says your patient is here." He closed the door.

Darn, she was early. Maybe this is the Lord's way of telling me no. She did allow herself one more visit to the window, where she lifted the blinds up about halfway. She felt more than the sun on her face. "It's my imagination. No one is looking at me." The whispered words didn't stop her neck hairs from rising. She looked around seeing nothing out of the ordinary, yet she still felt as though she was in a low budget, horror movie with the music getting louder and louder. Right on cue, she recoiled as something smashed against the window.

Shadow praised himself for his diligence. He wasn't wasting time by continuing to follow Dr. Howell. He felt very close to her, beyond affectionate, as if he was inside her and could predict her moves. She was a beautiful bird, not meant for Mr. Security's captivity. It was only a matter of time before she came to him. As he watched her peek out the window the second time, he felt her; licking his lips, he could almost taste the expression on her face. Having her aware of him was a heady experience. And he believed he truly was what made her tremble, not that bumbling Weasel with his sloppy pranks. He watched Dr. Howell look around and he whispered, "Don't give in to second thoughts. Come on, baby, come to me. I'm ready for us to be together, as well."

Their psychic connection was interrupted. Some kid egged the building. Again Shadow praised himself for not swooping in and destroying the boy. He played it cool as he watched Mr. Security storm from the entrance and catch the kid after a brief chase. The man handled the boy as if he was a fly, managing to survey the area and drag the kid into the clinic at the same time. Then Shadow caught something that had him cursing. Too bad Mr. Security didn't know what he was looking for, because they weren't alone. Weasel slipped out of Starbucks with a snide smile on his face. The death of the special moment rested squarely on Weasel's shoulders.

Chapter 7

The kid looked about fourteen to Malik, and he was tough. Still, he was no match for Sergeant Ross. Malik had called her as soon as he'd dragged the kid back to the clinic. Fifteen minutes later, she was there, reading the boy his Miranda rights. All the kid would say was, "A middle-aged white guy gave me twenty bucks to egg the building."

The sergeant's eyebrows rose before she said, "You better tell me something. You've got warrants, kid, so we're going to lock you up. We just put a whole bunch of gangbangers in juvy last night. It's not a pleasant place right now, and it would be unfortunate if you were put in the wrong cell."

The boy's hard eyes shifted from side to side a few times. Then, he said, "Look, if I help you, I get to keep all the money and you put me in a red cell, okay?"

Red. Malik wasn't surprised the kid was a Blood gang member, considering he was wearing enough red to be mistaken for a Coke can. Even his sunglasses were tinted with the bright color, making the brown skin around his eyes orange.

"Help me how?" Sergeant Ross's arms crossed her chest.

The boy started talking fast. "The guy said I could have twenty more if I did it right. I'm supposed to pick it up under a big rock at this phone booth. I figured, even if he stiffed me, I'd still be up $20 bucks just for throwing some dumb eggs." The kid dug in his pocket and handed Sergeant Ross a dirty scrap of paper, which she wouldn't accept until she put on rubber gloves that she retrieved from her purse. Malik looked over the sergeant's shoulder to see street names written on the paper.

"'Twenty-six and Jackson,'" Sergeant Ross read out loud. "That's about three blocks away." She asked a uniformed officer to get her briefcase from her car. When the officer returned, she took a manila folder from the case and pulled out a photograph, which she studied before handing it to Malik.

He stared at the picture of the writing that had been left on Dr. Howell's kitchen door, then his eyes shifted to the note that was still in Sergeant Ross's hand and he commented. "Different material was used as a writing utensil, but both of these could have been generated by the same person. Both are printed, and look at the capital *T*s, they sort of slant the same way."

Sergeant Ross nodded and put the scrap of paper in a plastic bag she'd retrieved from her briefcase. "Maybe the techs can figure it out," she said.

Leaving the clinic protected by four uniformed officers and two of his guards, Malik left Dr. Howell to her patients and drove to the phone booth with Sergeant Ross and the kid.

Sergeant Ross parked the car about twenty yards away and turned to the boy who sat in the security-locked backseat. "See any one you recognize?" she asked.

Glancing around, the kid shook his head.

"I'll go and you watch junior, Malik," she said. Still wearing the latex gloves, Sergeant Ross left the car. She was back in two minutes, waving the twenty. Using the money as incentive, she continued to question the boy, mainly about the appearance of the man.

Frustrated, the kid almost shouted, "I don't know what he looked like. He had on sunglasses and a baseball cap. I already told you he was a white guy with a little gut. He asked me and I said, 'sure.' Then he left. Can I just have the money?"

"Nope. It's evidence. There might be fingerprints on it, but I will make sure you're put in a red cell," Sergeant Ross said, then she radioed one of the officers to come book the kid. After the boy was gone, she turned to Malik. "It's a real long shot, but I'm going to fingerprint the door handle of the phone booth and a few other choice spots. I'll have to take the rock and money to the lab, though. The techs will have to use chemicals on the rock's porous surface to see if there's a print. By the way, they didn't find anything usable on the rocks thrown through Dr. Howell's windows."

Malik nodded and said, "Mind if I look around?"

"Nope. Just wear the rubbers and stay out of my way." She handed him the latex.

Malik watched Sergeant Ross spread the messy, black fingerprint powder, hoping it would make an invisible print appear. Glancing around the booth, he saw nothing out of order except the soccer-ball-size rock resting in the far right corner. Malik walked around the perimeter, seeing only street grime and dust. He wandered over to a nearby trash can and peered in while holding his breath against the smell. Dented and multicolored from various forms of decomposing garbage, the metal can was half-full. *Nothing. The perp was here; he had to leave something.* A white flash on the side of the can caught Malik's eye. He picked up the crumpled piece of paper and opened it to discover it was a list of some sort and a piece was missing. He went back to the car and got the bagged note from Sergeant Ross's briefcase. Holding both up, he compared the writing and tear. They didn't seem to fit together, yet the writing on both notes was similar.

He walked back to the phone booth and said, "Hey, Ross, what do you think? I found this by the garbage can."

He held the items up, and she stared intently, reading the writing on the larger paper, "Milk, bread, wheat thins, cotton balls, Depend diapers?" She looked at Malik. "Why's he buying adult diapers?"

Malik shrugged, "Maybe he has a bladder problem."

"Could be. So, we should be looking for a guy with a wet spot, huh?" she asked.

Malik snorted and said, "We're in the inner city, Ross. I don't think that would narrow it down much."

The sergeant made a similar noise while nodding. Then, she said, "Well, the writing looks comparable, but it's not the same sheet of paper. I should have another plastic bag in my glove box. Put it all in my briefcase, and I'll have it analyzed. If it is the same writing, this guy is detail oriented. He could have just told the kid the address."

Malik agreed. "When the lab guys are done, I want a copy of both pieces of paper. Maybe Dr. Howell or somebody will recognize the handwriting," he said.

Malik searched a little longer, then told Sergeant Ross he

was walking to the clinic. Once there, he checked with his men, gave Dr. Howell an update, and then began asking questions at the surrounding businesses by himself. As he listened to everyone in the Starbucks, McDonald's, car wash and gas station tell him that no one had noticed anything, he reflected that Dr. Howell was a trooper. She'd had one hell of a scare, but she didn't let it interfere with her day. She was in the clinic, handling her last few patients as if nothing had happened.

Everyone had gone except Alice and his men by the time he finished. Alice sat at the receptionist's desk with her arms crossed. "Good," she said, standing up, "I can leave now. Make Dr. Roni rest. She's in there reading medical updates as if she didn't get the crapola scared out of her today."

Malik entered her office to the sight of her reading. Her lips were slightly parted and she tapped them with the long forefinger of her left hand. Her right hand was spread out like a delicate vine, shadowing the material holding her concentration. Glasses pushed up on her nose only enhanced the sexy rhythm of her eyes as they trekked across the page. Malik's greeting died in his throat as he watched her. That was the weird thing about Dr. Howell. His walls were high to fend off the attraction, yet often his emotions jumped the fence and caught him completely off guard.

She looked up and said, "Find out anything new?"

"Not yet, but we will. Ready to go?" he asked.

She nodded, took off the glasses, and silently prepared to leave.

Sunday, Malik found his respect growing by the minute. If nothing else, the woman had stamina. She maintained her own practice and still took the time to help out at Harborlake, the best trauma center in Washington State. According to Dr. Howell, summer in Seattle turned hospital emergency rooms into MASH units. "Increased heat brings increased violence," she'd said, "not to mention all the festivals. There's Seafair, Bumper Shoot, The Torchlight Parade, and Soulfest to name a few. The system gets flooded, and that's why I agreed to help out just about every other weekend for two months." So, they were slated to spend Saturday and Sunday at Harbor-lake.

Fortunately, it was such a big hospital that the administrative officials didn't even stutter when they found out Dr. Howell came with her own posse. In fact, they were relieved since it meant less liability if something happened to her on their premises. And given that the place was a maze of secret doors and elevators, it was a distinct possibility that a nut could reach Dr. Howell.

Also, it didn't help that every other person spoke a different language, making Malik feel as though he was at the Tower of Babel. A kidnapping plot could be occurring right under his nose, and he would have no idea. It was hellish trying to keep abreast of things in the middle of controlled chaos. His stomach was in knots, even though he had Carl and two other experienced guys stationed near the closest entrances.

The ambulance wail was constant, making silence foreign by Sunday afternoon. He bet the staff would fall in shock if it were suddenly quiet. In his periphery, he acknowledged another stretcher whizzing past. He focused more when he saw Dr. Howell rush to the old woman lying there. She would have captured his attention even if it weren't his job. Underneath her open lab coat, she wore a formfitting tunic, over a skirt that stopped right above her knees. Both were auburn and brought out the richness of her skin. She was confident in her element. He couldn't imagine her being anything other than self-assured. She quickly examined the woman, who looked pretty bad to Malik, then she immediately began shouting orders and led the way into the examination room. As Malik continued his visual sweep, he noticed two police officers standing near.

"It's a shame," one of them said, "kids who starve and beat their parent like that should be shot."

"I agree." The other officer shook his head. "Unfortunately, elder abuse is on the rise. Work all your life and your reward is to be dogged by your kids."

Malik whispered a short prayer that he knew was answered when he saw Dr. Howell come out some time later. Although she was red eyed and ashen, she smiled when she spoke to the policemen. Malik heard one of the officers tell her that he was relieved it would be an assault charge, instead of murder.

By the end of the day, Malik had suppressed the incident. A feat made easier when Sergeant Ross brought photocopies of the writing samples to Dr. Howell's house. "The lab guys are still going over this, but I think it's the same handwriting," she said. Dr. Howell didn't recognize it. Malik used her fax to send a copy to Samantha, so she would have it when she went through the files at the clinic.

That evening, Dr. Howell's crying reminded him of the elderly woman. He'd knocked on her bedroom door when he'd first heard her and she'd said, "Go away, Malik." When he'd pressed and asked if there was something he could do to help, she'd said, "No, I...I'm just releasing the bad feelings I have from the day."

The encounter through the door had surprised him. Sure,

she'd been quiet on the way home, but he'd attributed it to the fact that the last few days had been stressful. Harborlake was a rough trauma center, and she'd done her residency there. Why didn't she have impenetrable walls against the inevitable ugliness and suffering?

Speaking of barriers, his were slipping. He felt her tears as he lay down on his couch bed. They washed the dust off a memory of another woman crying in his arms, those extremely rare times when his mother showed weakness. She would climb into his narrow bed weeping and saying she was sorry. Young Malik didn't understand her tears, didn't fully comprehend why she was apologizing. He did know that his momma was hurting, so he'd wrap his thin arms around her neck, press his small hands to the sides of her face and whisper, "It's all right, Momma." He'd been a scared little boy who knew he had to be strong, just as now he knew he had to be there for Dr. Howell. That knowledge didn't make deciding what to do any easier. Go to her or stay away as she'd told him to do? Time provided the answer when the noise quieted and sleep finally came to Malik.

Monday evening, Veronica sat in a gold pantsuit at a table in Mortons of Chicago with her three girl friends: Samantha, Belinda and Shane. She'd followed Malik's suggestion that they meet at the popular steak house once he told her there were only two ways in and out. He sat at a separate table, in his khakis and white shirt, where he could see the women and the main entrance. He had a guard stationed at the other door located just outside the kitchen.

Samantha had made the arrangements and had given everyone a skeleton version of why there had to be a change in time, place and day. Still, the women pummeled the tired

Veronica with questions. She was exhausted, but no way would she miss this outing with friends.

Belinda was the most petite and the most vocal. According to Samantha, who had gone to college with her, she'd always been that way. The two had met during a protest of the university's involvement with apartheid South Africa. Waving a small hand, and being anything but inconspicuous, Belinda asked, "Now, which table is he sitting at? The white guy behind us, or the big, strong brother who looks like he would've cost a pretty penny back in the day? And he's got good teeth, too. Look at him handle his meat."

Veronica blushed and looked at the three-quarters of Malik's face that was visible. If he heard, he deserved an Oscar because he was stone-faced as he looked around the restaurant. Veronica clutched the cloth napkin in her hand and contemplated gagging her loud friend with it. She could use Belinda's long hair to hold the gag in place for the rest of the evening.

Samantha answered the question. "Oh, that's him, and considering their proximity to each other, since he is her houseguest, I suggest we ask Roni all questions about his abilities, meat handling or otherwise."

Veronica gasped, eyes flying to Malik again. He sipped from his water glass, his face blank. She couldn't help chuckling with the other ladies as she wondered if his ears were burning. Hers were. If Samantha didn't behave, she'd muzzle her, too. If she yanked her curls straight, Samantha's hair should be long enough to use as rope.

Shane joined the fray, shifting her heavyset frame in the large chair. "It's his body that's got me starstruck. It's always been a fantasy of mine to be completely covered in chocolate. I imagine it feels pretty secure, huh, Veronica?" The women knew they were embarrassing the hell out of her, and they were thoroughly enjoying it. Veronica's frayed nerves struggled not to tatter more.

Belinda poked Shane in the arm. "Take a number and you better clear it with your husband, because I'm sure you're not the only woman wanting his personal protection."

"I'm not married," Shane said, frowning.

"Shane, after living together for seven years, you're his common-law wife, right, Sam?" Belinda asked.

Samantha just laughed at Belinda's question.

Belinda swung back to Veronica and said, "Does his hair always stick up like that, Roni? It makes him look like such a bad boy."

"Oh God. You're going to make me sick if you don't stop," Veronica protested, and the truth was she did feel a little queasy. Maybe it was a combination of too much laughter and being very tired. She sipped a 7-Up, hoping it would settle her stomach and continued picking at the Caesar salad she'd ordered.

Belinda held a big bite of filet mignon on her fork as she asked, "So, is he married, single, any kids?"

Veronica snapped, "I don't know the man's personal business."

Unperturbed, Belinda said, "Why not? I'm sure he knows all of yours."

Veronica realized she had a point. Malik knew a heck of a lot more about her than she knew about him. She wondered exactly how much he did know.

Shane added her two cents. "That man looks too good to be single." She patted her short Afro and batted her eyes.

"Well dang, Shane, why don't you go ask him?" Veronica said, putting down her fork and crossing her arms.

"I just might, Roni, but won't I blow his cover?" Shane asked.

Veronica responded, "He's a bodyguard, not a spy, Shane!"

The women laughed again and Shane said, "You guys know I'm just joking. I'm quite happy with Bobby, even though we've had our ups and downs. I heard this woman on one of those talk shows say that love is like labor. You go through all that agony, but you forget about it once you have the baby in your arms. Is that right, Roni?"

"I wouldn't know. I've never been in love, or had a baby," Veronica answered.

"No, but you've delivered plenty. Don't those mothers just smile and make goo-goo eyes, although their bottom half has just gone through…" Shane paused, then said, "trauma."

Samantha grimaced and said, "Ohh, Shane that's a little too much. Before you get more graphic, could you please remember I'm trying to enjoy my food here."

"I'm just talking about natural stuff, Sam. Right, Roni?" Shane persisted.

Belinda answered before Veronica could open her mouth. "Girl, why are you asking Roni? As much as she's messed with Mother Nature, I wouldn't be surprised if she was struck down by lightning before the weirdo got to her." All of them looked at Belinda.

Samantha recovered first and said, "Belinda, this isn't a meeting at Microsoft where you can be just as rude as you want to."

Belinda actually looked a little sorry for her outburst before saying, "Hey, sometimes I get caught up in work mode and forget to shut off. Roni, that just popped out and I was too harsh. I'm sorry, but I think science has gone too far in manufacturing kids, like one would customize a car. It's too nonchalant. I know we've had this debate before and have agreed to disagree." She shrugged. "I'm still learning to control my mouth, and I'm sorry if I've offended you."

Veronica sighed and said, "It's okay, girl, since I know you don't have manners. And you're right, I don't want to rehash the fertility issue with you again." Veronica paused, then said, "But I do want to share what's been driving me crazy lately, and it's at the complete opposite end of the spectrum. Elderly abuse—kids mistreating their own parents in a complete perversion of the natural order. I see too much of it. Just yesterday, I had to document injuries for a police report. I'll spare you the gruesome details, but the adult son is being charged today." Veronica's hand ran down the front of her face. "He was cashing her checks and manhandling her or leaving her to fend for herself."

Veronica was still looking toward Belinda, but seeing the malnourished body. "I…I was so angry. Still am." She blinked and came back to the table. "There are lots of bad things in this world, Belinda. I suppose there always have been and there probably always will be."

"But that's just it, Roni," Belinda said as she sat forward. "That's exactly why I think with fertility—"

"Ladies, ladies," Samantha interrupted, "enough for one evening. Darn, I'm tired of these serious subjects. Let's get back to men. Anybody see that rerun of *Sex and the City*?"

They all laughed and Belinda said, "All right, Sam, point taken, but before we move on to bigger and harder things, I have something to say." She threw her arms around Veronica and Shane who sat on either side of her. "Ya'll are my sisters. We are educated women of the new millennium, and we can agree to disagree as I have done with all of you at least once.

I get to say my piece without any of you trippin' too much. As you know, I'm not a sister who's used to keeping things bottled up. I tend to go pop when I try." Belinda lifted her arms from their shoulders and into the air. "I feel good being with my girls. I just wanted to say that before we delved into Sam's fantasyland being played out on TV. You like to pretend you're the Samantha in the show, don't you, Sam?"

"Of course, my namesake always ends up bedding the hottest guy in the room," Samantha quipped.

Then, with a devilish grin, Shane said, "I suppose if you really were the Samantha in the show, by tomorrow we'd be asking you all those personal questions about Malik because he's definitely the sexiest man in this restaurant."

A hard spike of jealousy made Veronica's humor sputter, and she sipped water to hide her reaction. She needn't have worried, because no one noticed as her friends continued to laugh and the jokes became more ribald.

Chapter 8

Dr. Howell fell asleep during the car ride home. Malik glanced at her slack features, and they told him how truly tired she was. This was a first. Usually, she was very alert and looking around when they were in the car together. Malik had heard the entire dinner conversation. Initially, he'd been morbidly curious to see how Dr. Howell responded to the comments being made about him. *Why do I care?* He'd fussed at himself, because even if she thought he was God's gift to women, he would do nothing about it.

His thoughts shifted to the old lady Dr. Howell had struggled to save, and it made him remember his mother's funeral. She'd overdosed a few months after he'd gone to live with his father's family. He'd been stiff and expressionless throughout the entire ceremony, unable to shed a tear. On the car ride home, his stepmother sat in the backseat with him.

"Remember how you broke the lamp playing football in the house last week?" she'd asked.

Malik remembered, nodding.

"Once we got you to tell the truth, do you recall what I said?" his stepmother had asked.

"Yes, ma'am. You said nobody's perfect, important thing is to tell the truth."

"That's right. We all have faults, and your momma had them just like everybody else. But one thing I can guarantee is that your momma loved you."

"No, she didn't," he recalled screaming. "She was mean to me!"

"Oh, Malik." His stepmother had wrapped him in large, loving arms and said, "Don't say that. Your mother was a little disabled and sick. It's a lot like when your daddy had that bad infection last month."

"You mean when he kept mumbling about the jungle and secret tunnels?"

"Yes, little Malik. The high fever made the war real to your daddy again. Now, your mom had a different type of illness, but she was sick just the same, maybe even sicker. That disease made your mom say and do things that she really didn't mean."

"What did she have?" Malik had asked.

He remembered his stepmother had been quiet for a moment, then she had said, "She wasn't right in head, not because of anything God did, but because of all the junk she put in her body—alcohol, drugs."

"You mean that stuff in the needle I saw her put in her arm?"

"Exactly," his stepmother had answered. "All that garbage made her say ugly things to the people she loved the most. And I know she loved you because she gave you your daddy's last name. She was proud of you and wanted your daddy to be able to find you. I think she did those things because she knew she was ill, and your daddy would be able to do better for you." She'd hugged Malik tighter. "Don't hate your mommy. In her own way, she loved you more than anything else in her life."

Malik remembered holding his stomach tight, scared to let the big knot inside of him loose, scared he'd fall apart if he relaxed his muscles. Something about his stepmother's words pulled the knot apart. He burst into tears. His father, who had been driving, took the nearest exit, parked in a lot and joined them in the backseat. Malik had cried until he fell asleep between his parents. Later, he'd learned that his father had found him because his mother had called his paternal grandmother and hinted she'd had a kid. Learning this made his stepmother's words ring even more true.

Carl pulled into the driveway and opened the garage door. The automatic lights lit the night. Malik glanced over at Dr. Howell. Her coloring wasn't good, a little grayish. He gently rubbed her shoulder until her eyes fluttered open.

As they walked into the kitchen through the garage door, Veronica noticed Malik staring at her. He rushed to the alarm and shut it off. That was her job. He let Carl check the house and continued to look at her funny. He was getting on her nerves, and she just wanted to go to bed.

"You barely touched your food at dinner," he said, standing in the doorway, blocking her path.

She couldn't decide if it was a question or an accusation. Either way, she was too tired to care.

"All you had was sushi at lunch. You must be starving. Do you have any soup I can fix you?" he asked.

Veronica shuddered and said, "No, I'm not hungry." They both said bye to Carl. She was about to push Malik from the doorway when she remembered something she was supposed to tell him. "By the way, Samantha's going to start on the patients' charts tomorrow evening. I suppose she'll let you know if she finds anything."

"Great. Are you sure you're okay?"

"I'm fine. Just a little headache. I could use some Tylenol," she responded.

He advised, "Not on an empty stomach, doctor."

She glared at him.

"Hey, I'm just trying to keep you alive until I can figure out who's stalking you."

The man decided to have a sense of humor at the oddest times!

Veronica moved to leave the kitchen and swayed a little. Malik grabbed her arm. "Dang. I guess I'm ill, huh?" she said.

He answered, "Yes, Dr. Howell. I believe you are."

Malik escorted her to her room where he left her to get dressed for bed. He hadn't been gone long when she made a mad dash for the toilet. At first, she was too busy being sick to notice his hand at her back. Gratitude filled her when he was there with a wet cloth when she finished. She didn't know what to think of his behavior, nor could she get rid of him. He sat with her through the night, helping her when she needed it, putting damp cloths on her head. By four in the morning, she was spending most of the time in the bathroom.

She could see the concern in Malik's face. "If this keeps up, I'm taking you to emergency, Dr. Howell," he said.

"No," she croaked from her position on the bathroom floor. "I think I know what it is. Food poisoning. Sushi Heaven is closed for remodeling, so I had Alice try that new place. Big mistake, I think. I have specimen containers under the sink. I can collect some and have it tested in the morning. Just go away for a minute."

Malik left and with sheer will she managed to get a sample. However, as she washed her hands, she bumped into the items on her sink, making a lot of noise. She knew he could hear the commotion and hoped he would stay away. Of course he didn't. He knocked before saying, "Dr. Howell?"

"I'm…fine." She stood, bracing herself against the counter, fighting the dizzy spell that had just hit her. When it passed, she realized how soiled her nightgown had become. Pulling it away from her skin, she knew she needed a bath. Malik knocked again and she ignored it as she slowly made her way to the tub. He came through the door, startling her and she stumbled. He was there with steadying hands at her back and arm. She told him, "I need to clean up, Malik."

He responded, "It's not that bad, Dr. Howell. Why don't I just get you a change of clothes?"

"No," she answered, "being clean will make me feel better."

"Okay, if you insist, but let me help you." He must have felt her stiffen because he said, "I'm just going to run the water and get you towels." He slowly helped her move to the tub where she sat on the edge as he turned on the spigot. A short while later, he handed her a towel and said, "It's time to get in, Dr. Howell. Can you manage?"

She nodded.

"Just leave your gown on the floor. I'll get it later," he ordered while he turned off the water and left the bathroom. Veronica still closed the curtain once she managed to sit in the warm water.

Not fifteen minutes later, there was the knock again, and then she heard the door opening. "Dr. Howell?"

"Yes, I'm done," she answered. "I just need to rest a minute before I try to get out."

She reared when his big hand burst through the curtain, holding another towel. "Wrap this around yourself, and I'll help you get out," he said.

"No," she answered as she stood and took the towel.

Instead of responding to her statement, he asked, "Do you have the towel around you?"

"Yes." Before she could say anything else, the curtain moved to the side.

Malik knew what he was about to see, and still, his heart leaped. She was dark, sweet chocolate wrapped in an orange towel. It only took five seconds for the image to be imprinted in his brain. Flushed checks, damp skin, wet tendrils of hair clinging to her face, half-soaked towel clutched to her breasts, and the clean fresh scent wreaked havoc on his nostrils. He knew he was in trouble because her hands alone were enough to arouse him. He imagined bringing her fingers to his lips and beyond. The urge was strong to test his theory that she tasted as good as she looked.

She swayed and lowered her head, which was just enough movement to jolt him out of his stupor. Not trusting himself to speak, he helped her step from the tub onto the rug. He had her sit on the closed toilet seat and, recovering his powers of speech, he asked, "Are you ready to move to the bed."

"Yes, but I think I can make it on my own. As I thought, being clean has made me feel better. Maybe the worst is over." She attempted to walk as she talked. She whispered, "Ohh," and started to sway.

Malik was there instantly. She yelped when he lifted her in his arms. He noticed her skin was hot and she was shivering. Those were clear signs of fever. He sat her on the bed where he had already pulled back the covers and asked, "Which drawer are your nightclothes in?" He moved to the dresser.

"Middle," she answered.

He pulled out a large T-shirt, and when he turned to her, he noticed she was staring at him. "Your shirt's wet," she said.

Malik looked down at his skin showing through the soaked material and replied, "So it is. Here's your shirt, Dr. Howell."

She blinked, took the clothing from him and struggled to put it on over the towel. He helped when the towel got stuck underneath her shirt, and he inadvertently caught a glimpse of the top of her bottom. The yearning was sharp, and Malik bit the inside of his cheek, so he wouldn't make a sound. He felt bad wanting to ravish the ill; kind of like taking candy from a baby, or a trike from a toddler. His thoughts didn't stop the substantial warmth of arousal from rising toward his stomach. He breathed a sigh of relief and regret when her shirt was finally on, and his fingers didn't have the excuse to brush her midnight skin anymore.

Dr. Howell lay back and her eyelashes rested against her cheeks. Malik looked at her, and as a defense against his lust, forced himself to remember the times he was sick and living with his father. He recalled the loving hand of his stepmother was always there to soothe him. She'd sit beside his bed and sing him Spanish lullabies while wiping his head with a damp cloth. She'd hold his hand and give him liquids through a long straw. It was kind of corny, but even now when he was ill and had to drink liquid, it made him feel better to do it through a straw. He wondered if Dr. Howell had any. He went to look.

Five minutes later, he returned after a successful hunt, holding a glass with a long straw. "Here, drink this," he ordered.

She shook her head, and he believed she acted out of sheer orneriness, so he said, "Dr. Howell. Either you drink this, or I'm taking you to emergency."

"What is it?" she asked, glaring at him with one eye.

He answered, "It's Jungle Rehydration juice. You said you're suffering from food poisoning, and the way you're spitting stuff out, I believe you. I'm worried about dehydration, so I made you a special drink with your own straw."

Dr. Howell looked at the half-full glass suspiciously.

"Look, Dr. Howell. It's a pinch of salt, a teaspoon of sugar, water and a dash of fruit juice." He moved the straw to her lips.

She sipped slowly. After a few minutes, she pleaded, "No more."

About a quarter of the liquid was gone.

"Okay, but every time you hit that bathroom, I'm going to be bugging you to drink when you're done."

Dr. Howell rolled her eyes and flopped back into the pillows. Malik noticed her skin was even clammier than before, and he decided to do something about it. He got a fresh washcloth and wet it. At the first touch of the cool towel on her forehead, Dr. Howell cringed. Opening her eyes, she stared at Malik leaning over her with a washrag.

"You're hot," he explained and continued to stroke her face with the cloth. "I'm just trying to cool you off. Shush, Dr. Howell." Her mouth closed. "You won't let me take you to the hospital, so let me at least do this, okay?"

Veronica didn't answer the question. Against her will, she began to relax and think. *Good Lord, the man is driving me nuts.* Earlier, when he'd lifted her in his arms, the bathroom had performed a stomach-turning revolution. Even though she'd been fighting the urge to retch, it had been intriguing to be picked up as if she weighed no more than a feather. And then he'd put his hand on her bare back! His palm and fingers had been rough, warm, full of strength and totally male. She still felt as if it she'd been branded, and he was continuing to mark her with the rag.

The slow, smooth movement was hypnotic as the cloth drifted over the edges of her face, down her cheeks, along her throat, and across the skin revealed by her nightshirt. This was new to her. Her parents didn't coddle. When she was ill, her mother made sure she had everything she needed, but she wasn't one to rub heads or sit there for any length of time; and her father was too busy working to baby her.

Malik's movements had a certain rhythm and where her head and stomach roiled with sickness before, the two began to churn with gratitude mixed with desire. The man possessed the softest touch she'd ever encountered. She fought hard to remember she didn't like him, which was especially difficult when she looked at his muscular forearms. Even the sight of his tattoo didn't interfere with the strong urge to cuddle into them. Turning away from temptation, she encountered his chest. The deep brown contrasted sharply with the wet, white shirt. It gaped while he worked, revealing way too much. She licked her dry lips, and wondered if the sparse hair there was as soft as his touch. Then she noticed a dark ridge of skin to the left of the hair. Focusing, she whispered, "Knife?"

The rag kept moving, yet she felt him stiffen as he said, "Yes." With his other hand, he closed his shirt.

"Don't," she ordered, tapping his hand away. "Whoever stitched you up did a fine job."

Malik chuckled. "Thanks, Doc. Now shush. Let yourself relax."

She did and her guard melted away. She closed her eyes and imagined nuzzling against the springiness of his chest hairs. Goodness, could a man with such a magic touch be capable of the extremes that may be necessary to protect her? In her current state, she wondered if it mattered. Did anything matter beyond the comfort he provided? Veronica's insides were turning into Play-Doh and her mind was just as mushy. When he raised the towel and moved to leave, her lids lifted, she reached out and whispered, "Don't go." Malik turned back and stared into her eyes.

His lips pursed, and she braced for rejection. Instead, he said, "Let me change my shirt." Minutes later, he was back and before climbing into bed, he turned off the overhead light and turned on the lamp resting on her nightstand. Then, he tucked his fully clothed, long body next to hers, so that her back was to him. She looked at the arm that landed on her waist and found herself focusing on his tattoo. As before, she wondered why the sight no longer repulsed her. Lifting his arm, she pulled it up for a closer look.

"I'm sorry," Malik whispered, "I forgot to cover it."

"No, it's okay," she answered, "it doesn't bother me as much as it used to." Then she asked, "Lots of guys get this particular one?"

"Yes," he answered.

"Why did you?" she questioned, finger tracing the anchor.

He shrugged. "Young and gung ho are the only excuses I have."

"I wonder if that's why the animal got it?" she pondered out loud.

"Excuse me," Malik said.

With a deep sigh and a shudder, Veronica explained, "My brother, one of the creatures who attacked him had this tattoo." Malik was completely silent as she told him about the worst event in her life. His only reaction was to hug her tighter when the tears began to flow. As her eyes dried and her story ended, she felt drained, emotionally and physically. She whispered, "Thanks for listening, Malik," and he murmured something unintelligible against her hair. A profound sense of relaxation filled her, and her breathing became slow and heavy.

She entered a surreal world, between dreaming and wakefulness, when he whispered, "Are you asleep?" She was too comfortable to answer.

The next morning, Veronica woke with a start. The first thing she saw was Alice, in full color, inches from her nose.

"You poor thing," Alice said and tried to rub her forehead, but Veronica swiveled, looking for Malik, wondering if the previous evening had been a dream. "Don't worry, dear, he's still in the house."

Veronica felt her eyes getting wider.

Her head nurse laughed and said, "Sorry if I embarrassed you. You're hot enough already with the fever you have. Do you think your stomach can handle Tylenol?"

Veronica shrugged. She realized that she hadn't thrown up since she sipped Malik's Jungle Juice.

"Well, then we'll try some." Alice patted her large purse before saying, "I've got the sample, and Dr. Kroger is going to cover for you. We've rescheduled all the nonessential appointments. Ahhh." She wouldn't let Veronica talk. "You rest. Don't worry. I've got this handled. I'll get the sample tested, and we'll know what this is in an hour or so."

Veronica saw Malik for the first time, smiling in the doorway as Alice left. He didn't seem uncomfortable at all.

She was, and with hot cheeks, she lowered her eyes. When she raised them, he was gone. A minute later, he returned with a glass and straw. The man was completely at ease, and for some reason that irked Veronica. She took the glass and looked at it defiantly.

Malik said, "Look, Dr. Howell, you're not good to anybody sick. Here, drink, and maybe then you can keep down these pills."

Silence ruled as she sipped and obediently swallowed the two tablets taken from his hand.

Veronica wet her lips and tried to put the irritation aside. She was awfully curious and so she asked, "Why are you doing this?"

She felt relief when he didn't pretend that he didn't know what she was talking about. However, he answered her question with a question, "You want to be by yourself, don't you?"

She nodded as she sipped a little more from the long straw.

"You'd probably lie here all alone, and eventually, you'd get up and get yourself water, maybe even some soup. Someone else from your office would come and check on you and you'd shoo them away. You wouldn't take care of yourself nearly as well as I'm taking care of you. Doctors are notorious for being horrible to themselves when they're sick, and you know what, you'd probably still get better."

"For goodness' sakes, Malik. What's your point?" she asked.

"You hired me to make sure you're safe and that's what I'm doing. In sickness and in health—"

She interrupted him, "Good God, Malik. Just go away."

His smile mocked her. It reminded her that last night she'd asked for the exact opposite. Her breath caught; she waited for him to ridicule her, or worse yet, mention what she'd told him about her brother.

As if reading her mind, he hesitated, holding her in suspense a tad longer before saying, "All right. I'm leaving the door open, and I'll be in hollering distance."

The breath eased out.

Veronica slept most of the morning. At midday, Dr. Kroger and Alice dropped by. The round, middle-aged man entered Veronica's bedroom and announced "Vibrio Parahaemolyticus, Dr. Howell. I hear you suspected the sushi and you're right. Raw seafood did you in, and you're so lucky," he said sarcastically, "that you encountered a particularly nasty strain. Not wicked enough to admit you, although I am prescribing antibiotics. And, oh yes, you are officially banned from the clinic until Monday."

"Monday!" Veronica shouted.

"Yes, that's only three working days, and I'm handling things quite well. You need rest!" Dr. Kroger yelled right back.

Turning from the heavily frowning Veronica, Dr. Kroger faced Malik. He began complimenting him on his caretaking abilities and giving instructions. Alice sat on the edge of Veronica's bed and said, "I called the health department. They're starting an investigation of the restaurant, and they may call you with a few questions."

Veronica nodded.

"Well—" Alice patted her shoulder "—we're off. We have an office to run. Don't worry, you'll be back in the fray soon enough. Really relax, okay, Dr. Roni."

Nodding seemed to be the only response she was capable of.

Chapter 9

Two days later, on Thursday, Malik got up and did his usual perimeter sweep. Nothing out of the ordinary, except that Dr. Howell still slept. Normally, she would have been up an hour ago. He looked at her and remembered when she asked him to stay and how she'd spoken of her brother. It was a tragic incident that he'd already been aware of because it was in the file Graham had provided. However, he'd been unaware of the connection to his tattoo. "An unfortunate coincidence," he whispered.

Malik didn't necessarily want to, but he couldn't help recalling how her body felt, back pressed up against him. He told himself it was all about making her feel secure, which was his business. He was a watchdog for others' comfort, and that's all she was really asking for, and that's all he gave—a sympathetic ear and human contact while she was sick to help her sleep. Absolutely nothing was wrong with that. His cell phone rang and he answered it quickly, hoping not to disturb Dr. Howell.

"Malik?"

"Yes. Hi, Sergeant Ross. Do you have something for me?" he whispered as he moved to the living room.

"Sure do," she responded. "A sketch. The artist met with the neighborhood kid."

Malik was overjoyed. He was tired of sitting around waiting in defensive mode. He was ready to do something proactive.

The sergeant continued, "That's the good news. Here's the bad—white male, five seven to six feet, dark hair, and chubby or husky, wearing dark pants and shirt. How many folks in Seattle fit that description? I don't think the sketch will help you."

"Did you show it to the egg thrower?"

"As soon as I got it," she answered. "I'm leaving the juvy jail right now. He couldn't identify it."

Malik sighed, then said, "I still want to see it."

"Okay, I'll be there in about an hour." Sergeant Ross replied and hung up.

Veronica was just stirring when the doorbell rang. She heard voices and when no one came to her room, she whispered, "Who in the world is in my house?" She struggled to the living room, where the beautiful Sergeant Ross assaulted her eyes. Clear brown skin, bouncy ponytail and clothes so orderly she looked as if she'd just stepped out of a cleaner's. *How did the woman drive and not crease her pants? The eighth wonder,* she mused, feeling like a hag in her tattered, cotton robe and nightshirt. She used both hands to clutch the rags to her chest.

Veronica swore she saw a brief smile cross the woman's

lips before she nodded in her direction and asked about her health. Veronica made some innocuous comment, letting her know that she'd been ill, all the time wishing she'd stayed in bed. She was about to excuse herself and return to her safe haven when something occurred to her. *The sergeant must be here for a reason.* She shuffled toward the couch. From the look on his face, Malik wanted to assist her. Veronica shook her head slightly, thinking the interaction had escaped Sergeant Ross until the woman said in a stage whisper, "You should go help her."

Despite Malik's low voice, Veronica heard him reply, "No, she's all right."

She made it to the couch and sat down. Back straight, she looked at them expectantly, determined to stay informed.

In a louder voice, Malik said, "I know your time's valuable, Sergeant, so show us what you've got."

The sergeant handed Malik a sheet of paper. He sat beside Veronica and held the paper between them.

"It's a sketch." Surprise rang through her voice.

"Yes," Malik answered. "The neighborhood kid provided the details."

"Oh." Veronica tried to focus, but a tingling distracted her. The problem was Malik's leg kept brushing against her thigh. The heat shot right through the material of her robe and gown, giving her fever of a different sort. If Malik felt a similar sensation, he was good at hiding his emotions. She loosened the collar of her robe.

"You feeling all right?" Malik said, his hand touching her forehead, making her flinch. "Hmm, you're not hot enough to have a temperature."

She wiped the place he'd touched and replied, "I probably just need a bit more rest."

"Finally!" Malik shouted. "We agree on something." His smile was broad, like sunshine cutting through rain, and it took Veronica's breath away.

She turned back to the sketch and forced herself to concentrate. She saw nothing distinguishing in the average eyes, which were neither wide nor close set. Equally nondescript were the Nordic nose, thin lips and short hair. Veronica said, "This could be any white guy in Seattle."

"Yes, that's the problem," Sergeant Ross said. "I assume the man doesn't look familiar to you, Dr. Howell?"

"About as familiar as any Tom, Dick or Harry," she quipped.

"Well, at least we know his race," Malik said.

Sergeant Ross chuckled, saying. "That's certainly looking for the positive. Your mother taught you well."

"Believe me. It wasn't her," Malik said and viewed the drawing from different angles, and Veronica stared at him.

Did he have problems with his mother, too? she wondered.

"Maybe he's Asian. Do his eyes look a little almond?"

"Malik," Sergeant Ross said, "stop looking for things that aren't there. The picture's too vague."

"Yeah, you're right," he admitted.

Something caught in Veronica's throat and she coughed.

Malik went to get a glass of water from the kitchen.

Veronica felt the sergeant's eyes on her. She looked up and said, "I appreciate the extra help you're giving us. Thank you."

"You're welcome," Sergeant Ross answered. "I owe Malik."

"Why?" Veronica asked.

"I had a tough, unsolved case. We got a tip the suspect had thrown the weapon, a gun, into the Puget Sound. Malik had been hired to provide advanced training for our divers. I told him my problem and, free of charge, he agreed to look for the gun."

Malik returned and handed Veronica a glass of water before saying, "Why're you guys talking about that?"

"She asked," the sergeant said. Then she chuckled and shook her head. "I still don't know how you found it in all that water."

"Currents and an educated guess," Malik said.

"Oh well, that explains it then. Anyway, Dr. Howell, the suspect claimed he'd sold the gun to some friend who had moved to Europe. Supposedly, he'd lost contact with the friend. Malik's find proved him a liar. The matching serial numbers and the ballistic report sent the guy away for life without parole. So when Malik asked, I was more than willing to help."

Before Veronica could comment, Malik clapped his hands and said, "Okay, back to business. Any luck with the car?"

"Car?" Veronica said.

"Yes," Malik answered her. "Remember I told you the kid saw the guy get in a tan car?"

Veronica nodded.

Sergeant Ross crossed her arms and said, "Pretty much another dead end. The kid said it was like an undercover cop car. After I questioned him, I figured out that he meant a government-issue car. You know, Malik, a boxy, older model sedan. It could've been a Ford, Chevy, Plymouth. Who knows? The kid didn't remember any logos on the side to help us narrow it down." The sergeant uncrossed her arms and put her hands in her pockets. "Sorry, there isn't much to go on, folks. We have a chubby, white guy that drives a tan sedan and has animal guts on his shoes. The best we can do is wait for him to make his next move."

No, I can do more than that. Time for the tedious work to start. Malik thought as he walked Sergeant Ross to the door. By the time he returned to the couch, Dr. Howell was gone. The copy of the sketch still lay on the coffee table. Sergeant Ross was very meticulous, and he knew the fact it had been left was her way of giving it to him. Malik shook his head and went to knock softly on Dr. Howell's bedroom door and entered.

The robe was on the floor and she was just slipping under the covers. "Geez, I haven't been this tired since my internship," she said, curling into the pillow.

"I have to go," Malik told her.

Her eyes flew open.

"Now that we have this information, I want to check some things out. Carl is on his way. I'll be back tomorrow morning." His tone was very professional. Then he walked to the bed and pulled the sheet up to her chin. Next his hand brushed her cheek in what could have been a caress as he moved a piece of hair out of her face. Her brow furrowed in what looked like puzzlement. Malik could relate. His attitude toward her had him just as confused as she was.

Malik went to the garage, where the brain of the security system was located. He gathered up all the tapes that had been used while on this job, some from the house and some from the clinic. His habit was to watch the cassettes within twenty-four hours of recording, thus he'd viewed all of them before— however, today was the day for repetition.

By the time he finished packing, Carl was there. His gut overruled his brain, and he went to check on Dr. Howell one last time, even though he knew she was fine. The bed linens were bunched at her feet as she slept on her side, legs drawn upward, and hands near her face. The nightgown had gathered and hit her midthigh. Seeing her shapely calves and slender feet were entrancing and the sight of her hand against her face stopped him in his tracks.

More specifically, her right thumb barely touching her slightly open lips. The view was enough to send Malik's imagination into overdrive. He wondered if she'd sucked her thumb as a child, and then he began wondering things that made his lower body immediately respond. Very soon, he was as hard as the World War II helmet his father kept as a memento. As a boy, he took a flying leap and broke two ribs when he landed on the thing. He'd gladly give a rib to see Dr. Howell's tongue in action on him.

He placed a newspaper at the end of the bed for her to read when she woke up. Then, moving quickly before he could change his mind and telling himself she was asleep and would be none the wiser, he walked to the head of the bed and bent to gently press his lips against her forehead. Somehow, being able to touch her eased his anxiety about her safety in his absence and just made him feel good.

"Watch yourself," he whispered as he left her room after checking the windows.

His father's words came to him, making him feel guilty about the brief kiss. "Learn to control yourself now, or someone, or something will control you later. Drugs, a jail cell, it doesn't matter. The point is it won't be you calling the shots. Self-discipline. If I teach you that, then I'll have done my job." He shouldn't let desire for Dr. Howell drive him no matter how lovely she looked sleeping. Taking deep, even breaths, he checked all the other windows and doors in the house. When he reached the living room, Carl was coming through the front door. He told Malik, "I did a perimeter check and everything is secure outside."

"Thanks," Malik said. "I should be back before the doctor wakes up tomorrow. Call me if anything happens." Malik left, circling the house once just to be sure before getting in his Pontiac.

When he reached the clinic to pick up the few tapes there, his equilibrium was back. He ended up staying longer than he anticipated, fielding all the questions about Dr. Howell's health and showing the sketch around. The receptionist stared at it a long time, raising Malik's hopes. Then, she gave it back saying, "Sorry, it doesn't ring any bells."

The setting sun was at his back when he opened the front door to his house on Mercer Island. The house was nestled in trees about two miles from the water. He enjoyed the rural environment that was only ten minutes from downtown Seattle.

However, Malik wasn't pleased at the moment. He stood in the front doorway of his house a second, analyzing why he felt odd. It came to him in degrees. His three-bedroom home was nothing like Dr. Howell's. His place was impressive with its high ceilings, tiled floors, Danish furniture and circular stairway that led to the second floor. Not an item out of place; it was clean and efficient, which had always appealed to him in the past. It contrasted sharply with Dr. Howell's small home that exuded warmth with its luxuriously upholstered couches and chairs.

He sat on his beautiful, hard, black couch and realized no one could relax on it for two minutes, much less all night. Dr. Howell's couch was as comfortable as his bed. Looking around, he admitted he missed the vibrantly colored throw pillows and rugs that created an environment of relaxed messiness. His place was like a display model, and Dr. Howell's house was a home.

Shaking his head, he told himself to stop being silly. Since he'd been on his own, his spaces were always sparsely furnished and neat. So living with Dr. Howell had taught him appreciation for a different style. He'd buy a few throw pillows and be done with it.

Hours later, a blurry-eyed Malik rubbed his temples, hoping to ward off a headache. Putting his hands down, he arched his aching back and cursed the hardness of the couch for real. Viewing security tapes ranked right up there with seeing an anthill being built: slow and monotonous. He forced himself to stay focused as he watched the whole set of tapes for the third time. Boredom had caused more than one investigator to miss an important detail.

His finger reached out to pause the video, so he could take some aspirin when he caught something in his peripheral vision. Malik rewound the tape. He pushed Play and then Pause. At the top, left corner of the television screen, the camera had caught part of a brown car. It was an older model sedan and a white person sat at the wheel. Malik leaned back on the couch, feeling as though he was missing something. Why did his brain tell him to stop and rewind the tape? He closed his eyes and tried to relax, knowing that the answer would come to him, and it did. He'd seen that car before!

Malik pushed Eject and put in a tape from another day. About fifteen minutes later, the same car rolled through the clinic parking lot. Headache forgotten, Malik rewatched all the tapes. He found the car four times on three different days, all at the clinic. The driver never stopped, nor looked directly into the camera; and, whether by chance or purpose, the camera always caught a side view of the car, so the license plate wasn't visible. Malik thought the driver was male, but he wasn't positive. The car matched the general description the kid had given: a tan, boxy sedan that looked as if it belonged to the government. Brown was close to tan. Malik's gut was on full alert, demanding that he check this out.

Although the clock showed 3:00 a.m., he phoned Graham. After grumbling and calling him everything but nice, his old friend agreed to call his contacts first thing in the morning to have the cassettes analyzed. Malik returned to the tapes with renewed vigor. He fell asleep some time later as the film rolled on.

The shrill of the phone ringing startled Malik awake at 8:00 a.m. Slightly disoriented, it took him five rings to find the cordless among the couch cushions. After Malik croaked hello, a cheerful Graham yelled, "Oh, were you asleep? Payback is difficult, isn't it?"

Malik grunted.

Graham laughed. "You have four hours to wake up fully. Be at the Federal Building by noon. An old colleague is willing to go to work on his off day to enhance video."

Malik assured Graham he'd be there before clicking the receiver to off, and then back on. He dialed Carl, who told him that all was well with Dr. Howell. She was still sleeping and nothing unusual had happened during the night. Malik told Carl to look at last night's cassette to see if there were any white men driving midsize, brown sedans. He promised Malik he would.

When Malik put the phone on the coffee table, his joints popped like a rusty tin can. Groaning, he knew more than the long hours on his couch caused the problem. He hadn't exercised properly since he took Dr. Howell's case. Hands at his lower back, he went to the bathroom and brushed his teeth and washed his face. Looking in the refrigerator, he realized everything was spoiled. The piece of bread he pulled out of the bread box was hard, but he didn't see anything green, so he dropped it in the toaster. He ate it dry and it scratched the roof of his mouth, helping to chase the grogginess away.

Next, he went into the spare bedroom he'd converted into a gym. Body creaking, he stretched, wearing a white tank top and army-green shorts. Ignoring the weights, he did five hundred sit-ups, two hundred push-ups and fifty pull-ups. His joints protested less when he began a series of light jabs that developed into complicated punching and kicking patterns. "Pop, pop, pop," he whispered sounds as if he was hitting someone as he kicked the imaginary opponent's butt. A half hour into it, he felt loose and started adding back kicks and sliding kicks. Sweat poured when he stopped an hour later.

Wiping the perspiration from his brow, he moved to the window, opened it and stuck his head out. The sun was glorious, even if it made the breeze hot. Bringing his head back in, he ripped off his soaked tank top, feeling good; his muscles gliding as if he'd oiled them. He moved his torso and arms, stretching in the hot breeze from the window. After extending his arms far above his head, he closed the window, looking forward to the cold shower he was about to take and hoping he had enough time to eat before he headed downtown. He wanted a huge steak sandwich.

"Bingo!" Phillip Washburn said. "That might be your driver."

Malik's heart raced.

Graham's contact had examined all the tapes containing the car, and he'd enlarged several side views before zeroing in and trying to capture the driver. Malik prayed this was it.

Washburn played with a keyboard connected to a large screen. "I think your guy looked in the camera's direction long enough." The technician sounded like a kid who'd found his favorite surprise in a Cracker Jack box until he muttered, "Oh no."

Malik stared at the enlarged picture and whispered a curse.

"Sorry, guys. He's wearing a hat and sunglasses. Do you still want me to print this?" the technician asked.

"Yes," Graham answered.

Feeling dejected, Malik pulled out the sketch Sergeant Ross had given him and placed it beside the hard copy of the driver. "Do you think that's him?" he said.

"Could be, could not be," Graham answered. "They're both white and we know the driver is male."

"Yeah." Malik looked at the pictures of the car and said, "What kind of car is this?"

Graham shrugged, "Could be a Ford, Chevy or Chrysler. All of them put out boxy sedans like that."

"Yeah, but look at the wheels." Malik pointed. "The hubcaps don't match—one's a pancake and the other has spokes."

"Hey, you're right," Washburn said staring. "I've got a friend who's a car buff. He can identify this thing in seconds." He reached for the phone and fiddled with the fax machine. Five minutes later, they knew that it was a Plymouth Acclaim.

Malik turned to Graham. "I bet you know what I'm going to say."

"Yes, I do," he responded. "Where do you think the teams should circulate the pictures?"

"Everywhere," Malik said. "Start in the neighborhoods around the house and clinic. Then hit the meat processing plants, grocery stores, taxidermist. Can you think of anything else, Graham?"

"No, I think you've just about covered it. I can probably put four people on it."

"Okay, I'll help you for the rest of the day," Malik said, then called Carl to let him know he wouldn't be back until tomorrow. He also told him about the printouts from the film, and explained that Graham would be e-mailing them to him to show to Dr. Howell. He instructed Carl to call immediately if she recognized the car or the person.

Veronica awoke on Friday still feeling a little drained. She looked at Thursday's newspaper lying at the foot of her bed and smiled. She'd been so surprised when she'd seen the paper late yesterday evening. She remembered whispering, "Malik," and then reading most of the local section before falling asleep again.

Stretching, Veronica got up, brushed her teeth and ate a banana for breakfast. Looking at Carl pour a cup of coffee in the kitchen, she wondered where Malik was. She was up and down most of the day, and by early evening, she was feeling a lot better. Yawning, she sat up from her latest catnap on the couch. Carl sat across from her reading a book, which meant that Malik still wasn't back. Carl smiled and put the book on his lap. Veronica read the title, *The Art of War.* "Darn, is that all these people think about," she muttered as she made her way to her room.

"Dr. Howell."

She turned back to Carl.

"Mr. Graham e-mailed me a couple of pictures he wants you to look at," he said.

Veronica walked over and knelt in front of the coffee table where his computer sat.

"We think this is the perp's car."

"Perp?" Veronica said, frowning at Carl.

"Sorry, perpetrator," he explained.

"Oh." Veronica stared at the screen. "I don't know this car."

"All right." Carl pushed a few buttons and said, "Here's the driver."

Veronica looked at Carl sideways before saying, "I'd have to have X-ray vision to recognize him behind the glasses and hat. Is this the only picture you have?"

Carl shrugged and said, "I guess so, because it's the only one they sent."

With a frustrated sigh, Veronica got up and went to her room. Once there, she stripped off her long nightgown and fought the fact that the joy she'd experienced about feeling better was diminishing. Strange as it was, she feared her bad humor was directly related to Malik's absence. *Dang, I have issues. This is not a man I should miss. I should rejoice that he's gone, and I have some space.*

Her body paid her mind no attention, and in defiance, Veronica yanked her hair into a ponytail before putting on a shower cap. The sharp pain didn't overshadow her feelings about Malik. Something inside her found his presence comforting, and she wasn't happy with the substitute bodyguard.

Since the feeling wasn't going away, she tried to rationalize it as she stepped in the shower. Some attachment to Malik was natural since he had been her almost constant companion for a number of days. All it meant was she was used to him. *Oh, yeah?* her conscience taunted. *Then why doesn't his tattoo bother you anymore?*

"Oh, be quiet," she muttered. "It's a good thing he's gone because I need to face these silly emotions and get them out of my system because there is no way Malik is going to be a part of my life beyond this current crisis."

Veronica stepped from the tub, dried herself and applied lotion vigorously as her mind continued to mull over the situation. The man's reaction to her was as puzzling as Seattle weather. One minute he seemed attracted and the next he became distant, an extreme professional on the edge of being cold. She didn't have time or patience for a man who didn't know himself.

Veronica wandered out of her room. Now that she felt better, she was restless and tired of being cooped up in a dark house. She complained to Carl, "Can't we at least raise the shades from hell?" She stood in front of him, arms crossed at the chest. The two hadn't really spoken besides the conversation about the pictures.

From his seat, Carl answered, "Sorry, ma'am. You know it's not safe." He looked around her, trying to see the cameras showing on the television. She moved with him until he sighed and sat back. "Would you like to watch a show? I can see the cameras from my laptop. In fact, I'll go in the kitchen and do that now."

Carl's modulated tone bugged her, as if she was an angry child needing to be soothed. Her upper body hurt. It felt as though a defibrillator paddle had been smacked down on her chest, and she shuddered in frustration. She was too keyed up and watching television wouldn't do a thing for her.

By evening, Carl actively avoided her, a difficult task in the small house. She wondered if her bad temperament would make the man call Malik for help. She looked at her watch and knew Carl would be doing his routine house check soon. Veronica didn't miss the opportunity to glare at him when he cruised through. As far as she knew, Malik hadn't even called to check on her. He was unpredictable and irritating as heck.

At eight, Samantha dropped by to return the clinic key and to let her know the search was fruitless. She was surprised to learn about her friend's illness, and even more surprised to hear who had played nurse. "All right. I'm not mad at you for not calling. My caretaking abilities can't compete with the angel disguised as a hunk. Where is he anyway?" her friend asked. Veronica had introduced Samantha to Carl at the front door.

She snapped, "I don't know," as the two women sat facing each other on the couch. "He's been gone since yesterday."

"Ouch! Now I see why poor Carl disappeared so fast." Samantha screwed up her face and punched Veronica in the shoulder. "Stop being so mean, girl."

Irritated as she was, Veronica couldn't help laughing. "Sorry, Sam."

"He's only been gone a day, huh? And you're as feisty as a porcupine. Have you analyzed these feelings?" Samantha asked.

Veronica whined, "Sam, did you come over here to torture me?"

"No, not until you nearly bit my head off, but since we're on the subject of men—"

"We're not on the subject!" Veronica interrupted her.

"Yes, we are! I think you're avoiding your feelings for Malik for a variety of reasons. You have commitment anxiety," Samantha concluded.

Veronica protested, "What! I dated Neil for three years."

"Oh, he was just a safe place to shelve your emotions. You were both workaholic residents using each other as a release every once in a while. Admit it, Malik has reached another level. I think you care about him, and you're not even getting any, or you wouldn't be so edgy."

Veronica considered whether she was strong enough to lift Samantha, so she could throw her out. She wondered if Carl would do it if she ordered him to.

Her friend wouldn't let up. "Have you had a serious relationship since before your medical school days? I always assumed it was because you were too busy finishing school and setting up the clinic. But as I watch you fighting yourself over Malik, I wonder if something else is affecting your view of men? No, seriously. Stop being mad and think about it."

"I have thought about it." Veronica's hand ran down her face. Deciding that talking to her friend was better than sitting around stewing in her own foul mood, she answered the question. However, she got her dig in first. "Are all attorneys like a dog with a bone when they want something?"

Laughing, Samantha said, "No, only the good ones."

Veronica's lips curled into a smile and she said, "Because you're such a good friend, I agree to this cross-examination. While I was an undergraduate, I dated my share of eligible men. There was even a guy I thought about spending the rest of my life with until Mitchell asked me the crucial question. 'Would you be with this man if he worked at Burger King?' I protested and we argued before I saw his point. I wouldn't be with the guy."

"Veronica!"

"Calm down, Sam. I said no, not because I'm a snob, but because I didn't love him. I was settling for a pleasant man with the right credentials. Mitchell pointed out that some of my mother's programming had reached a subconscious level. Although my parents had managed to find a form of true love, she'd be all for a marriage of convenience to the *right* kind of person. I was disgusted, and promised myself on the spot that I wouldn't really commit to someone unless I loved who he was on the inside, not what he does, even though he has to do something. I can't imagine myself with a freeloader."

Veronica paused to take a deep breath, then said, "Sam,

what I really want is a man who thrills me with his body and his mind. I want to look at him, hear him talk and feel the urge to do nice things for him. And when he looks at me, I want see the same desires reflected in his eyes."

Veronica smiled wearily. "So, you're right, Sam. I never felt that way about Neil, and who knows what he really felt about me because he was so commitment shy. However, I didn't care because I knew I wasn't serious about him." She shrugged, "I still call him when I want male company, although we've never been intimate since we officially ended it. It was a perfect fit then and now. At least it was."

Samantha perked up and said, "What? You're not satisfied with the arrangement anymore?"

"I didn't say that!" Veronica objected.

"Not in so many words, but maybe you've felt that elusive, spontaneous spark with someone living in your house. That kind of unpredictable love you're looking for."

"Samantha, stop it."

Her friend persisted, "Why? Am I making you think about your feelings too much?"

"Look, Sam, it will be a cold day in Hades before I fall for a self-centered man who can't even call to check on you when you've been ill."

When Samantha stopped laughing, she said, "Have you asked Carl if he's phoned?"

"No."

"Stop pouting and ask the man, Roni," Samantha ordered. Out of sheer stubbornness, Veronica didn't.

Chapter 10

Saturday morning, Veronica woke to a ringing phone. Someone picked up at the same time as she did; however, only she said hello. The voice that said, "Hey, Doc," was easily recognizable.

"Deirdra?" She'd given her young patient her home number over a year ago along with an offer to phone whenever she wanted to talk. Deirdra had never called, making the present call extremely startling.

"Yeah, Doc. I know it's early. Sorry, I really need to get with you," the young woman said.

She heard a soft click and knew whomever was listening had hung up the phone.

"What's the matter?" Veronica asked.

"I don't want to say over the phone. You got time to meet today?"

Her curiosity demanded one answer. "Yes." Rather than

deal with endless security measures, she gave Deirdra her address and told her to come by in an hour, which would be eight o'clock. Then, she quickly showered and dressed in shorts and a nylon T-shirt. She found Malik staring at his computer in the living room. Although her heart jumped a little at his return, she planned to ignore him.

"All's well at the clinic," he said. "Do you want to see the security cameras?" Nosiness made Veronica detour and sit on the couch. She knew how to check the cameras from the TV, but not from his laptop. She had to scoot closer in order to see the screen. She looked at the clinic's parking lot.

"You can check these from anywhere?" she asked.

"Yes. Technology is incredible," he answered. "I can access all the security cameras here and at the office via the Internet. So I can look wherever I can log on, which is just about everywhere because my computer has a built-in, wireless modem." Malik proceeded to show Veronica how to access the different cameras at her house as well as the office. He left her to it and went into the kitchen. After satisfying her curiosity and deciding there wasn't much happening this early on a Saturday morning, Veronica went to get a cup of coffee. As she stood, Malik returned with two cups in his hands. She accepted the steaming offering, and the fact that Malik was a hard man to stay irritated with.

"Carl was correct." He sipped before continuing to speak, "Each time I called, he said you were looking better and better. How do you feel?"

Dang, Samantha was right. "Um, I'm feeling pretty good, thanks. By the way, a young woman's coming over—" she looked at her watch "—in about fifteen minutes."

"The same one who called?" he asked.

"Yes." Veronica didn't elaborate and Malik didn't pry. She picked up the newspaper from the coffee table, then looked at Malik. "Thanks for leaving the paper the other day."

He just nodded and smiled.

They were silent until the doorbell rang. Malik looked through the peephole first and said, "Oh, I remember her from the office. I promise not to burst in if ya'll get rowdy again." Veronica couldn't help noticing that the thick accent went well with the playful tone.

He unlocked the door and moved to the knob when Veronica's hand covered his. She said, "Please, I'd prefer to keep your presence private."

"I don't like you opening doors, Dr. Howell." The accent receded behind the professional attitude.

The bell rang again, making Veronica jump. Her eyes pleaded with Malik. He uttered a curse before saying, "Let the door shield you when you open it. I'm going to stand by the kitchen, and I'll slip inside before she sees me." Malik grabbed his computer and moved into position.

Veronica stood as instructed and let Deirdra in. After the door closed, she glanced to see that Malik was gone.

"You live real close to the bus stop," the young woman commented.

"I know. Comes in handy when my car's acting up. Would you like something to drink?"

The long braids Deirdra had gathered into a scrunchie bounced as her head shook. She wore gray sweatpants and tennis shoes. Very relaxed clothing that contrasted with the red eyes and nervous movements as the woman shuffled about. Veronica began to be concerned about a relapse. She led the way into the living room, where Deirdra said, "Dang,

Doc. Do you know the sun is shining real bright outside? Why's it so dark in here?"

Veronica felt like shouting, *my sentiments exactly!* Instead, she told a polite lie, "I just like it that way."

"Oh. You never struck me as the dark and gloomy type," Deirdra said, sitting in the armchair Veronica had just vacated, unaware that she was being examined. Despite the dark circles under her eyes, her coloring was good. Veronica sat on the couch and studied her arms, revealed by the short-sleeved shirt she wore. There were no fresh track marks. After about another thirty seconds of watching the young woman fidget, Veronica said, "Deirdra, what's bothering you?"

"Well, remember when I asked for the pills?" she said.

Veronica nodded.

"Um…I didn't get the prescription filled fast enough."

"Oh!" This was the last thing Veronica expected to hear.

The woman stood up and began pacing. "A wonderful evening, wine, music," she said and glanced at Veronica. "Well, you get the picture, Doc, but I don't get it, though. The man wore a rubber. Anyway, I don't want this baby."

"Hey, hey. Wait a minute, Deirdra!" Veronica said. "Are you saying you've taken a home pregnancy test?"

"I'm real regular, Doc. I can almost tell you the exact time it'll start."

The girl wasn't answering her question.

"I'm three days late. I don't know how this happened."

She looked at Veronica's expression.

"Well, of course I know *that* part, Doc. I just don't get it. Like I said, we had protection."

"Unfortunately, condoms aren't a hundred percent effective," Veronica said as she stood and put her arm around

Deirdra to stop her from ping-ponging around. "Sit. You're giving me a headache." The young woman allowed herself to be led to the couch.

"Doc, I just got my stuff together. I can't have a baby. You have to help me take care of this."

"Does your friend know?" Veronica asked.

She looked at Veronica as if she were crazy before answering, "Heck no!"

"Deirdra, you like this man, don't you?"

"I like him a lot. A baby would kill that, too," the young woman said in an obstinate tone.

Veronica questioned her. "How do you know? If you are pregnant, he has a right to know and be involved in the decision."

Deirdra laughed—a hard, harsh sound. Then she said, "All telling Roy will do is make the brotha run. He's going to say I been with you one time and you're trying to trap me. I ain't trying to hook nobody, and I don't need to hear the crap he's going to hit me with. I just need you to get rid of this for me, Doc. Can you open up on a Saturday?"

"Goodness no," Veronica answered. "Even if I could, I wouldn't do it. I prefer not to do terminations. I would have to refer you to someone else. But we're getting ahead of ourselves. The first step is a pregnancy test. If you are expecting, then we talk about options. I strongly suggest you tell Roy, Deirdra. He has a right to know."

"Right? That's a funny word, Doc. Life hasn't been that fair to me, so I don't feel much of an obligation."

"Oh, that's not true, Deirdra. You're sitting in front of me drug free, right?" It didn't hurt to ask.

Deirdra gave her double confirmation. "Uh-huh." She nodded.

"I agree, Deirdra, you weren't presented with a bed of roses, yet you've evolved into a wonderful, vibrant woman. A baby isn't the end of the world. You're working and you have health coverage. A strong will can make a way."

With her head down, Deirdra didn't answer. Veronica repeated the question she'd asked earlier. "Have you tried one of the over-the-counter tests?"

"No, I've just been freaking out since my missed period. Last night, I had the idea to call you. I made myself wait until seven this morning." Deirdra looked up and smiled. "I didn't wake you, did I?"

"Of course you did," Veronica responded. "What person in their right mind would be up at seven on a weekend?"

"I guess I think you doctors are superhuman, you never sleep. You're killing my image by wearing shorts, Doc." She smiled for the first time. "Hey, you have a lot of muscle in your legs for an old chick!"

"I'm not old." Veronica laughed and lightly popped Deirdra's leg. "You're just young, and we're both only human, Deirdra. So is Roy. Let the man know what's up before you make an irreversible decision. He is half of what may be happening."

"I don't know, Doc," Deirdra replied. The two women were silent for a moment. "I feel better than when I first got here, though." Deirdra leaned back into the couch and released a sigh that circled the living room twice before settling on her shoulders. At least she wasn't jittery anymore. After a time, she opened her eyes and asked, "Is this your home?"

"Yes," Veronica answered.

"Do you mind if I just walk along the beach for a while?"

"No, of course not," she said, wanting to add, *I'd give my right arm to go with you, though.* Instead, she told Deirdra, "Just a minute."

Veronica went to the kitchen where Malik sat at the table looking at some papers.

She told him, "Deirdra wants to go for a walk. I'm going to open the shutters, so she can go out the sliding doors leading to the deck." She walked to the panel on the wall by the garage door. "Is the alarm on?"

"Yes, disarm it while I let her out," he said. "I won't allow you to open the shutters. That's too much." He moved through the door into the other room.

Veronica uttered a curse as she punched buttons on the keypad before following him.

Deirdra rushed to her side as soon as she entered the living room. She smiled so wide, Veronica swore she could see her throat. "Isn't that the guard from the clinic?" she asked while they both watched Malik manipulate the controls for the shutters. Before Veronica could answer, she said, "I see he's providing more personal protection now, the kind that puts him in your bed at night. I feel guilty busting in here on a Saturday." Veronica didn't bother explaining. She tried not to grimace and bore the impish comments as she stood outside the line of sight while the shutters rose. The sunlight streamed through and reached her standing in the dark corner. Her face lifted to the light like a dying plant.

Deirdra turned to her and said, "Can I come to the clinic on Monday?"

"Of course," Veronica told her.

Deirdra hugged her and said, "Thanks, Doc. I'll head to the bus stop when I'm done communing with nature, so you two feel free to do whatever you want. Just don't end up like me." With a harsh laugh, she disappeared into the light; and

Veronica drifted after her, chasing the warmth until she ran right smack into Malik's voice.

"Please stay back, Dr. Howell."

Her chest tightened in frustration and she retreated into shadows. "I wasn't meant to be a mole in a dungeon," she said.

The rustle and clicks of the shutters and locks closing were the only answer she received.

Monday morning, Veronica's staff welcomed her back with flowers, and she responded by hugging each of them. Malik went around showing the pictures of the car and the person. As far as Veronica knew, no one recognized them. Then the busy day began. Noon had come and gone, and Veronica sat at her desk in a lab coat and black slacks going over charts for the afternoon patients when a knock interrupted her concentration. "Come in," she said, not bothering to look up.

Veronica was vaguely aware of another person when a delicious smell assailed her nose and she lifted her head. Malik stood there holding two bottled waters and a long brown bag. Veronica's stomach growled, reminding her that she'd only had coffee for breakfast.

"Sounds like I'm right on time," Malik teased. "I had a cheesesteak delivered from Philly Fevre and it's way too much food for me. You want half?" He put the items on the corner of her desk and began neatly stacking the charts.

Veronica had seen him eat and doubted his story; however, she didn't challenge him. Instead, she helped make space. She told herself the smell of warm onions, cheese and chicken was just too much to resist. She thought he'd sit down and join her, yet after dividing the enormous sandwich, he took half and disappeared back through the door. Veronica didn't have long to ponder his behavior because Alice marched in without knocking. She caught her in the middle of a huge bite.

"Hey, where'd you get that?" Before Veronica could answer, she said, "Deirdra's here. She claims you told her to come in today."

Veronica chewed, taking time to enjoy the wonderful taste. After she swallowed, she said, "I did. Sorry, I forgot to mention it. Stop frowning at me—it's just a pregnancy test. It won't take long. Can you put her in a room and draw the blood?"

Scowling, Alice replied, "I will if you share. That smells wonderful. It's making me forget I already ate lunch." She rubbed her stomach. "As much as you have me running around, it's hard to maintain my girth."

"Of course you can have some," Veronica said, laughing. "Let me put them in a room, and I'll be right back."

When Alice returned and sat down, Veronica handed her half. "Them. Who's with her?" she asked.

"A handsome, young man," Alice answered.

"Oh yeah! That's interesting."

Alice took a bite, "Mmmmm delicious." She stared at Veronica and said, "Did Malik bring you this slice of heaven?"

Veronica nodded.

"I think he likes you," Alice said, smiling.

Veronica scowled.

The expression didn't deter Alice from saying, "His eyes gave him away at your house when you were sick. Now, my question is, what're you going to do about it?"

Veronica choked on her sandwich. Grinning from ear to ear, Alice said nothing while Veronica coughed, then sipped her drink. When she could speak, she said, "Nothing! There isn't anything going on."

Alice's head shook from side to side as she said, "Oh come now, Dr. Roni. Don't tell me you're not interested in him. He's the type of man who'd stir the most frigid of women, and Doc, I don't think you're that cold."

A ripple of shock passed through her. Veronica knew her head nurse was blunt, but this was a bit much. She tried to change the angle of the conversation by saying, "Even if there was something going on, why's it up to me to do something?"

"It's always up to the woman, don't you know that?" Alice asked.

"No!" Veronica shouted.

"That's why you have an empty bed while an attractive gentleman is in your house," Alice quipped.

That comment stunned Veronica into silence.

Alice had just celebrated her twentieth wedding anniversary and was considered the office expert on relationships. Her nurse finished the last bite and left with the last word. Elbows bent, she shook her fists and said, "The man's yours. All you have to do is get in there and take him."

Alice's words were still resonating in Veronica a little while later when she felt Malik's eyes on her as she breezed through the office handling four patients at once. She slipped into Deirdra's room, physically putting the door between her and Malik. She was determined to place the same type of barrier in her mind as Deirdra hopped off the examination table, talking before Veronica could say hello. "I don't want to know yet, Doc, not until Roy gets back, and he just went to the john."

Veronica slipped in a nod seconds prior to Deirdra's mouth

moving again. "It was hard, Doc, I almost peed my pants while I did it, but I keep thinking about what you said, and, well, I told him." She released a small laugh. "The amazing thing is he ran toward me, instead of away, ya know?" Veronica smiled at the teary-eyed woman. "He didn't blame me. I guess 'cause we both knew we had protection. He just said this must be God's way of showing us that we were meant to be together."

Uh-oh, Veronica wondered if what she thought was positive news would now be something else. There was a soft knock right before the door opened and a tall, thin man in his late twenties came through the opening. He sported a wild Maxwell Afro and an engaging smile that stayed on his face while he said hello and went to put an arm around Deirdra. They both looked at Veronica expectantly.

She watched their eyes dull and their features slacken when she explained that the test was a hundred percent accurate, and it had come back negative. The expressions didn't change much during the fifteen minutes it took her to explain all the reasons why Deirdra's period could have failed to show. Veronica suspected it was stress, yet she went through the other possibilities like a pituitary tumor or a thyroid problem. They'd know in a couple of days after a blood test. When Veronica left them with Alice and a needle, she felt absolutely terrible.

By the time they got home that evening, Veronica's mood hadn't improved much. She felt drained and tense, a weird combination. She was tired, yet too agitated to rest. She convinced herself that her disposition resulted from illness and work stress rather than anything else, mainly Malik. Regardless of the cause, she craved release. She had an operation to perform tomorrow, and she needed to be at her best. She decided only one thing would help. Something she hadn't done since this madness had started, but she usually did it at least three times a week. It was time to dance away the stuff burning inside of her.

She grabbed compact discs from the entertainment cabinet and headed to the spare bedroom that doubled as a workout room. She put numerous discs in the boom box and programmed it to play the songs she wanted to hear. Soon, the smooth sounds of Seattle's own Kenny G. filled the air. In her room, Veronica changed into red shorts and a white, short-sleeved top. As she pulled her hair into a scrunchie, she walked out of her room, and passed Carl, who was studying security tapes in the living room. After making sure the house was safe, Malik had disappeared, saying he needed to talk to Graham. Carl barely lifted his head when Veronica told him what she was doing.

In the spare room, she grabbed Malik's large gym bag off the hardwood floor and put it in the closet. The small twin bed rested in the far corner, creating more than enough open space for her purposes. She started out slow, doing mostly stretches to the soft jazz tune playing until she was sure her stamina matched her desire. By the end of the set, she felt good. Her body transitioned smoothly into faster movements when the music changed to an energetic tune with Latin rhythms. She started with a basic step: right foot crossing over the left while her hips swiveled and twisted on the next three beats.

Veronica's mind wandered as her body boogied barefoot. She recalled the words of her favorite dance teacher, Rosetta Rees. In a heavy Spanish accent that went well with her deep, throaty voice, she'd yell, "Real Cuban motion isn't just shaking your bottom. The movement starts here." Her hand would slap the area between her breast and stomach. "Your stomach is the key. Get it going in this spot and your shoulders, knees, and everything else will follow!"

Veronica smiled and remembered Ms. Rees also yelling, "Don't overcomplicate, just feel."

"Just feel," she said out loud. "How do I feel about Malik?" She admitted to herself that most of her preconceived notions were wrong. Malik was nothing like the animals that had hurt her brother, although he could be intensely forebidding and not the type to put people at ease. Oh sure, he was a protector, and others were drawn to him for that; but they also feared him, and gave him his distance. She'd seen it with the men who'd installed the security system; seen it in the eyes of people they came into contact with; and she remembered her own initial reaction to him. However, Veronica now knew his secret, the one truth that went totally against his soldier persona. The same truth that Veronica suspected was responsible for the fact that she was no longer repulsed by his tattoo.

He was kindhearted.

Completely violent people wouldn't have cleaned anything from her porch. Nor would they have noticed how she liked her coffee, and rubbed her head when she was sick, or listened to her as she grieved.

Although, there was one thing that was disturbingly similar between Malik and others that lived by violence: both could make her blood boil, even if for vastly different reasons. Malik was a caring man in a fierce world. Could she separate the man from the world? She nodded, answering her silent question. There, she'd admitted it, allowed it to be in the forefront of her mind that she was attracted to Malik, and just maybe that was okay.

Veronica relaxed and found her spirit soaring. She didn't have to focus on the steps because her feet took over and turned her into an instrument of the music. This blessed feeling wasn't bestowed on her every time she danced, but when it coursed through her veins, she went with it. Her midsection gyrated, her hips rotated, her arms coiled upward twirling as her feet glided through syncopated steps. Her dancing was controlled abandon. Turn pattern after turn pattern, she executed complicated moves until sweat poured, taking away all the bad feelings, worry and stress.

Soon, she entered that magnificent state she called the dancer's high. Instinctively she felt the music, sensing every accent as it built and executing a move that punctuated the break perfectly. Each time she hit it, she got a thrill, an intense feeling that she could only describe as WOW!

Malik's heart thumped and quit beating altogether when he reached the doorway to the spare room and stopped short. He'd followed the music that reminded him of his stepmother until he'd found her. Before Carl left, he'd said, "Dr. Howell is exercising in the back."

What a misnomer! This wasn't working out. It was art, poetry in motion, not to mention spellbinding. Malik stood there mesmerized by the silky movements, the hips that undulated confidently. She was pure liquid, and he wasn't thinking about the water glistening on her dark skin, making the spandex shorts cling as though they were a part of her body.

As he watched, he now remembered why she was so special as a jazz singer. Something about her was electric. When she performed, you didn't want to take your eyes off her. She was fire personified, and he suffered like hell trying to stay in the periphery to avoid getting burned.

Of course, his lower body responded to the sight, yet Dr. Howell's dance went beyond physical. She gave life to the music, making it romantic by interpreting it through her movements and facial expressions. Dancing was her focus. That was clear. She wasn't trying to get a rise out of a non-existent audience. The sensuality was subtle, suggestive and totally alluring.

She had what his stepmother would call *flavor*. Years ago, the woman would watch the Latin dance competition on TV and complain that all they had were steps with no heart, no zeal. No way would she say that about Dr. Howell. She had technique combined with her sense of soul, and style. The woman had enough *flavor* to start her own spice island. He had to lift his shirt collar because he was baking in the amount of seasoning flowing from her.

When her hair came out of its band, it didn't help his situation. Strands began whipping into her face, and Malik had to lean against the doorjamb, trying to settle himself as he watched the damp tendrils swing about. The music changed to a fast, swing beat and Dr. Howell went with it. She bent forward, and the hair falling in her face prevented her from seeing Malik standing right in front of her. He watched her work her shoulders and turn in a tight circle before straightening with her back toward him. Then, with legs bent and arms waving, she shimmied with such vitality, Malik caught himself leaning toward her. His eyes strained painfully when she did a move where her fingers reached her toes.

He was in actual physical agony, trying to hold himself back. Breathing shallowly, he tried to ignore the ache in his chest. "Thank you, Jesus," he silently mouthed the words when the music ended soon after. His relief was short-lived because her wet clothes clung in all the right places. He swore that the slightly spicy scent wafting off her body called his name; or maybe, it was the half smile on her mouth he heard. When Dr. Howell's tongue darted out to wet her lips, Malik's jaw clenched, his feet shuffled. Then her generous lips came together, creating a perfect oval. Malik stared at her abundant mouth and almost cried out loud, the desire to kiss her was so strong.

Veronica was oblivious to the fact that she had an audience. She tingled all over, basking in the warm glow of the dance. She stood there with her head back, eyes closed, savoring the experience, trying to prolong the high. She opened her eyes to Malik standing in the doorway. It stunned her so much, she couldn't move. She stood there while questions whirled through her head. *How long has he been standing there? What did he see? What did I just do?* She'd been so caught up and now she was so discombobulated, she couldn't recall how she'd moved her body. *Did I shake my rump toward the doorway?* From his slack jaw and glazed eyes, she suspected she did.

Her body responded to his hot stare. Goodness, the man appealed to her. Veronica hated to admit it, but she wanted him, badly. Surprisingly enough, her mother's words kept her rooted to the spot. "There's love, and then there's lust. You give up your good stuff every time you lust, and you'll never find love, plus your stuff won't be that good anymore."

Another woman's words overshadowed her mother's advice.

"Yours for the taking." Alice's declaration propelled her forward.

"Enjoy the show?" she asked, advancing on him.

A slow smile spread across his face—lots of teeth, and very mischievous. The look was new, sexy as hell, and not at all comforting to Veronica. "Immensely." His voice was a throaty rumble. He leaned away from the doorjamb and walked toward her.

They were almost touching when they both stopped. Malik lowered his head and brushed his lips against hers. They were firm and soft. Veronica sighed, waiting for him to kiss her more deeply. A delicious tingle ran through her when she first felt the tip of his tongue. The thrill was cut short when a vicious pain gripped her calf.

Separating her mouth from his, she yelled, "Oh, cramp," and fell into him. His hands flew to steady her and he lowered her to the ground. Strong fingers kneaded her calf firmly in a comfortable, even rhythm that contrasted sharply with Veronica's pounding heart. The sensation was strange. Her pulse continued to race, but her body relaxed, ready to melt into the phenomenal fingers.

The tenor of the massage changed from squeezing to stroking. She was raw and eager with anticipation. His touch made her feel new, as if she'd never been aroused before. It reduced her from a woman to a sixteen-year-old virgin, experiencing her first hot kiss that heated new and unmentionable places. His caress journeyed longer in distance, swiveling around the inside of her thighs as it came back down. Veronica braced herself, expecting his fingers to brush over her shorts into uncharted territory with the next pass.

He stopped.

She lifted up on her elbows and mere inches divided them. They breathed the same air, and they were close enough for Veronica to see the gold specks in his eyes, yet she knew they might as well be miles apart. The pained expression on his face made his struggle clear. Following his eyes down her leg, she swore his nostrils flared. She barely bit back a growl and lay back on the hard floor. In a strained voice, she spoke, "You know, I don't get you. One minute you're Mr. Freeze and the next you're snuggling up against my back in bed."

Malik sighed heavily and stood up. "Hey, you asked me not to leave."

Veronica pushed away the hand he offered when she stood, as well. Glaring, she said, "Sure I asked you to stay, and I appreciate the fact that you listened when I spoke of my brother, but did I ask you to put your hands right here?" Her fist pounded her chest. "Did I ask you to stroke my cheek, or kiss my head? Did I ask for the response I felt right here, Malik?" Her fist thumped her back this time. Her eyes lowered to the evidence that he was having a similar reaction now.

He didn't answer her, or try to hide his present arousal.

"Was that just part of the service, Malik? Was I wrong to think something more was going on here?" she asked.

At first, he was distressingly quiet, and then he said, "Would you have preferred me to leave?"

The man kept avoiding the real issue. "I'd prefer you to be honest."

"Honest? Okay, you stir certain…feelings that I'd prefer to lie dormant. I thought you were asleep the other night." He shrugged and said, "A few stolen moments are complicating the hell out of things now."

His bluntness surprised her and anger was replaced with curiosity. She asked, "Why, Malik? Because I'm paying you, or because you don't like some of the services I provide?"

"Both," he answered. "Also, they hamper my ability to protect you. That's what I was hired for, not for…intimacy. It's the wrong time, wrong place, wrong everything."

Veronica didn't expect his words to hurt as much as they

did. Her face burned as though he'd slapped her. She took a deep breath and said, "Well, I asked for the truth, didn't I? Thank you very much. However, the next time I ask you to punch me in the gut, feel free to say no." She breezed past, headed to the kitchen.

Chapter 11

Malik followed, and as soon as he turned the corner, he knew he was in trouble. He watched in silent agony while Veronica's bottom angled up as she bent into the refrigerator and came out with bottled water. She popped it open and took a long drink, chest arched, throat working. Malik wasn't thirsty, but he asked for a bottle anyway. She glared at him. Then, without a word, she bent again and the next thing he knew an object was flying at him. Instinctively, his hand covered his face.

"Nice catch," she uttered. Then she left, disappearing into her bedroom. Right after the door slammed closed, it opened back up. "You know what you are, Malik? A tease." The door slammed again.

A tease! Talk about the pot calling the kettle black. She's the ex-singer, driving the crowd crazy with love songs.

Malik drank the ice-cold water, willing it to cool him down quickly. He could hear the shower and his imagination went into overdrive. He downed the liquid and rushed to the fridge for another one.

Malik had a bad night. He doubted if an ice bath would have helped. Knowing an unlocked door was the only thing separating him from a *willing* Dr. Howell had his teeth grinding. He couldn't get her out of his mind. Every time his lids lowered, he saw her and ached with the need to touch her satiny, tar-black skin. The image drove him from his prone position on the couch. He sat up and rubbed his out-stretched legs. Then he suffered a thought so horrendous that he threw off the light blanket covering him and swung his feet to the cool floor. He was ready to blast off the couch, rocked by the question reverberating between his ears.

What if she called that Neil guy, her last boyfriend?

Hell, if she was anywhere near as horny as him, then she needed *companionship and friendship* right now! He squirmed, imagining the man leaving Veronica's room and thanking him for getting her so riled up. The pillow his fist slammed into was too soft to give relief. The back of the couch did the trick, though. He flung his head into it, relishing the pain, hoping it would restore perspective.

The fact that she'd been restless also made him concentrate. He reviewed the sounds he'd heard: a toilet flushing, water running, bed creaking. No murmuring or other indications she'd used the phone.

He heard a click. Looking behind him, he saw light squeezing out from under her door. Twisting awkwardly, he leaned toward the brightness. He almost climbed over the back of the couch when her moving around the room interrupted the light. *Go on*, some part other than his brain urged, *she's not the woman you once thought she was.* Yes, indeed. All his first impressions had been blown away.

He told himself it was lust-induced insanity. Just go beyond the door, give in, and you can think clearly again. His hand drifted downward when he realized he was danger-ously close to doing something he hadn't done since he'd made love to his first woman. He yanked his arm back up. "Dammit." He could survive months at sea without stimula-tion, so he could for sure survive Dr. Howell. Maybe he should have Carl relieve him, so he could go relieve himself. He threw the thought out as soon as it was formed. The idea of Carl watching Dr. Howell do her dancing-exercise made him clench his fists.

The irony was that in the past, he'd used casual sex to keep serious relationships at bay. Now he was getting no sex, and he could feel himself falling into something he didn't care to name. Wanting her was like being in quicksand, the harder he fought, the deeper he fell.

Chuckling, he remembered his stepmother's often repeated advice, "Don't judge a book by its cover." Or hell, it should have been, "Don't judge an issue by your view of it." That's what it really came down to. He heard the word fertility, and his brain filled with ugly images of his own neglect. In the past, that's when the wall went up, shutting it all out, no reason to think about it any further. But being around Dr. Howell gave him reasons to reflect. He'd seen the old lady at Harborlake and couldn't deny that neglect and abuse did come in all shapes and sizes. So maybe it wasn't the process, but the people who used it, like weapons. A gun was a piece of hardware. Depending on whose hand it was in, the result could be good or horrific. Good Lord, he'd certainly seen the truth in that most of his adult life.

An image of his mother crying and him trying to soothe her flashed through his mind; and it hit him, like a blinding light turning on in his brain, helping him to see things more clearly. The thoughts were so shocking his erection wilted and he sat straight up.

Yes, my mother had issues and I suffered because of it, but she did the best she could do. She wasn't mean to me because she hated me. In fact, it was just the opposite. She'd loved me! That's why she cried sometimes and told me she was sorry for no reason.

As a kid, he didn't understand, but now he was putting it all together. The ultimate proof was that she'd let him go to his father without a fight. She'd loved him enough to release him to go to someone who wouldn't abuse him!

It was a powerful idea, and he wondered why it hadn't occurred to him earlier. Or maybe it had. Perhaps it'd been a real low humming he was now able to hear. Deep inside, Malik knew the reason why. He'd actively avoided thinking about the subject because it made him mad, or maybe what he'd been feeling was really sadness. Whatever the right label for the emotion was, he'd reasoned at the time that his birth mother didn't matter because she was sick, and he had his stepmother and his dad. So many people grew up without any love, and he had two wonderful people who told him often he was important.

However, dealing with Dr. Howell—no, not Dr. Howell, Veronica. Yes, calling her by her given name sounded right to him now. Dealing with Veronica, made him revisit his feelings for his mother. That old hurt created a chasm between him and Veronica. The gap was narrowing, though, with the epiphany he'd just experienced. His mother and childhood hurts had no place in his feelings for Veronica.

Veronica stood at her window in the dark, listening to the waves she wasn't allowed to see when she heard the creak of the door opening. Turning, she saw Malik wearing only boxers and a tank top. It was an alarming sight. The skimpy white clothes revealed too much and contrasted sharply with the deep brown of his skin. He stood with his muscular arms extended slightly from his sides, powerful legs spread apart, and long feet balanced on the floor. She felt his heat, even though several feet separated them. It was the fire she'd always sensed was there, but he'd kept tightly covered.

He moved, coming closer. The bathroom light sneaking around the partially closed door allowed Veronica to see his face clearly. His eyes burned and his nostrils flared. Drawing deep, she used every ounce of self-control she possessed not to fling herself at him. The sting of his rejection was too great. Looking as hard as she could under the circumstances, she said, "Why are you in my bedroom?"

Her cold attitude had no affect. He kept coming forward as he said, "I'm living up to your declaration. Let me show you how I tease."

The way he said *tease* made Veronica's stomach clench. His tongue and lips drew the word out, caressing it with a sexy Southern drawl, right before his mouth accented it perfectly with a crooked smile.

Breathing deeply, she stood straighter and said, "You have some nerve coming in here and expecting me to open up and be intimate with you."

"Oh, I expect a lot more than that," he proclaimed.

He didn't attack her and that threw her off. Instead, he moved in close, and she experienced his breath warming her forehead right before he rubbed his slightly crooked nose there. The gentle friction was deliciously soft, deceptively captivating. Her nose became enraptured by his unique male scent mixed with freshly laundered cotton. She breathed shallowly, afraid of getting drunk off the intoxicating fumes.

Taking half a step back, he imprisoned her with his eyes. He moved his hand up her robe-covered arm to the back of her head. Veronica felt herself being drawn into the face bent above her, all resistance obliterated by the desire flaring from his eyes. When they were inches apart, his other hand moved to her smoldering neck, just inside the robe.

How in the hell does he do this to me? Veronica searched the dark brown eyes and wondered if the answer really mattered because he was leaning in closer. She instinctively knew that the brief kiss they had exchanged earlier would be nothing compared to what was about to happen. She held her breath for what seemed like forever, waiting for the man to completely bridge the gap between fantasy and actuality. Double thick, deep-piled lips pressed into hers, locking Veronica in, and rendering her mentally mute. All she could do was savor and feel. Instinctively, she matched every delightful stroke of his luscious mouth. When his tongue touched her lips, she zealously greeted it, and wrapped her arms around his waist. Their tongues intertwined: searching, exploring, then dancing. Veronica couldn't breathe, couldn't think, and for darn sure couldn't move. She didn't care. All she wanted was his crushed velvet mouth, his profound tongue that was already driving her to the edge of climax. She'd never been so thrilled by one kiss, never been so ready to explode from the inside out.

"Sugar," Malik whispered in his hot lava voice, and then peppered her lips with kisses before pulling away slightly. "Forget timing. Something strong is between us that may conquer all our differences. So I'm here to do what we've been meant to do since we first saw each other in your office. Are you ready to experience what our eyes have been talking about?"

She gasped, still trying to get her breathing under control from that first kiss. She'd never been asked before, if you could call his declaration a request. How could he be so manly and courtly at the same time? It was both confusing and erotic as hell. Under the circumstances, how could she not be with this man? Besides, it was a foregone conclusion. Rather than use words, she answered with her lips and tongue. A language she was sure he understood very well.

Everything seemed to be happening in slow motion: Malik's hands at the belt of her robe, slipping it from her shoulders, leaving her naked and exposed. His words, "You are absolutely magnificent," being pronounced separately and distinctly. His hands, gently laying her on the bed; and his eyes, gazing at her lustfully before stepping back.

Veronica watched in admiration as Malik's shirt went up and off to reveal stomach muscles that were mesmerizing as they undulated with each move he made. She wanted to reach out and trace the ripple and roll, but his hands moved to his boxers. Her eyes were riveted, and he disposed of his shorts just as quickly as he had his T-shirt. The bulge his jeans had hinted at was nothing compared to seeing the real thing. The sight that jutted from below his waist was too erotic for verbal communication, and all Veronica could do was stare.

"I have scars." He stood in the glow of the bathroom light, looking like her dream come true.

"You're perfect as any specimen I've seen in my medical books. Your scars make you wonderfully human," she responded.

He came to her, dousing her body in kisses while tantalizingly avoiding several key areas as his mouth skimmed over breasts, his hands glided over buttocks, and his lips hovered over her pelvis. She withered as he drew each of her fingers into his hot mouth and gently sucked. However, the worst teasing was the part of him that dangled. It rubbed here and there as he traveled along her body. Every time she reached, he evaded. She was only allowed to feel it as it brushed her skin, causing ripples of indescribable pleasure.

She was on the edge of surrendering pride and begging for what she wanted when he devoured a breast. Veronica arched her back and willed him not to stop. "Just right," he uttered before the other disappeared into his mouth. A blast of pure heat erupted from within Veronica centering below her stomach. She'd always been self-conscious about her small breast size, but in his mouth she felt perfect. Malik's hands were never still. They traced and retraced her body, making sure that all of her remained at a fevered pitch.

When his finger glided between her legs, she actually yelped. The sound surprised her, yet Malik seemed unperturbed. He simply began moving downward, stopping at her thighs to kiss deep within while his lower half tickled her calf. She looked down and met his eyes as his tongue ran along her inner leg.

She whispered, "Please, no more teasing."

A hint of a smile graced his lips before his mouth disappeared from view.

She waited with bated breath.

Nothing happened.

"Malik," she growled, "if you stop now, I swear I'll hurt you!"

He was close enough for her to feel his warm breath when he chuckled. "Oh, don't worry, sugar, a team of wild horses couldn't stop me now. I'm just admiring the view."

Her eyes slammed shut when she felt the first sweep of his tongue; she stopped breathing with the second; and the third made her clutch so tightly she was afraid of the pending release. Nothing so strong could be survivable. So she held out against the inevitable, squirming in his grasp, alternately avoiding and seeking what he offered so skillfully. In an attempt to find an anchor, her hands flung out. One throttled the mattress edge and the other strangled the sheet. Veronica held her own until he switched tactics. He went from warm, moist and gentle stroking to sucking.

She reasoned that her center had been weakened from the time it'd spent steeped in its own desire, and now it was being treated to *this*. Her back arched and there was simply nothing she could do to stop him from siphoning the pleasure that had settled at the tip of her right out of her body. Before Veronica could reach in and yank it back, her mouth opened with an embarrassing, earsplitting cry that she was sure left Malik with no doubts about what had just happened. The joy was so astoundingly splendid that tears leaked from Veronica's eyes.

It took her a minute to recover. She licked her chapped lips, wiped the sweat off her forehead and gulped, trying to relieve her dry throat. She was too drained to believe that she could respond to anything else. But something about the butterfly kisses trailing along her stomach made her want more.

Her desire fought against the fact that she knew she should reciprocate and make him suffer the firestorm she'd just survived. However, he was positioned and toying with the entrance when he asked, "Am I still a tease?"

Veronica decided this man could bring the dead back to life if he wanted to. "Yes," she answered, arching her hips upward, trying to encourage him to enter her, to no avail.

"I supposed I should have asked this earlier. Please tell me you have protection." The desperation in his voice caused her to smile. She wasn't the only one suffering.

She told him, "The medicine cabinet. I don't know the shelf life. They've been there for a while."

Before he lifted from her body, he seared her with a kiss. He quickly returned, whispering, "They're good as new." Then he came to her. She saw his wide nostrils flare as he moved to bury his lips in her neck. Simultaneously, he eased himself along her body, prolonging the moment before he would enter. Despite herself, Veronica began to lightly throb.

She gave him incentive to make them one when she whispered, "It's time. Malik, give us both what we want."

He needed no other prompting. A hard thrust later, Veronica moaned, "Yes," along with a stream of other encouraging words.

Malik groaned and kissed her. He couldn't control his hips and he didn't want to stop how she was moving with him, but the words were too much. If he didn't stop her encouragement, he feared he'd almost do something else he hadn't done since high school: release way too soon. Her mouth was as hot as the erotic phrases that came from it. She'd run her tongue along his lips before darting inside, and the way she cradled his head with her hands and arms while she did it, made him feel as if she wanted all of him.

Taking a deep breath, Malik lifted and balanced on his knees, so his hands were free. A thumb vibrated between her legs, and the other hand filled with her right breast. His mouth felt denied. Soon, he came forward and swallowed her breast again. While his thumb continued to move, he felt her tremble and knew she was tumbling over the edge once more, even though this time she didn't yell. He waited until she quieted before lifting his head and looking at her. She was so beautiful and wore such an expression of satisfaction, he closed his eyes for a second just to experience the rapture of lifting them to see her looking at him in such a way.

Soon, Malik pressed back down and his hands gripped her curvaceous bottom. An act he'd fantasized about since he'd first seen Veronica in San Diego. The firm, full flesh he kneaded was far better than anything he could have imagined. Malik burrowed in, intending to treasure every sensation before letting go. He quickly learned she had other plans. He lifted a hand and caressed her cheek while his lips enjoyed her neck. She moaned in his ear, thrilling him right before she whispered, "This is what I do to teasers." She tightened her muscles, torqued her hips up and jerked down.

Malik was paralyzed. This thing with Veronica was wild and exciting, way beyond anything he'd experienced before. The third time her hips lifted, he lost the control he never really had and released with a loud groan. He knew he was in trouble because it was too intense to be casual. He feared that for the first time he was actually making love. He searched her expressive face, hoping that he'd see the same thing reflected. All he saw was deep satisfaction that stroked his ego, but not his heart.

Fighting disappointment, he rolled onto his back, and she followed, curling her face into his warm chest hairs, then draping a leg over his thighs as if she'd been doing it all her life. Malik realized he wanted her to do that for the rest of his life. He wrapped his left arm around her waist.

"Malik," she said.

"Hum." His nose nuzzled her scalp.

"You know what this means, don't you?" she asked.

"You love how I tease and want me to do it again?"

The soft chuckle made her head vibrate, tickling his nose before she said, "Yes, I truly do. If I didn't have an operation in the morning, you could tease me all night long. That's not what I'm talking about, though. You don't have to call me Dr. Howell anymore: Sugar, honey, baby, or sexy will do just fine."

He laughed hard, ruffling her hair with his breath while his heart complained. She hadn't mentioned love or even lover. His right hand began stroking her hair. Soon, her breathing slowed and her weight settled, leaving the wide-awake Malik alone with his thoughts. He didn't want to hear himself, so he cleared his mind and listened. He heard waves crashing and the house creaking. Before he'd come to her, he'd checked and rechecked the house, alarm system and cameras. Maybe he should check them again. Veronica sighed and her thigh brushed his groin, her lips tickled his chest. Possibly he could stay a minute or two more.

Chapter 12

The next day Veronica was in the operating room. At the end of the surgery, she took a deep, cleansing breath, which was a contrast to the shallow panting she subconsciously did during the entire procedure. She never noticed how she breathed until that final deep breath. With it, came fatigue. A bone-deep tired, resulting from last night's lovemaking combined with an early-morning operation.

"Okay, we've done our best here," she announced to her surgical team. Alice handed her a towel, and she used it to wipe sweat from her forehead while she surveyed her handiwork.

"Excellent job as usual, Dr. Roni," Alice said, patting her shoulder. "I don't know how you do on cloth, but when it comes to needles and flesh, your stitches look as delicate as the lacework on my Victoria's Secret underwear."

That drew a chuckle from everyone, even the exhausted Veronica. "I assume you're trying to compliment me," she said.

"Sure am," Alice confirmed. "This woman will barely have a scar, and what is there will be covered by her body hair." Alice began cleaning and dressing the incision in a sterile bandage. Another nurse took care of the numerous tools that had been used.

As her staff worked and Veronica supervised, the word came from the pathology lab. Having operating privileges at Harborlake was wonderful to Veronica because the large, competent lab produced quick results. The grapefruit-size cyst they'd removed from Mrs. Gans's ovary was benign. They all smiled, happy to hear the good news. The procedure had taken four long, grueling hours, and Veronica was extremely proud of her two nurses and anesthesiologist. She stepped back until she leaned against the counter and pushed her surgical cap away from her forehead. She rubbed her temples, where a slight headache was forming.

The tough part was over and, God willing, the woman would make a full recovery. However, Veronica couldn't relax yet. She had to face the family, Mr. Gans. A draining task regardless of the outcome in the operating room because so much raw emotion flowed, and she was the focal point. Usually she didn't mind, especially when she had good news like today, but she was tired. All she wanted to do was sleep, preferably in Malik's arms. However, a person was in suspense out there in the lobby, and his need to know was paramount.

Malik was waiting when she left the operating area after cleaning her hands and face. His grin boosted her adrenaline. She resisted the urge to kiss his cheek and settled for brushing his tan pant leg with her hand as she passed and went into the lounge. A raised eyebrow was Malik's only acknowledgment. He followed and took up a post in the doorway, which was the only way in and out of the room. Dark drapes covered the windows, and Veronica assumed that Malik knew the lone man waiting on the couch wasn't a threat, because he turned his back on them and focused on the busy corridor.

She approached the sitting man. His ashen, brown skin made his coloring worse than the patient she'd just left. With slack features, he stared at the blank television; one hand gripped a rolled magazine while the other hung limply, palm up. The limbo of waiting had taken its toll on this man. He looked as if he'd assumed the worst, had already given up hope. Veronica knew so much emotion could be hard for those who didn't have coping skills to deal with it.

She cleared her throat and said, "Mr. Gans."

The man got up stumbling, as if his feet forgot how to work. She rushed to meet him. Before she could say a word, he blurted out, "Just between you, me and the Lord, I promise she won't have to lift a dish or push a vacuum ever again if she's okay." The man painfully squeezed her hands. "I've been a fool for thirty years, and I'm so sorry. She's worked way too hard, and I haven't let her know how much I appreciate it."

Veronica squeezed back and said, "Well, you better buy some rubber gloves and get ready for housework because, chances are, that your wife is going to be just fine."

"Oh, thank you, Doctor." The man almost pushed her down with his weight. In her lab coat and black slacks, Veronica spread her legs and braced her clog-covered feet to support what had to be close to three hundred pounds. Mr. Gans sobbed his relief into her already aching shoulder. Veronica patted his back and was filled with a strange sense of sadness.

Here, she'd performed a successful operation and should be filled with joy, but instead she felt sort of melancholy. She turned her head to look at Malik's back and knew the reason why. She wanted what Mrs. Gans had, and she wanted to give it back tenfold. She wanted a man to clearly adore her, and she wanted to worship him just the same. Sure Malik had thrilled her body, but how did he feel about being a lifelong partner? Although her parents weren't her favorite people, they had a deep love and commitment to each other. What did she have? She wanted more than a bed warmer. She wanted a soul mate, a significant other whose life would be left hollow without her, not someone just proficient at *teasing*.

Stop it! She scolded herself as she managed to place Mr. Gans back on the couch. *You are being way too premature. Let this thing have a life before you kill it with unreasonable expectations.* Then her subconscious threw in the kicker. *Maybe you're so keyed up because you love him. Love?* She called herself all kinds of names as she remembered just yesterday she'd decided it was okay to *like* him.

Using supreme control, she shut off her thoughts and turned her complete attention to Mr. Gans. "Thank you," seemed to be the only thing he was capable of saying while Veronica explained the recovery process and when Mr. Gans would be able to see his wife. As she gently extracted her hand from his grasp, he said, "There's no way my wife will overdo it because she's going to be treated like the queen she is until the day she dies."

Standing in front of Mr. Gans, who was still talking, Veronica looked beyond him and froze, fear straightening her spine into perfect posture. A black purse that looked an awful lot like hers sat on a small table behind the couch. Dread bubbled inside her, because her purse shouldn't have been here. She'd placed it inside the desk of the tiny office that was provided for visiting physicians.

"Excuse me," she interrupted Mr. Gans and walked around the couch to pick up the bag. She opened it and immediately knew she was the owner because her tattered wallet rested right on top. Intending to make sure she still had her credit cards, she grabbed the wallet and her heart jumped into her throat.

"Malik." Her tone must have communicated what she was feeling because by the time she'd whirled in his direction, he was there. She thrust the purse in his arms. "He…he's been here," she whispered so Mr. Gans wouldn't hear.

Malik looked into the purse to see a clear, plastic storage bag. He picked it up, peering at the long black strands it contained.

"It's my hair." Veronica said, touching the bag. "I cut it off when I opened the clinic, and the beautician gave it to me. I put it in that bag and shoved it in the kitchen junk drawer." Veronica hissed, "He must have taken it that first night, and I didn't notice it missing. The creep has been here, Malik!"

"Where did you leave your purse?" he asked.

"Not in the lounge," she assured him. Veronica quickly explained.

Malik shifted his attention to Mr. Gans and spoke louder. "Did you see anyone come in here, sir?"

The clearly puzzled Mr. Gans said, "I'm sorry, I don't know. I was sort of out of it until Dr. Howell called my name."

Looking back at Veronica, Malik said, "Stay put." He returned to the doorway speaking into a small communication device.

"Are you okay, Dr. Howell?" Mr. Gans asked.

She swung to see he was staring at her. Veronica assured him all was well. She shifted the topic to his wife, telling him he'd be able to see her soon.

Mr. Gans nodded and surprised Veronica by grabbing her hand. He patted it and said, "Don't worry, Dr. Howell. Whatever's happening, your friend looks like he can handle it."

Sergeant Ross arrived, people were interviewed and no answers surfaced. Veronica was relieved when she finally left the hospital surrounded by Malik and two other men to quickly get into the car being driven by Carl. No one spoke during the ride to the clinic, and then to Veronica's house.

After the house was checked, Veronica fixed tea while Malik and the men secured what seemed like the entire neighborhood. Malik came into the kitchen just in time to rescue a full cup from Veronica's shaky fingers.

"Thank you," she murmured as she sucked the back of her hand where some of the hot liquid had splashed. "Please put it on the table. No one would believe I sewed perfect stitches just a few hours ago."

"Milk?" he asked.

Veronica nodded. She watched, noticing his movements were even more brisk and efficient than usual. It didn't prepare her for his next words. "You can't go back to Harborlake." He poured milk into her tea and put the carton back in the refrigerator as if he hadn't just made an important decision for her.

She felt as though her whole brain was shaking, instead of only her hands. She sat down and sipped the hot tea, trying to control her nerves. She was proud when she spoke calmly. "That's not possible, Malik. Mrs. Gans is there, and I'm working emergency in two weeks."

"Get that doctor who helped when you were sick. I can't allow you to go back," he said.

"No!" she yelled and reflexively gripped the hot cup and instantly regretted it. She set the cup down and put her scorched hands in her lap, softly rubbed them together. In a lower voice, she said, "I won't let this interfere with my work in such a way. I will not abandon a patient so soon after an operation."

"This isn't a discussion, Veronica," he said in an even tone.

"The hell it isn't!" she was shouting again.

Malik's blank expression spread into wide eyes and flared nostrils before he said, "Don't you get it, Veronica?" His large hand slapped the counter. The loud crack made her jump. "Harborlake is a maze—too many doors, too many ways in and out. I can't protect you there."

Seeing this strong man's raw emotion was truly daunting, yet something clicked inside Veronica. He wasn't like her mother trying to control her for control's sake. She saw beyond the anger to its source. Malik was scared. Someone had gotten behind his shield and it unnerved him. She wondered if it was a professional affront, or something more personal?

"Malik," she said, "I know we can compromise through this. I should be able to release Mrs. Gans in a couple of days if there are no complications. I won't need to spend more than a half hour there. I'll cancel all other obligations at Harborlake until this is over." A glance revealed that his expression had calmed. She continued talking. "I'm just tired, Malik. I want peace, just a little, so I can recharge and face another day." She waved her hand. "Living this way is…it's driving me nuts. I want the sunshine with no bars or cameras. I want fresh air and birds singing. I want uninvited guests to stay out of my house!" She laughed bitterly. "This is my *I Have A Dream* speech."

Pushing the tea out of her way, she laid her arms on the table and her head on her arms. She sighed deeply when she felt Malik's warm hand on her head and back. His lips graced her cheek and he whispered, "I can make part of it reality, sugar. The first weekend after Mrs. Gans is released, I'm going to take you to paradise. Graham owns property on an island, and I'm sure he won't mind us using it. How does that sound?"

"Like a dream come true," she sighed.

Veronica immediately began to pray that Mrs. Gans would make an uneventful, speedy recovery.

The next day, Veronica didn't complain when five people accompanied her to the hospital. Malik and Carl stood outside the door as she examined Mrs. Gans. Mr. Gans was at his wife's side, still thanking Veronica profusely. Mrs. Gans was groggy from the pain medicine, but healing just fine. Veronica continued to pray, and by Friday, her pleas were answered and she was able to release her patient.

Later that same day, Veronica had a special glint in her eye when she explained to Alice that she'd be unavailable for the upcoming weekend. Veronica was in such a good mood she'd ordered pizza for the entire office. She, Alice and Malik were enjoying their slices on the couch in the lobby. Alice, a nurse practitioner, assured Veronica that she could handle any emergencies, and then the wily, old woman winked at Malik. Veronica pretended not to notice. She wasn't ashamed of her burgeoning relationship, but that didn't mean she was ready to discuss it with her head nurse. Alice doubled in laughter when Malik winked back with each eye.

Then Alice said, "Tell me about yourself, Malik?"

He murmured, "Not much to tell. I'm a country boy that joined the service."

"Any siblings?" she asked.

Veronica's eyes widened, yet she didn't interrupt Alice's inquisition. Heck, she'd slept with the man, which was something she wanted to do a lot more. So, she supposed these were things she should know.

Malik smiled before saying, "I'm an only child."

"Oh. What made you join the service?" Alice questioned.

"Trying to be like my dad, I guess. He was a Marine in the Vietnam war."

"A military family." Alice obviously approved. "You look young to have served a full twenty years," she added.

"I left the navy after fifteen years for personal reasons," Malik said while his hand smoothed out the front of his thin, white sweater, which was a change from his standard uniform although he still wore the khaki pants.

Veronica felt a little bad. The first time she was learning about Malik's family and career was through her nurse. She looked up to see Malik smiling at her. He crossed his long legs.

Alice showed some tact and didn't pry into why he'd left the navy. However, that didn't mean she was done being nosy. "Are you married, divorced?" she asked.

Malik answered, "Nope, I've never been hitched."

"Ever been close? Live-in girlfriend, engaged?"

Malik laughed and said, "You're in the wrong career, Alice. A lot of unsolved mysteries could use your touch." He took a bite of pizza. "It was easier to have friends with special privileges."

"Privileges?" Veronica's shout surprised everyone, including herself. Alice's hand covered her mouth, but it didn't contain her giggle.

Malik smiled big, then he focused on Veronica, capturing her with his eyes. "Yes. Kind of like *dates*," he replied.

She immediately knew he was referring to her arrangement with Neil. She felt herself blushing and looked down. She'd have to explain to the man that *dates* meant companionship, not sex.

Malik smiled, then said, "I wasn't ready for anything else. Plus, the sea would have drowned any relationship. I was constantly leaving for six, nine months at a time. It was easy and convenient to just have friends. Of course, some were better friends than others."

Veronica's head shot up and met his wide grin. "Have I told you how nice you look in that emerald skirt and silk shirt, Dr. Howell?" he asked. "In fact, a little green looks good on you."

Is my jealousy that obvious? She wanted to pinch him for teasing her so. Instead, she muttered, "No, you haven't." The man was a master at trying to keep her off balance.

They both turned to Alice when she announced, "I see now." She'd fully recovered from her giggling fit. Crossing her arms, she said, "You just haven't met that special one yet. The one that makes you forget your own name." She seemed unaware of what was going on between Veronica and Malik. Veronica doubted it. The crafty woman just chose to overlook it for some reason.

"I don't know about that." Malik smiled into Veronica's heart. Then he winked and turned back to Alice before proclaiming, "I've met you, head nurse."

"You scoundrel. You know I'm married. But," her eyes twinkled with mischievousness as she said, "you've also met

Dr. Roni." Alice's hands joined in a loud clap. "Look, Malik. I think we've embarrassed her. Dr. Roni is becoming purple."

Veronica was hot. The cause wasn't all embarrassment. She was more than slightly resentful of her frumpy nurse and his special friends.

Alice wasn't done digging facts out of Malik. "How old are you?"

"I'm thirty-seven, ma'am," he responded.

"Just because I'm grilling you, doesn't mean that you have to be so polite. Call me Alice and tell me to mind my business if I'm getting on your nerves."

Malik laughed and said, "You're too cute to get on my nerves, Alice."

That seemed to catch Alice off guard. Her face turned bright red. She patted her brown hair that was pulled into a bun, and Veronica doused common sense on the green-eyed monster gnawing at her belly.

Alice was momentarily silenced, and Malik took the opportunity to say, "If I remember correctly from the file, you're thirty-four, right Dr. Howell?"

Veronica nodded.

"Soon to be thirty-five," Alice added. "Her birthday is next month. When's your birthday, Malik?"

"Today, actually," he said.

"What! Why didn't you tell us?" Alice shouted.

Malik just shrugged.

She took off, mumbling something about getting everybody together.

"Well, what would we do without Alice to cover the basics for us," Veronica said as she stood and began clearing the remains of their lunch from the coffee table.

Chuckling, Malik grabbed her hand when she was near

and said, "Believe me, we'll know everything about each other long before this is over."

The other two nurses and the receptionist crowded the small lobby. "I couldn't convince your hardheaded security guards to leave their post," Alice complained.

"Good," Malik replied.

With Alice leading, they all sang "Happy Birthday" to the gracious Malik. Afterward, Malik followed Veronica into her office. Glancing at her watch, she realized she had about fifteen minutes before the next appointment. Feeling naughty and more than a little possessive, she locked the door and turned to Malik. "So, it's your birthday?" she asked.

He nodded.

She pushed him to the office chair and said, "Have any of your special friends called to wish you well?"

"No." A grin spread across Malik's face. "I wouldn't accept their calls anyway."

That made Veronica happy. "Well, I have about ten minutes to give you a preview of the gift you'll get once we get home." She saw the shock in his eyes as she shimmied out of her lab coat.

"Veronica, I want this, baaaad, but I need to get back to keep abreast of things." His voice was almost a whine.

"Interesting choice of words. I have two you can keep right here," she said pointing to her chest. Hiking her skirt up, she straddled him, making sure her chest was face level. "This will only take a few minutes. Besides, remember you said I get to be the boss sometimes? Well, this is one of those times."

"Goodness," he uttered, "you have me ignoring all the rules. I hope we don't regret this."

"We won't," she said. "Now be quiet and let me have my way." She didn't have any problem with Malik obeying.

Chapter 13

Early Saturday morning as they got into the car to start their trip, Malik reflected that, originally, he'd told himself this excursion was for Veronica. However, as he adjusted his jeans to sit comfortably in the car, he admitted the truth. A large part of him craved isolation, time to discover and make decisions about whatever was happening between them without the constant worries about her safety. He pushed up the sleeves of his loose blue, cotton shirt and began to drive.

To his surprise, Veronica continued the discovery process started by Alice when she asked, "You and Graham are pretty thorough, huh?" The slight drowsiness in her voice didn't fool him. Apparently, her impressive brain had been mulling things over.

Malik nodded as he pulled into traffic. Graham had graciously offered them the use of his pilot and seaplane, which was docked in Tacoma. They had about an hour's drive ahead.

"So, I suppose you have a file on me?" she questioned.

Malik spared her a glance. Her legs, covered in black sweat-pants, were tucked under her, and her loose T-shirt gathered where her arms were crossed. He shifted his eyes to the rearview mirror before answering her. "Yes," was all he said.

"I want to see it." Her tone suggested she expected him to object.

"Okay. Get my computer bag from the backseat and look in the side pocket. It's in one of the manila folders," he directed.

She located the file quickly. He stopped her when she moved to turn on the interior light. It was dark outside because Malik wanted a predawn start to have more time and also on the theory it was too early for the bad guys to be bothered. However, he didn't want to attract unnecessary attention with a bright light. "There's a flashlight in the glove compartment. Please keep the light focused downward."

He was silent as she followed his instructions and used the small light to thoroughly examine the file. Fifteen minutes later, she closed the folder, sighed and leaned back. Unsure of her attitude, he decided to wait it out. It didn't take long for her to turn to him and say, "Heck, Malik, you know it all. Why didn't you stop me when I told you about Mitchell?"

He shrugged and said, "It seemed like you needed to talk, so I let you."

Veronica sighed and said, "I suppose I shouldn't be shocked. Every major news agency in San Diego covered it, but how in the world did you unearth the quarrels between me and my mother?"

He looked straight ahead as he answered. "That's Graham's department." That would have been the end of the conversation as far as he was concerned if he hadn't glanced at her. She wore a pained look, one that spoke volumes about how she felt about her life being probed. The expression loosened his lips and before he realized what was happening, his mouth opened. "I agree with how you stood up for your brother. Who you lie with is nobody's business, but your own. It's too bad that it caused the rift between you and your mother. And some of the stuff in the file I already knew about. I saw you perform when you were a singer." A quick look revealed wide, shocked eyes. "San Diego's a navy town," he explained.

"What does that have to do with anything?" she asked.

He chuckled and said, "Navy guys gravitate toward beautiful women, and you happen to be one. Someone saw you singing and the word spread like wildfire. Everyone in my unit went to have dinner and watch the gorgeous woman with the microphone. Present company included. You even walked by me once and ran your hand along my shoulder."

She gasped. "I'm…I'm flabbergasted." Her voice shook slightly, and she seemed to be talking more to herself than him. "I don't remember seeing you, much less touching you, and considering that you have enough appeal to make a nun notice, I find that hard to believe."

"Oh, really? I think you're pretty cute, too," he responded.

Clearly, she was embarrassed when she said, "It's unnerving to realize how easy someone can get so much information on you." He nodded. "It seems as if you have an unfair advantage, Malik."

"Look, I'm not judging you because of that file," he answered.

"But you have in the past?" she countered.

"What's to judge, Veronica? You've lived a clean life. Even if you hadn't, I'd still be impressed with all you've done in a short amount of time. The files are irrelevant to what's happening between you and me."

Veronica sighed and leaned back into her seat. "Thanks, Malik."

My opinion matters! She didn't actually say it, but her manner suggested it. The idea made him smile and sit up straighter. He glanced, and she flashed him a huge grin. His heart thumped, and he found himself talking more. "I didn't get along with my mom, either." He cursed under his breath and slammed to a stop at a red light. A quick peek revealed she was looking at him as if he was a nut. "You know, something about you has me saying things I don't want to say." Her lips curled upward just a little. He turned to the road and began driving again as he spoke. "My birth mother wouldn't have won any awards. I got in the way of her lifestyle." Malik reduced the first seven years of his life into five minutes. It took him slightly longer to explain how his childhood related to his issues with fertility.

When he finished, she placed a hand on his knee and said, "Now I understand. Thank you."

Malik's shoulders relaxed. He didn't know what to expect, but he didn't want her pity. She didn't offer that and the short sentence let him know they were truly connecting.

So he went even further and said, "Despite what I've just told you, I still loved her. In her own way, she loved me, too. My father found me because my mother called his mother and implied that I existed." Malik took a deep breath, checked all his mirrors and continued speaking. "I think the contradiction would have torn me apart if it hadn't been for my stepmother and father. They explained the world isn't perfect and neither was my mother, but she cared. I didn't completely understand that for a long time, but now, I think I finally do."

Her next words only fed his belief that he'd done the right thing in telling her his story. "Just so you'll know, Malik, I'm on your side. You tell me your mother was awful and I dislike her. You tell me you loved her anyway, I believe you because I think you're incapable of loving someone who's completely bad. Just like I still love my mom. I prefer to have a coast between us, yet I still care for the woman, and I dutifully go home for Christmas every other year."

Malik stared ahead, unable to speak because her words were such a jolt to him. She was gouging out the last of the cancer, helping to make him whole. When he found his voice again, he said, "I've been thinking a lot since I met you. I'm a warrior and you're a healer. I fight against people and you usually fight against things, diseases et cetera, right?"

"Yes," she answered.

"I've been analyzing this. Maybe, it's not how you fight, but what you fight for. You're struggling to fulfill the God-given desire most of us have to procreate. I can see the good in what you do, even if I don't think that some people should be parents."

He glanced, catching her nod.

"I guess what I'm saying is I can be open on the issue." When he looked this time, he was happy to see a big smile on her face.

"Has anyone ever told you, you're wonderful?" she asked.

"Not lately," he responded.

"Well, I'm not telling you, either, because I suspect you're susceptible to getting a big head," she said, leaning over to peck him on the check.

The Lord acquiesced by providing another red light. He looked her in the eyes and said, "You know what this means, don't you?"

She shook her head.

"You're mine until we figure this out. No more Neils, dates, or anybody else," he demanded.

Her eyes widened and her lips tightened, and then she burst out laughing. "I agree only because I'm of like mind, Malik Cutler," she said before reaching out and placing a soft palm on his cheek, the tenderness in direct contrast with her voice tone. "But, let me warn you. I didn't reach this point in my life to be subjugated. The dominant male routine will only get you so far!"

The spicy expression and independence thrilled him. He wanted to stake a physical claim right then and there. He had a hard time listening when Veronica continued talking. "And just for the record, Malik, Neil and I are only friends now. When the romantic relationship ended, so did the physical."

"Good," he said, leaning sideways to kiss her.

The car behind them beeped.

Malik's heart jumped and his eyes flew to the review mirror. In the faint light of the dawn, he saw the female driver behind them throw her hands up. *Just a frustrated motorist,* he tried to soothe himself as he took in the green light and began driving. The feelings he couldn't control were already compromising his ability, and he was deeply ashamed. The woman zoomed past, almost clipping the Pontiac.

"She's got some nerve!" Veronica said as she sat up and glared after the car. She must have been completely unaware of Malik's mood because she settled back and asked, "By the way, I know we're going to an island on a seaplane, but exactly where are you taking me?"

"A small, private place called Decatur," he answered. "It's in the San Juan Islands. Are you familiar with it?"

Veronica yawned before saying, "No, but it sounds far enough away for me to get some peace." She put a hand on his leg and soon fell asleep against his shoulder.

The boatyard where the seaplane was docked was teeming with activity, providing focus for Malik's anxiety. He was mildly surprised at the number of people because it was the weekend after Labor Day, and usually the recreational boaters docked their boats for the season after the holiday. Malik chalked it up to the unseasonably hot weather.

As he maneuvered into the parking lot, the sensation struck him that something wasn't right. Refusing to just explain it away as nerves, he parked and left the engine running. His feeling was instinctual, a warning chill vibrating along his forearms and neck. The sun was up and promised another blistering day. He looked around seeing nothing but weekend warriors comprised of harried adults and joyous children. A small hand even waved to him as little legs skipped past the Pontiac. The premonition didn't go away and subconsciously his hand began stroking the grip of the nine-millimeter at his right hip under his loose shirt. Ten minutes later, he woke Veronica and locked the car. She was too groggy to notice his tension as he placed both of their light bags in her arms and hustled her toward the seaplane.

Pete Johnson, the pilot, was waiting for them on the dock beside where the plane was moored, looking like a military officer in his all-white uniform. He briskly shook Malik's hand and tipped his hat to Veronica, then took their bags as Malik tried to quickly get Veronica on the plane.

"My," he heard Veronica say as she went through the doorway, "the ski things are as big as the plane."

Pete laughed and asked Veronica if she'd ever been on a seaplane.

"No," she told him.

"Well," he said, "this Cessna Amphibian aircraft is first rate."

"I can see," Veronica said as she ran her hand along the plush, white passenger seats. "I'm getting the red carpet treatment." The toe of her tennis shoe toyed with the burgundy runner that ran down the aisle as she said, "Wow, Malik, every seat is a window seat."

"Yes it is," Malik agreed and pecked her cheek before slipping into one that faced the parking lot so he could look out.

"Once we are in the air, feel free to help yourself to food and drink," he heard Pete say and knew he was pointing to the cabinet at the back of the plane. "However, I must warn you, that it can be a little noisier than a commercial aircraft. It's not so loud that you can't have a conversation, but it bothers some people. Would you like earplugs just in case?"

Malik turned to see that the still-standing Veronica looked concerned as she took the earplugs. Before he could assure her, Pete said, "Don't worry, ma'am. The view you are about to see is so lovely, you probably won't even notice there's a little extra racket."

Malik nodded and rubbed her waist then turned to the parking lot again. Nothing.

"Ma'am, it's time to sit down," he heard Pete say.

He looked up to see Veronica at the front of the plane, poking her head out the entrance. His heart jumped and he rushed to her, taking her hand and leading her to the seat.

"I'm just looking around, Malik," she protested.

Malik nodded and said, "I know, sugar. I just feel safer with you away from doorways."

He sat her in the seat nearest him, smiled briefly and said, "The flight will take about an hour and a half." He turned back to the window and continued staring out of the plane, unable to shake the vibe that something was amiss.

Shadow was furious. He used his binoculars to watch the seaplane disappear over the horizon. He stomped back to his car so mad that he kicked the tire with his steel-toe boots. Then he restrained himself and slowly smoothed out his black jeans with both hands before running his fingers down the front of his pullover shirt. *Take a deep breath*, he told himself, *so you can decide your next move*.

It had been difficult tailing Mr. Security. He knew the man would notice right away if he followed too close; consequently he took advantage of the slow-moving traffic and hung about five cars back. Trying to outthink his foe, he sped past the entrance to the boatyard. He cussed a blue streak as soon as he realized the man's destination. By the time he'd turned around and made his way back, they were boarding the plane. He didn't know it until he'd left his car and lifted his binoculars to see Mr. Security look back before he had disappeared inside the aircraft.

It's okay, he attempted to console himself, *they'll be back soon because Mr. Security wouldn't take the good doctor away from her precious flock for long.* People dedicated to others amused Shadow because it helped them to be so predictable. Speaking of others, Shadow knew it was getting close to the time to act. He'd told his associates he would be gone for six weeks at the longest, and they were getting anxious for his return.

Shadow felt restless. He didn't like the feeling and the more he thought about the current turn of events, the more he blamed Weasel. He'd seen the man sneak into Harborlake a couple of days ago, then slink back out. He wasn't sure what Weasel had done, but within a few hours, that girl cop had arrived with other police officers. Mr. Security had practically been on top of Dr. Howell since. Yes, Weasel was responsible for his lady being whisked away.

Shrugging, Shadow told himself that he really should thank Weasel. Everybody's tension was high, awareness was peaking, and the game was getting hotter. All that equaled greater risk, one of the things he thrived on, he reminded himself. This was becoming a supreme challenge, more than worthy of his attention, and he loved the idea that he was about to do things that only an elite few could do. Without Weasel, there would have been no Mr. Security and winning Dr. Howell would have been significantly easier. Yes, Weasel had raised the stakes, and he should be grateful.

So far, he'd been an observer in the game, but now, *showtime* was approaching.

As the plane lifted in the air, Malik still searched the ground. His shoulders didn't relax until Pete announced over the intercom that they were at cruising altitude. Slowly the vicious tension holding his body captive began to ease.

"We're at cruising altitude?" Veronica leaned over, looking out her window. "I can still see the ground."

Malik smiled at the back of her head and said, "That's the beauty of a small plane. They fly low enough to see the landscape."

"I see," Veronica commented without turning to him.

Malik didn't blame her, because he knew the northwest coastal areas were dazzling, and he looked forward to enjoying the view through Veronica's eyes.

He didn't have to wait long. Very soon, Veronica shouted, "Look, Malik." She pointed out the window, and he bent over her to see what had her so excited. "Is that what I think it is?"

Malik looked at the big ship plowing out of the water. "If you think it's a submarine, then yes, it's what you think it is. Washington is rich with naval bases."

"I know," she responded, "but I've never seen a submarine moving before. It's intimidating."

Malik held back his chuckle and just smiled. "We hope our enemies think so, too."

Veronica nodded and then said, "Wow, I know we're thousands of miles up, but I feel like I'm getting a sneak peek at people's lives—farmers on tractors, kids playing in school yards, half-naked women sunbathing on boats."

"Where?" Malik pretended to look out his window desperately. Veronica slapped his arm playfully. He laughed and said, "I know what you mean about the view. We're blessed with sunshine today, but it's even astounding when there's a misty drizzle."

Time passed quickly and soon Pete's voice came over the intercom. "Decatur Island on our right, folks." Looking down, Malik saw a gravel beach, the dense green of the forest and the instantly recognizable A-frame shape of Graham's cabin perched between the trees and water. Malik knew that landing on water could be unsettling for those not used to it. He glanced at Veronica who held the armrest in a death grip as the plane buoyed from side to side before finding its balance in the water surrounding them. Pete pulled up to the dock and secured the plane before telling them it was time to disembark.

Malik helped Veronica, then bent to lift the bags that were near Pete's feet. "It's a hot day. I took the liberty of getting both of you some water," Pete said, handing them the bottles.

After hefting both of the light bags on one shoulder, Malik thanked him and took the waters, handing one to Veronica.

With a salute, Pete said, "Enjoy your time, and I'll be here at three sharp on Sunday."

Malik nodded before taking Veronica's hand and leading her to the house that sat about a hundred yards from the dock.

"Is that where we're going?" Veronica pointed.

Malik nodded.

"Take a plane and we're right at the cabin. No jeeps, taxis, or bus rides!" she shouted before dropping Malik's hand hugging his side. "Oh, Malik, this is wonderful, and it's so isolated. Are there other houses on the island?"

"Yes, last count, there were fifty-nine residents," Malik answered. The closest house is about a mile and a half away, and it's a summer home. According to Graham, the people are rarely there so we should have no interruptions, sugar."

Veronica squealed, "I guess I can take off my top then. I'm burning up." She ripped her T-shirt over her head to reveal a purple bikini top, as her sweats hung low on her hips. Placing the shirt in the crook of her elbow, she took a long sip of water, making her throat work. Desire kicked Malik in the gut. "Um, there's nothing like cold water on a hot day," she said.

Oh, Malik could think of a few things better. He took a sip of his own water, hoping it would cool him off as she literally skipped the rest of the way to the cabin.

"Oh Malik, it's made out of real logs—" Veronica trailed a hand along the polished wood "—and it has a wraparound deck and a porch swing attached from the rafters. How quaint." She practically pranced up the steps before plopping down in the swing, making the chains creak as she moved back and forth among the plush cushions. Malik was ready to drop the bags and join her, but he had chores to do before he could completely relax.

Her stomach growled loudly. "Oh," Veronica said, looking at her bare midsection, "I guess breakfast was a long time ago?" She sipped more water.

Malik's stomach rumbled, and she laughed, saying, "I'll take that as a yes." Next, she sighed, stretched and said, "But I don't feel like moving."

"Don't," Malik told her. "Relax while I put our things in the room, and see what the property manager stocked for us to eat." But he couldn't resist touching her. He put the bags down, and bent to run a hand along her bare stomach.

"Mmm, I like that. Join me," she said, then grabbed the hand at her belly and kissed the palm.

Her mouth was cold from the water. Malik enjoyed the sensation. He breathed deeply.

"Join me," she said again. "I'm hungry for more than food."

"Believe me, so am I, sugar, but I can't completely relax until I scout around a bit. Let me do my thing, and then I'm all yours," he placated.

The slight pout on her face softened, and she said, "All right. I'll just rest my eyes, until you're done." Her lids lowered, and she leaned her head back as she swayed gently on the swing.

It was quite a sight, her body stretched out and supple. Her breasts were covered, yet he imagined they were bare. The globes moved slightly with the motion of the swing, and it helped to fuel his fantasy. Although she was small in that area, she had been graced with very large nipples. He liked to think his look was enough to make them crest as they were doing now, poking against the material of her bikini. Malik jerked his head up. He couldn't watch anymore, or he'd be on the swing making her nipples do more than poke out. Whispering a prayer about good things come to those who wait, Malik unlocked the door and went into the cabin.

He dropped the bags near the front door and disabled the alarm system before surveying the spacious living room, making sure nothing was amiss. Then he went around the large, brown, soft leather couch which sat across from the stone fireplace and down the short hallway to scrutinize the only bedroom, and kitchen. After making sure the house was safe, he went out the back door in the kitchen and checked the perimeter. The back of the house faced the forest while the front rested near the water. He encountered nothing that raised his suspicions, and the last bit of tension eased out of Malik as he used the back door to reenter the house.

He retrieved the bags, took them to the bedroom and quickly exchanged his jeans for gym shorts and a gray T-shirt. Next, he looked into the refrigerator, not surprised to find it fully stocked with food and drink, including wine. "Thank you, Graham," he whispered and quickly made two ham and cheese sandwiches. Stacking them on a paper plate, he grabbed a couple of sodas, some napkins, and walked back to the front of the house. Before he went outside, he looked at the water out the large bay window and was happy to see it was clear of boats. After they ate, he had plans for Veronica that shouldn't be subject to prying eyes. He sat down beside her, trying his best not to disturb the swing too much. She sat with her legs tucked slightly underneath her to the side. "Veronica," he said, resting the items in his lap.

No response.

Leaning over, he saw closed eyes and a completely stress-free, relaxed face. He used his feet to swing a little harder. It had no effect.

"She's asleep." He muttered the obvious. His hand reached to stroke her cheek, so she'd wake up and love him. Something he'd been looking forward to since the morning. Guilt stopped him. He ate both the sandwiches and drank both sodas, a poor substitute for what he really wanted. Again, he focused on Veronica. She looked soft and relaxed, making him think of melted, dark chocolate. He longed for a taste; instead he got up, got a thin blanket from the closet and covered her. The sun was angled so its rays reached far below the overhang of the roof. He could just imagine his efforts being thwarted later because the heat had seared her too badly as she lay in bikini top and sweatpants.

The setting sun was loosing its grip on the day as it started to sink out of sight when Veronica's lids finally lifted. She noticed Malik was sitting beside her, and she smiled when his eyes left the fiery red glow to look at her. Veronica stretched, moving the swing, and disturbing the carefully placed blanket.

"Geez, I slept like the dead. It felt good," she said as she sat up straight, arms securing the cover to her front.

Malik tugged at it, trying to remove it. "I've been lonely while you got your beauty sleep."

Veronica chuckled. "Beauty sleep. I hope it worked." She let him take the blanket.

"Figure of speech. You're gorgeous no matter what," Malik said, leaning in until her stomach growled loudly.

"You'll have to feed me first," she demanded. "I haven't eaten since that toast at breakfast." His eyes showed his suffering, so she reached and caressed his face with delicate fingers. "Poor baby. I'll eat quickly." Despite Malik's pout,

Veronica got up and then stopped. She stared at the almost-set sun and whispered, "My God." She drifted down the stairs and stared at the beautiful scene before her.

Malik joined her and said, "I know. It's indescribable."

Veronica squinted and hopped around, grasping his arm. "Did you see that? What was it? That flash of yellow then green, did you see it?"

"I saw it, I saw it, babe." Malik seemed to wait for her to settle a little before he said, "It's called a Green Flash. I used to see it out at sea every once in a while. It usually happens when the horizon is clear and cloudless. Right before the sun goes down, there's a brilliant flash of emerald green."

"I've never seen anything like it. It was truly phenomenal! Now I know that God is real because things like that are too beautiful to happen by chance."

Malik wrapped his arms around her from behind and said, "Sounds like a song."

Veronica responded, "It is, with my paraphrasing. India.Arie from her *Voyage to India* CD."

Malik nuzzled her back, as her stomach growled once more. "Come on, baby. Let's put something in your belly so it'll stop fussing at us."

Veronica sat at the dinette across from the stove watching Malik prepare dinner as she sipped a glass of red wine. Looking around, she commented, "This is a pretty modern kitchen for a log cabin. A microwave, dishwasher, I suppose those things aren't much of a surprise, but a warming oven?" She waved her hand, "Come on, Malik, don't you think that's a bit much?"

He laughed and removed the rolls from said oven.

"I have to admit I'm impressed," Veronica said.

"Good." Malik pulled a dish out of the oven. "Dinner's

ready. Baked salmon, green beans and red potatoes." He fixed two plates and sat across from her.

"This looks great. I guess I expected cold sandwiches and beer," Veronica said.

Malik laughed.

"What?" Veronica asked, fork stopping midway to her mouth.

"Nothing, except that your comment sounds like my lunch, and I think you're wonderful," Malik replied.

When they were done eating, Malik stood and offered her his hand. After she was standing, as well, he said, "Close your eyes."

Veronica was suspicious. She withdrew her palm from his and crossed her arms. "Why?"

Malik laughed. "Because I asked you to. Trust me."

"There you go with that butter voice again. What if I ask you to let me put a blindfold on you and tie you up? Would you trust me?" she asked.

Without hesitation, he said, "Sure, but I should let you know that I'm double-jointed and can get out of just about any knot."

"No fair," she muttered. "That must have come in handy when you were a SEAL."

Malik shrugged. "Come to think of it, it never came up when I was in the navy."

"Then how did you find out?" she questioned.

He answered, "My mother used to tie me up when she didn't want to be bothered."

He said it so nonchalantly, as if he was describing the weather. Veronica still flinched. "Oh, Malik, I'm so sorry." Her arms uncrossed and coiled around his waist.

Malik chuckled, "Don't apologize, sugar. It wasn't your

fault. Besides, she stopped once she figured out it wouldn't work. Now, turn around and close your eyes."

Giving in, she let Malik move her, so her back was to his front. With their bodies pressed together, he said, "Everything in my past helped to shape me into the man I am today. There's no time for pity or regrets." Then he put a hand over her eyes and an arm around her waist. Veronica liked how that felt. With lips close to her ear this time, he said, "Don't you want to trust me, baby?"

"Only if you don't stop," she retorted.

He chuckled, and she felt him maneuver so he was in front of her. After pecking her lips, he began leading.

He instructed, "Lift your feet for me."

She obeyed and knew they were passing the doorway between the kitchen and living room. Malik told her to lift her feet again, and she sensed they were outside by the smell and the slight breeze on her face. Malik put her hand on the railing and she gathered they were going down the steps. "Last one." His lips were close to her ear. About thirty seconds later, Malik said, "Stop and keep your eyes closed." She did so, even when he helped her lie down. Once she was settled, he said, "Okay, open your eyes and see the show."

Veronica lifted her lids to a world filled with stars. She realized she was lying on a thick blanket in the middle of the small yard.

"Isn't it magnificent? A full moon on a cloudless night," Malik said as he lay beside her.

"Yes, it's beautiful," she answered.

Malik caught her hand and began speaking. "When I was a kid, my dad claimed we needed quality time. Only he didn't call it that. He called it our time. Anyway, he knew I had a thing for water, and he had this little speedboat. After he got off from work, ate dinner and stuff, we'd get in the boat and go for a ride. He'd always stop in the middle of nowhere, and we'd lie back and look at the sky. I was amazed at how much he knew. He'd show me Orion, stars shaped like a guy holding a bow." Malik pointed and moved his finger about. "Can you see it?"

Veronica tried to no avail.

"And there's Taurus, the bull. He's one of my father's favorites." Again, his finger moved in the air as he tried to show her. Veronica felt her face drawing in as she concentrated. Malik looked at her, his smile as bright as the stars he talked about and said, "You can't see a thing, can you?"

Smiling shyly, Veronica admitted, "Just lots of pretty lights in the sky."

Malik's laughter boomed around them. He leaned over and gave her a full body hug before saying, "Well, my pops used to say my opportunities were endless like the heavens. I could be anything I wanted to be if I worked hard and stuck to it."

Veronica lifted to peck his lips, and then said, "Your father sounds like a wonderful man."

"He is." Malik's voice lowered.

Veronica looked up at him and saw desire glowing in his eyes.

He squeezed her hand and said, "You know, we haven't had dessert." His warm breath graced her neck before she felt his lips. "I'm in the mood for velvety-black, dark chocolate." Softly, he licked and sucked. It was so splendid that Veronica arched her neck and tilted her head to the side. A small groan escaped when his mouth toyed with her earlobe. She turned to him and captured his lips. The man was too sweet and too good to be true. Veronica couldn't have said the exact moment, but she knew she loved him long before he showered her with tender kisses on the grass on beautiful Decatur Island.

Malik stood and stripped off his shorts and T-shirt. His body wore the moonlight as if it was custom-made for him. Even his chest scar glowed majestically. The serious expression on his face thrilled Veronica. She knew she was about to be taken, possessed and fulfilled in the most primitive way. She could hardly wait, but first she wanted to do some of the taking herself. Something she had yet to do, which made the desire even greater. She rose to her knees, and found she was positioned perfectly.

She had barely started to do her thing when she sensed him trembling. Her eyes lifted to see his head roll back when all of him disappeared between her lips. He seemed to struggle for breath, but managed to say, "Baby, I've been a sailor for too many years to be this excited, so quickly!"

Pride boomed through her. She was happy to have brought him the type of pleasure he rocked her with. Feeling extremely confident, she made sure his eyes were on her as she slowly reached out with her tongue to capture the pearly drop that had formed at his tip. She felt his knees buckle, and she leaned in to steady him.

Veronica understood when she felt his trembling palm at the side of her face. She slowed her motion and allowed him to gently detach her fingers. Then, he bent to help her remove her clothing, and they lay back together. He began planting kisses all along her face and neck before joining their mouths, making her dizzy with anticipation. His lips moved downward as he meandered to a breast. "One day I'll draw sweet nectar from here, as well, when your belly is full of our child," he said while his rough hand grazed her stomach.

What?

Before her question could reach air, he sucked a nipple making her essence clench tightly. When he lifted his head to move downward, she was able to think for a second and said, "You did bring a condom?"

He chuckled handsomely before saying, "Of course. I'll put a ring on your finger before I fill you with anything other than me."

"Malik," she said, "is that your idea of a proposal?"

"Only if you want it to be," he countered.

Dammit. Why can't the man give a straight answer?

His tongue touched her lower abdomen and all worry of their future flew right out of her head. All issues could be resolved after *this. Oh God,* she thought, *I'm so excited I could melt into this blanket!*

Apparently, Malik was having similar thoughts. He licked her stomach and uttered, "So slick."

"I've never been this big of a sweater," she gasped. "I suppose my condition is a testament to your skill."

"Mum," Malik murmured against her skin. His tongue stroked her abdomen clean of the thin layer of perspiration. Then he said, "Just enough salt to make me real thirsty."

He gently nudged her legs apart. She didn't feel anything but breeze. Learning from last time, she lifted on her elbows before commenting to see Malik staring.

"So beautiful," he said right before his mouth merged with her flesh.

Air caught in her chest, tension seized her muscles. Malik's tongue was absolutely wicked, she decided. She'd thought the first time was a pentup-induced fluke, yet here she was climaxing again as she never had before.

When she could interpret the world once more, she realized why it was so different with Malik. She watched him, still between her legs, and it came to her. This man really liked what he was doing. It wasn't just to please her, and then he was done. He really seemed to enjoy it. Her suspicions were confirmed when he moaned and went at her with new fervor. She couldn't take it. Her hand to his head stopped him. He smiled, crawled up her body and planted a big kiss on her lips. She reached for him when he moved away.

He grabbed his shorts, retrieved protection from his pocket, and quickly rolled it on. Then he flipped her, so she lay on top of him and his back was pressed against the blanket-covered grass. *Okay*, she leaned down and caressed the slight bend in his nose with her lips and thought, *now I'm in control*.

She found out how wrong she was when she sat up and he slipped himself in. Veronica barely moved, letting the motion of her gently rocking hips do all the work. Then, she squeezed the wonderful thickness and emitted a gasp of pure pleasure. His feet gripped the ground and his hands gripped her hips. He said nothing, yet Veronica felt him willing her to put a palm on each pec, so she could rise and give him more access. She did so. The strokes were long, hard, and getting faster. She met them with deliberate, pleasure-seeking movements of her own.

Malik was in heaven. He watched as moan after moan rumbled from Veronica's throat. His eyes traveled down her body and he saw arms encasing breasts that moved with their motion. The sight held him spellbound. His hands shifted from hips to buttock, and he kneaded her bottom.

"Yes, Malik," she hissed and he watched her enter the next dimension. Her thighs gripped and her torso arched tight as a bow. Soon she was squealing and the sound corresponded with the hollowing of her stomach. Back bent, she gyrated against Malik's pelvis. That did it. Malik gave in and released enough liquid to rival the water that lapped beyond them. Veronica collapsed on his chest, sighing from deep in her belly, and all he could do was hold her. Heavy breathing graduated into sighs and then no audible sound at all.

Malik had thought she was asleep until she leaned up and seared him with her eyes. If asked, he wouldn't have been able to describe the look, even though it was the one he'd been waiting for. It let him know this was more than a physical thing. But still, he wanted the words, although he didn't need them to know she was his.

Her face changed. He sensed her confusion and wondered if the depth of her emotions scared her. A hand traveled down her face, and he knew she'd try humor to ease out of the moment.

"Now I understand," she said.

"What, sugar?" His voice was a throaty rumble.

"If you ever do that to another woman, I'll do something really bad to you," she teased him with a sly grin.

Malik's smile split his face. He'd allow her to hide a little longer. She had to get used to the idea that she loved him. So he said, "Is this how you sweet-talk all your men?"

"No. Just the special ones," she answered.

The teasing words were just that, but he experienced a twinge of jealousy. He resisted when she moved to get up.

She kissed his chest, saying, "Your back must be killing you. Let's test that big bed in the master suite." She got up, stretched and offered a hand, which he accepted. When he stood beside her, Veronica pointed, "Look, Malik! The moon is sitting on the ocean."

It was a rare extraordinary moment because the water was completely still. The dark even surface shimmered like a royal blanket placed before them. From behind, Malik wrapped his arms around her as they stood admiring the beauty.

"This is what peace looks like," she whispered. After a time, Malik reached for her hand and led the way to the cabin.

Chapter 14

If asked, Shadow would have described his mood as peaceful, too. Hard to believe when he was about to commit an act that would make front page headlines. However, that's how it was for him. He knew his mission, he'd planned well, and now he waited to act. He was energized, yet far from frazzled as he stood in the corner of Weasel's dark room. Getting in had been a breeze. He'd broken the rusty lock on the cellar door weeks ago, and it had remained unlocked. It struck Shadow as funny that the victimizer never thought he'd be the victim. The house wasn't even equipped with an alarm.

A small part of him fretted. He was taking a chance dealing with Weasel in such a way. It might send a clue he existed. *Shush*, he told this part of himself. It didn't matter because it was time to perform. The temporary loss of Dr. Howell had frustrated him. He needed to do this to release tension. Shadow didn't want to accidentally soil the fruits of his labor when he faced Dr. Howell. No, he wanted to cherish her in his own special way.

The clock struck midnight, and Shadow suspected this particular wait was almost over. He knew Weasel's habits. Soon the man would be leaving the neighborhood bar and returning home…to a house where his old mother slept upstairs, and where trouble waited inside his basement room.

Almost on cue, he heard a creak and the yawn of a door opening from above. Weasel was home. Shadow gripped his knife and stared at the bedroom door, mentally calculating how long it should take the man to come downstairs. As he waited, he stood to the right of the bedroom door and knew that he'd have to travel approximately three feet to reach his target. He listened to the groan and rasp of the stairs as Weasel came to him. When the door finally opened, Shadow felt exhilarated. That special joy that came at the last second when he knew his plan had come together. Weasel was unwary and in Shadow's zone, and Shadow glorified in the knowledge that he knew this man's fate before anyone else.

Weasel didn't see him because he was too comfortable to suspect anything in his own home. His target smiled as he turned to close the door and presented his back to Shadow. Lightning quick, Shadow struck. He grabbed Weasel's forehead with his left hand and as quick as that he had accomplished his mission. The deed was swift, and Weasel's demise coincided with Shadow whispering, "Thank you," to the still-smiling man. He lowered Weasel to the ground before removing his weapon, doing his best to avoid the spreading mess. He changed his rubber gloves and put the soiled items in his pocket before leaving as silently as he'd entered.

Veronica slept under a sheet on a rug in front of the fireplace in the living room while Malik sat on the couch and doggedly stared at the television screen, determined to watch all the surveillance tapes from the last couple of days. He had brought them with him because he hadn't had a chance to view the tapes before leaving for the trip. Carl had already examined them and said they contained nothing new, but he wanted to be sure.

Earlier, he and Veronica had left the bedroom to raid the kitchen, and once one hunger was satisfied, another grew until they ended up making more passionate love on the living room rug where Veronica now slept. Not wanting to interfere with their day, Malik disengaged from her luscious body at 4:00 a.m. and started the VCR in the only place where the equipment was available, the living room.

It'd been extremely hard to uncurl from that body, and the memory of it had him sighing while he focused on the tedious task that excited him about as much as dripping water did. "Only one more to go after this, Malik," he consoled himself. Veronica moaned, and he turned to the delight of seeing her naked breast play peekaboo with the sheet he'd covered her with. That opened his eyes.

"You can do this later," he whispered. Suddenly something on the screen grabbed his attention. His thumb was hovering over the remote's off button when he saw the car. More specifically, it was the wheels—mismatched in the exact same way. Instead of Off, he pressed Rewind, then Play. He hadn't seen the car since he'd had Washburn analyze the tapes. So he stared hard. Sure enough, it wasn't a mirage. It was definitely the same car, and it turned right before it left camera range.

Malik pressed Pause, halting the sedan in midturn. He stared at the blurred license plate. He could make out the letters U and S. They spoke volumes because it meant that the car probably belonged to a government worker. *The neighborhood kid was right!*

Malik rushed into the bedroom, grabbed his laptop and hurried back. Veronica stirred as he plugged it into the wall near the television. He glanced, seeing that she'd flung her right arm over her face and her snoring had slowed. Malik connected the cables between the VCR and the computer. After opening his editing software, he copied the thirty or so seconds of video. Then he fired up the wireless modem attached to his laptop and clicked on the phone at the same time. The Globalstar phone was expensive, but extremely flexible. It was designed to switch from cellular to satellite as required. Out on this remote island, he'd be using the satellite portion at about a buck fifty per minute.

After the third ring, Graham growled, "This had better be important."

"It is," Malik answered. "I got the car on tape again." He saw Veronica's face emerge from under her arm. She blinked blearily.

"I suppose that's good enough reason to wake me up at this ungodly hour," Graham grumbled.

Malik responded, "Well, if it isn't, how about this? I see the letters US on the license plate."

Veronica's eyes closed. She looked drowsy and sexy as hell.

"That certainly makes it interesting," Graham admitted.

"Yeah, I thought so. With better equipment, we might be able to get the whole number. I'm e-mailing it to you right now."

"Okay, you know I can't get anyone to look at it until later," Graham said.

"All right," Malik replied. "I'll be waiting for your call."

He clicked the off button. Veronica watched him once more. She seemed more awake as she leaned on her elbows, making an alluring pose.

"Don't tell me I have competition, sailor," she said.

Malik laughed. "You're in a class by yourself, sugar." He put his computer on the ground and crawled to the rug to charm her breast with the length of his tongue. "It was Graham. We've got the car on video again."

His full mouth made it hard to understand him; however, Veronica didn't seem in the mood to complain.

"I sent it to Graham, and we may have a license plate number."

Veronica lay back, taking Malik with her. He could see curiosity battling passion on her face. He pressed against her to ensure that lust won. He knew it had when she said, "I want all the details as soon as you're done convincing me I'm your only woman."

Sometime later, after the yelps, groans and sighs, Malik explained his discovery more fully. Then something else occurred to him and he said, "We need to call Samantha."

"Whatever for? It isn't even dawn yet." she protested.

He grabbed his phone off the floor near his computer. "I know she finished reviewing the charts last week. I want her to go over them again to see if anyone's a government worker and if they have access to animal parts."

Veronica answered, "Geez, tons of my patients have insurance through the government. Besides, Laura can probably tell you the answer faster. She does all the billing. A computer check will tell you who gets insurance from where."

Malik smiled, saying, "Brains to go along with that body. Let's call her."

Veronica didn't know Laura's home number, so she called

Alice to get it. After a short conversation with Laura, she hung up the phone and told Malik, "She'll call and e-mail the information as soon as she has it."

Malik sighed and lay back in front of the fireplace as if to say they'd done all they could for the time being.

Veronica stood by the television and wall, looking down at him with a question quivering at her mouth's edge. It had been on her mind for some time, yet fear of the answer made her hesitant. She didn't want the idyllic state of their relationship to change.

"What is it?" Malik asked.

His ability to read her was truly becoming annoying.

"Come on, honey. Bottled up things tend to go pop," he coaxed.

She smiled at the characterization. It reminded her of Belinda's outburst at dinner. Then she said, "All right. What's in your head, Malik? What were you getting at when you mentioned pregnancy and proposals?"

He smiled and said, "I want you, Doc. I was a sailor for a long time. I've traveled all over the world and learned a thing or two about women."

Despite herself, Veronica's heart wrenched. She didn't like to think of him with other women.

He continued, "I know lust and momentary attraction that lasts as long as a firecracker. I've lived with another, and believe me, I know that boredom is much worse than loneliness. You—" she watched him struggle with the words "—you're with me all the time, even when I sleep. I try to shut you off and all I get is insomnia." He crawled across the living room rug toward her. "Violent colors of jealousy flash in front of me at the thought of you with another." Standing, he pinned her against the wall with his naked body. "I'm not an easy man, Veronica, and I want you to think before you respond because once I've got you, I'm not letting go. I love you with parts of me that I didn't know existed."

She surprised both of them by pulling his head down and kissing him deeply before saying, "I'm not changing my practices at the clinic."

"I know. Like I told you in the car, I'm willing to compromise and be open-minded," he answered.

She arched up, and he eagerly met her for another kiss. When her grip around his neck lessened, he lifted his head. He searched her face, and she knew what he wanted to hear. She said, "How can I not love my houseguest, my personal protector? You stormed into my life and brought confusion, heat and compassion. I'm yours for the taking." And take he did, until they both collapsed into exhaustion.

"Your right bicep is bigger than your left, Malik."

"Mmmmm, probably because I'm right-handed," he said, his voice weighed down with sleep.

Veronica awoke with the urge to examine the man who meant so much to her. She'd unintentionally awakened him in the process. He seemed to be content, stretched out letting her have her way.

"Big strong veins." She traced the lines that ran the length of his forearm. Although she didn't know the time, she knew that the sun was up because light streamed through a crack in the living room blinds, allowing Veronica to see. Even relaxed and quiet, he was so strong; a long man with broad shoulders, narrow hips, lengthy legs and a hard torso. Veronica gently rolled him so he lay on his side, face turned away from her. She felt him tighten when her fingertips brushed the uneven, crisscrossing lump of scars at the top of his back.

"Please," she whispered, "you are so beautiful I just want to know all of you. Your scars are mere beauty marks to me." She sensed the tension leaving him slowly. Then, she touched his entire backside, leaning forward at times to let her lips stroke the thick, rounded tissue that dotted the surface from his upper back to his bottom. Buckshot was Veronica's guess. She didn't want to ruin the mood by asking. Hopefully, they'd have plenty of time for those types of questions later.

"You know, at night when I wasn't careful to block it out, I dreamed of doing this," she whispered.

"Mmm." His muscles shivered.

She fitted herself to him: breast rubbed against back, groin shifted against buttock, and Veronica savored being pressed against his solid, secure, arousing strength.

He turned and when they made love this time, it was different, much slower as if they were reaffirming their knowledge about each other. Afterward, Veronica lay in his strong embrace, watching the pulse throb in his neck. She reached out and touched it with her lips. Next, she pressed her forehead against it, sighed, and fell into a deep sleep.

The phone rang just as she and Malik finished packing later that same day. Veronica stood at the large window in the living room, staring out at the water. She knew it had to be either Graham or Sergeant Ross calling, and she was resentful and irritated because she wasn't ready for the lovemaking and relaxing to end. Calls represented problems, her problems to be exact.

Earlier, Laura had e-mailed the information they were waiting for. Approximately twenty-five percent of her patients received benefits from the government. The billing information didn't specify which agency the party worked for. Veronica usually noted occupations in the charts as background information, so they had to be searched. Samantha was called to see if she'd help since she'd already been through the charts once. Her friend agreed, but she insisted on grilling Veronica about where she was calling from and who she was with. Veronica admitted she was somewhere in the San Juans with Malik. Something in her voice must have told Samantha she and Malik were on friendlier terms because her friend's tone changed to annoyingly playful. She wouldn't hang up until Veronica promised to call her first thing Monday morning. An hour ago, Samantha and Laura had e-mailed a list of five names. Malik had called Graham and Sergeant Ross with the information.

Sighing heavily, Veronica turned from the view and accepted that her fairy tale was over. Would the newly acknowledged feelings between her and Malik be just as brief? Crushed by whatever evils awaited them back in Seattle? A memory, just a flash really, tripped through her. His strong arms wrapped around her, and her forehead feeling his life pulse through him. She opened the front door and inhaled the pungent marine air as the shudder passed. Turning back to the inside of the house, she could see Malik's bare back while he stood in the kitchen, holding the phone to his ear. As she admired him, she realized it wasn't just the physical part she loved, although that was certainly wonderful—it was how she felt when she was with him. She felt respected, whole, electric, and she wanted him to feel the same way.

Malik turned and smiled. Next, he put the phone down and rushed toward her. She squealed with delight when he picked her up and swung her around. She was about to insist he lie down, so she could check his head when he said, "Bingo!

That was Graham. He just got the full license plate, and it matches one of the names on the list from the clinic: a couple named Shawn and Joan Hailey."

Something tickled at the back of Veronica's memory. Then she shouted, "I know that couple! When I told them I couldn't help them conceive, the wife left very stoic, and the husband sat in the lobby and cried. We almost had to call the police to get him to leave. Good Lord, he's the person responsible for all this?"

Malik nodded and hugged her before saying, "I have more news. The man is a health inspector for the Department of Agriculture. Do you know what that means?"

Veronica was assessing and putting it all together. "That's right." Malik watched her. "He inspects meat houses, which means he could have animal remains on the bottom of his shoes."

A cold spike of memory reminded her of her kitchen. "The bastard," she whispered.

Malik wrapped her in another hug and continued explaining, "We're going to get him. The address at the clinic didn't match the address from the Department of Motor Vehicles, so Graham did a little more digging and discovered the couple is now divorced. She lives in New York, and he's still in Seattle at what appears to be his mother's house. Sergeant Ross is in the process of getting a warrant as we speak."

Veronica was elated. Could it really be so simple? Go out to an island, make love until you're silly, and your biggest problems melt away? She looked into Malik's smiling face and willed it to be so as she heard the distinct whir of the seaplane that she assumed was the pilot coming to pick them up.

* * *

Neither of them were happy several hours later. They were having a heated exchange in Graham's living room. Sergeant Ross had called to let them know that Hailey wouldn't be a threat to anyone anymore.

"Malik, if the man is dead, why can't I go?" she asked.

"We don't know if it's safe," he responded.

"Safe?" Veronica shouted. "What can be more safe than dead!"

Malik explained, "Veronica, it's a crime scene. I may not be able to get inside. We're not sure if this is the right guy, or if he was working alone. There are too many ifs to let you come. Graham's house is like a fortress—you'll be safe here."

She didn't answer him, just glared with arms crossed and a face that was taut with anger. He must have taken the muteness as silent acceptance and headed for the door. She followed. The door was open, and he was about to slip through when he turned and kissed her forehead. "Just bear with me, sugar, and soon you'll be able to go anywhere you want." She didn't answer. Her arms left her stomach, and she pressed their torsos close in a tight hug before letting go.

An ambulance was pulling away just as Malik drove up to the house in West Seattle. He wondered who was in it. The information he received said the guy was dead. Police cars and vans from the Medical Examiner's Office choked the small driveway and part of the street. Malik had to park a block away from the house. Police tape had been erected, and a uniformed officer blocked the only entrance to the property.

Malik approached, noticing that the cop was young. He began talking immediately. "Hi, I'm a detective down in

Pierce County. Your situation here sounds just like a case we had last month."

"Wait, sir." The uniform put his hand up and said, "I can't let you in."

"Isn't Sergeant Ross in charge?" Malik asked. "Radio and let her know Cutler is here."

The young man looked at him for a second, and Malik feared he'd ask for identification. He internally sighed when the man detached the radio from his hip.

"Sergeant Ross. There's a plainclothes here from another jurisdiction that says he knows you." The man listened then replaced the radio before saying, "She'll be here in a second, Detective."

It was nighttime, and the porch light reached out to them where they stood near the end of the driveway, but visibility was minimal. Still, he could tell that Sergeant Ross's eyebrows formed a fault line the minute she saw him. She looked as efficient as ever in crisp brown slacks and a yellow silk shirt.

"Brady," she yelled.

The uniform turned to her.

"Let him in," she instructed.

They met near the porch and Sergeant Ross said, "Telling lies, are we? You know you're not allowed here."

"I just want a peek, Ross. I'll owe you big-time," Malik answered.

"You already owe me," she mumbled. Then she looked at him as if she wanted to kill him. After about ten seconds, she nodded and handed him latex gloves. "Don't touch a thing," she ordered.

The house was old and poorly kept. Malik's eyes took in the sagging couch and newspapers piled high as they passed through to the dirty kitchen and down the stairs to the musty basement. He stepped around technicians, officers and photographers being careful to stay out of the way.

"The victim's room is down here. That's where we found him," Ross said over her shoulder.

They stepped into a small room off the large cluttered basement. Malik blinked from the glare of the bright lights. He saw the source was a large floor lamp placed in a corner of the room. Looking down, he saw Shawn Hailey. The man's legs and arms were straight, which indicated to Malik that he had been placed on the floor, instead of being allowed to crumple down naturally.

A thin, wiry man with curly, salt-and-pepper hair was circling the body, taking pictures from every conceivable angle. Malik assumed he was the medical examiner. He and Sergeant Ross stood to the side and watched. The man put the camera down and studied Hailey a long time, talking to himself and making notes. When he bent down with gloved hands and touched Hailey's head, Malik inched closer and crouched, as well. He heard Ross's frustrated sigh behind him, but she didn't stop him. They both looked until the examiner glanced at Sergeant Ross with narrowed eyes before saying, "She looks like she should be in a boardroom of a cosmetics company, instead of lead investigator of this mess."

Malik was mildly shocked. The old man hadn't even acknowledged his presence, and now he was speaking to him as if he were one of the boys. He just grunted in response. The examiner was in his late fifties, early sixties, and evidently still adjusting to the new world order. Besides, he didn't want to anger Ross further if she'd heard the man's comments. The examiner finished looking and stood.

Malik stood, also, before saying, "This type of action took

strength and skill." Then, he went on to explain how he believed Hailey meet his demise. Both the examiner and the sergeant stared at him.

"You know forensic science, son?" the examiner asked.

Malik shrugged. "A little."

"Well, you're right." The old man wiped his forehead with the back of his gloved hand and asked, "You know when this happened, too, son?"

Malik smiled slightly and said, "No."

"Good, I still have some use here," the old man grumbled. "It's been a day or two. I can be more specific when I get him back to the lab."

Sergeant Ross nodded and said, "Follow me, Malik. I may need to know where you've been the last couple of days," Sergeant Ross said.

Malik stopped walking, taken aback, "Am I a suspect?"

Sergeant Ross asked, "When exactly did you find out the license plate number?"

"Ross, I've been on an island the last day and a half with Veronica. I didn't have the full license number until Graham sent it to me today. You can verify that with him," Malik explained.

"Okay. You're my friend, Malik, but I have a job to do." She stared at him intently before saying, "I'll bust you if I find out you've crossed the line."

"Check away, Ross. I had nothing to do with this. Call Graham's house now. Veronica's there, too." Malik gave her the number. She pulled out her cell phone and moved a few feet away.

Several minutes later, she came back and said, "Thanks. Graham and Veronica corroborated your story."

Malik nodded. They both paused and moved out of the way to allow the people carrying the stretcher to pass.

Malik turned to Ross and asked, "Who else lives here?"

"Just his mother," she answered.

"Where's she?" Sergeant Ross looked at him. Malik answered the unspoken question, "I'm just curious. I'm not going to tie her down and question her."

"You'd have to go to the hospital to do it," Ross commented.

So that's who was in the ambulance, Malik thought.

"The sad thing is that they probably do have her tied down in monitor wires." Ross continued explaining, "When we showed up with a warrant, she assured us sonny was gone because she hadn't heard him moving around. We asked her to sit on the couch, but she kept following us like a lost puppy in her robe and slippers. She was right behind us when we found him. She lost it, went into cardiac arrest, and I had to perform CPR. Just another exciting day at the office. She had on Depend diapers. Explains why the perp had adult diapers on the list."

Malik nodded, looking around.

"Did I mention we know how he got in?" Ross asked.

"No."

"Over here." The sergeant led Malik to the cellar door and said, "There's a rusty broken padlock on the outside. He unhooks it when he wants in and remembers to rehook it when he leaves. No sign of prints, foot or finger. I'm sure our killer wore gloves." Sergeant Ross turned and faced Malik, saying, "Okay, you've got to go. I could get into a load of trouble having a civilian on a crime scene."

"I'm an expert, remember?" Malik quipped.

"Yeah, at finding guns in water, not this," Ross countered. "Really, Malik, you have to go."

"All right, but can I see his car first? Then I'm gone. I promise."

As they walked up the stairs to get to the garage, Malik asked, "You haven't found anything concerning Veronica?"

Sergeant Ross smiled mischievously, "That's the second time you've used her first name. So it's no longer Dr. Howell, huh? Are you two on more friendly terms?"

Malik decided he could tolerate the teasing since she was helping him. "You could say we're getting to know each other better," he conceded.

"Well, that's good since you live together," Ross chuckled softly.

A uniform was going through the brown sedan when they reached the garage. Malik looked at the hubcaps and saw they were mismatched. This was definitely the car he'd seen on the tape.

"Oh, Sergeant," the uniform said soon after they entered, "I found a briefcase. I was just about to bring it to you."

In the kitchen, Sergeant Ross emptied the contents on the table. Most dealt with work issues, but then Malik picked up a notebook with gloved hands. "Look at this," he said, holding it open on the table, so they could both read. "It's the same handwriting." Malik knew because he'd spent hours studying the samples and the weirdly slanted *T*s were a dead giveaway. "It's a log of Veronica's activities." Flipping to the front of the pad, Malik noted that it began about a month before Veronica called him. "This is our guy all right." The knowledge didn't bring the relief Malik expected.

Sergeant Ross turned the pages. She stopped, pointing, "Uh-huh, this perp sure liked lists. I think this confirms it," she said.

Malik read,

No alarm
    Work at 6:30/home by 7pm

Enter back door
Present on kitchen table
Words on door

Both of them knew what they were looking at. The man's plans for the first assault on Veronica's house. His motives were still somewhat of a mystery, yet he was definitely the harasser. *But who got to him?* The question thundered through Malik's brain.

He was at the front door when he said to Sergeant Ross, "So this is the guy, but both of us know that something is wrong."

Ross nodded and answered, "This man was disposed of quietly by someone who's trained to kill. The question is why. However, as I'm sure you know, Malik, this may have nothing to do with Dr. Howell. We need to do a full investigation to determine what he was up to. He's a health inspector. Maybe he had some black market meat scam going."

Malik knew anything was possible. Still, his gut told him no. What happened in this house had something to do with Veronica. He wouldn't let his guard down until he knew what it was. Driving to Graham's house, he thought it through. He didn't have any concrete answers when his friend opened the front door, saying, "Goodness, I'm glad you're here. I feel like a bad talk show host trying to entertain the good doctor."

Malik chuckled and entered the house. Veronica put the newspaper down when Malik and Graham came into the living room.

Without preamble, she said, "Is that woman crazy? Why are you a suspect? You should have let me come with you?"

Despite the hard tone, he smiled because she was concerned about him. "Sugar, I'm not a suspect," he answered.

"You and Graham took care of that." He went on to explain all that he'd discovered.

"So what does it all mean?" Veronica asked.

"That we still have to be careful until we figure out why Hailey was murdered," Malik answered.

Tight lips and a scowl showed how much she liked that option. He expected an argument. What he got was a nod, then she announced, "I want to go home. It's close to midnight, and I have a full load tomorrow." She thanked Graham for his hospitality, gathered her purse and headed to the door. After speaking quietly with his friend for a few moments, Malik followed.

"So what were you two talking about?" Veronica asked as soon as the car was moving.

"Graham told me that his people would continue to dig into Hailey's background," Malik answered.

Veronica nodded, and they both lapsed into silence.

At her house, Malik parked his car in the garage. He got out, making sure the garage door was completely closed before moving to the kitchen door. He opened it and immediately knew something was wrong.

The alarm didn't buzz!

His right hand tightened on the knob and his left connected with Veronica's chest. He intended to push her back, out of the danger he sensed, but couldn't see. An arm snaked through the opening and clamped down on his mouth and nose. The motion was lightning quick, and before his fingers could twitch in defense, his body slumped, and he fell into oblivion.

Chapter 15

Malik awoke with a start. He felt dizzy, slightly nauseous.

"Do you feel horrible, Mr. Security?"

Malik's head jerked toward the voice coming directly across from him. He noticed he was sitting by a small lamp that only gave enough light for him to see a few feet. A man dressed in black stepped out of the dark. "I hear chloroform can have that affect on you. Is it true?" the man asked.

Malik was silent, too stunned to speak as a twist of horror formed and unraveled repeatedly, knotting his stomach even more.

"I was concerned I gave you too much. It took you a long time to wake up and play, Leek," the man taunted.

Panic joined the horror. All were emotions that Malik wasn't used to feeling, but then, it wasn't every day that one found himself tied to a chair directly across from a person known to be very bizarre.

"You're eyes are bugging out of your head, Leek. Do I make you nervous?"

Malik was more than nervous; he was scared. A rush of adrenaline made his heart skip a beat, and he had trouble catching his breath as things popped into his head. Unbelievable things, but considering his situation it made perverse sense. He knew the man sitting in front of him. Carol Williams, nickname C.C. for Crazy Carol, had gotten to Hailey. He didn't know the exact reasons why, yet he deduced it had something to do with Veronica. The man had always been very weird when it came to women.

Carol had been Malik's SEAL team member for his last five years of service. Being teammates was like being in a sardine can together. Whether you wanted to or not, you got to know a person when you ate, slept, fought and relaxed with them. Malik appreciated the irony and sickness that the crazy man goading him was the one who insisted that he go to the club where he first saw Veronica. All four members of the team, heck the whole unit, knew that Carol Williams was obsessed with Veronica. They also knew that he was strange around women. He seemed awed by nice girls and ended up spending most of his time with women he paid to keep him company.

Malik remembered how angry Carol became when Veronica disappeared. They'd all teased him, saying his *girlfriend* had fled, and when was he going to track her down, so he could ask for a date. All of them thought it funny Carol was so timid around the woman when he found her so fascinating. He always said the time wasn't right, and then, poof, she was gone. That had been years ago. Apparently, Crazy Carol had followed their advice and found Veronica. However, he was taking the date, instead of asking for it. The idea chased away the fright and made him seethe with anger.

Carol stared and Malik knew he was trying to read him.

"That's right, Leek," he said. "I've come to get her. I've been patient, and I know you've become…close with my future wife, but I ain't mad at you."

Wife! Did this nut plan on forcing Veronica to marry him? The idea was preposterous, yet it did mean Veronica was alive and most likely unharmed.

"You didn't know I was here staking my claim, Leek. I couldn't believe it when she hired you for security because of that Weasel!" Carol leaned in as if he was going to share a secret. "He annoyed me, too, Leek. I think Dr. Howell will thank me later for getting rid of him when she fully understands all I've done for her, don't you?"

Smirking, Carol leaned away and continued talking. "I'd been tailing her for about two weeks when you showed up, Leek. Talk about coincidences. I even know why Weasel was mad at her. Do you know why, Leek? Oh, of course you don't because you're much more stupid than me." Shadow's finger flicked Malik's head. "I heard Weasel talking on his cell phone in a restaurant, begging some woman to come to Washington, so they could get remarried or some mess. It seems his wife left him because they couldn't have children. I'm not sure of the man's logic, but somehow he blames Dr. Howell for this.

"I've been two steps ahead of you the whole way, Leek. I watched you install that state-of-the-art security system at the house from across the street, courtesy of her vacationing neighbors. I was also there when you did the same at the clinic. Remember the bum, Leek? Oh, revenge is sweet! Go ahead, man, I know you want to frown, give me a little grimace."

Malik remained stone-faced.

Carol taunted him more. "Gee, you were smart to bury the

power source at the house, Leek. Too bad your most dangerous enemy watched it being done."

A string of profanities went through Malik's mind. Keeping his face neutral was hard.

The man stopped laughing and leaned in close to say, "But I am still angry about the other incident. Remember, Malik? When you had to play hero. Did he tell you about that, Dr. Howell?" The last was said over his shoulder.

Malik searched the darkness, looking for Veronica. He could see nothing beyond the faint glow of the lamp that sat on the floor between them.

"I bet he didn't," Carol answered his own question. "Got our whole team in trouble because he wanted to save some girl."

Malik spoke for the first time, "Where's Veronica?"

"Oh, so you call her by her given name. I must admit that I still think of her as Dr. Howell, mostly. I had to investigate to get her full name." Carol leaned in close to Malik. "Do you remember the waitress that was kind of heavy and light skinned? She and Dr. Howell would always talk between sets. It was easy getting information from her. She told me Dr. Howell went to medical school. It's a shame she didn't know the state, though." The man sat back, crossing his arms and legs as if he were at a cocktail party. "Anyway, that tip was enough. The Internet is a wonderful thing. Once a quarter, I did a search for many years. When the clinic opened, I found her."

Malik didn't care. He wanted to see Veronica, assure himself that she was all right. Again he asked, "Where is she, Carol?" He knew the unisex name was a source of embarrassment for his tormentor.

He saw the hand rise, so Malik didn't even flinch when Carol slapped him. "We're no longer SEALs, Leek, and that's not my name. I'm known as Shadow now."

"Changing names doesn't make you invisible, or any less of an ass, Carol." The blow to his face came hard this time. Malik turned away to deflect the power. The chair almost toppled, something Malik didn't want to happen since his arms were tied to the back of it. He couldn't afford to break a limb now. Anger churned, but he knew he had to stop goading the man.

"It's impolite to change the subject, Leek. I was telling Dr. Howell about your wasted act of heroism," the man said, reaching into his waistband. Malik tensed expecting a weapon. Then he thought he'd feel an electric shock when Carol pointed a black square at him. Malik didn't know if he cringed out of expectation, or because he was suddenly showered with light.

Carol laughed bitterly. "It's just a control for the rest of the lights, Leek," he said.

Malik blinked rapidly, willing his eyes to adjust. Carol kept talking about subduing Veronica without using chloroform and without hurting her. "She put up a good fight, though, see." Malik's vision cleared just as Carol shoved his arm under his nose so he could see the scratches on his forearms. "I put her in the trunk of your car with you. That car is ugly, but the engine kicks. I may keep it after you're gone."

Malik tried to ignore Carol as he looked around. His breath caught when he saw Veronica tied to a chair on a raised platform. Her mouth and arms were bound and her feet appeared to be free. A full-length robe covered her, and he couldn't tell if she was injured.

Carol turned from him to Veronica. "Did he tell you about that night, Dr. Howell?" he asked.

Veronica didn't respond. Malik watched her stare at Carol expressionlessly. When Carol turned his back to her, Veronica looked at him. Trying to be encouraging, he smiled and lifted his chin. Amazingly, she smiled back. Carol continued speaking as if his victims hung on every word. "Did he tell you how his career path in the military was abruptly interrupted by his hero complex?" Warming to his audience or to hearing his own voice, Carol stood between them and continued the story. "See, Malik here has always tried to protect women. Maybe, 'cause he couldn't save his own momma from an overdose. Didn't know I knew that, huh Leek? I snuck a look at everyone's personal file. It was always such interesting reading."

Malik disregarded him because the rest of the room caught his attention. There were poster-size photos of Veronica attached to the walls. Most of them were shots taken during her singing days; however, some were more recent: Veronica sitting in her office, standing in front of her house, and one of her half dressed in her bedroom. *The pervert's created a shrine.* Malik prayed, *Please, dear Lord. If I don't make it, let me get rid of this madman first.*

Carol continued, "Me, I know what women are for and they aren't for saving. Unlike you, Dr. Howell. You're special. Worthy enough to really be one with me, and eventually you'll thank me for rescuing you from the real villain here." Carol glared pointedly at Malik.

Good Lord, the man's delusional! Malik thought.

"You, Dr. Howell—" Carol pointed at her "—you get the ultimate prize I know you've been waiting for, me." He rubbed his chest. "But I digress. Let me tell you the story. Our team is doing what we call a training mission, but what the DEA call information gathering. They tell us which boats to board in the harbor, we do it, find the drugs and report back to the suits. The DEA uses this illegally gotten info from a supposed unidentified source to get a warrant.

"See, Dr. Howell, that's how our lovely government works. There's usually only a skeleton crew aboard, and when they see armed men in black wet suits, they rarely interfere. Well, we're doing our thing when we find out there are girls on board. Apparently, we had stumbled into a kidnapping ring. The crew hadn't been very nice to these girls. Superman, here, couldn't take it." Carol's voice became very hard. "He wiped out the boys. I didn't mind that. I just wanted a chance to meet a few of the women before our commanders and the suits showed up. Hell, we were already in trouble for not following procedure. I go to introduce myself, and your boy tries to stop me. It took our commander and the other two team members to stop us from fighting."

Carol turned to Malik. "Isn't that why you decided to retire, Leek? Didn't like it when the navy brass told you your morals came second to the mission? You're lucky the DEA and captain stuck up for you, or they would've busted you down to private, or kicked you out with a dishonorable."

Malik didn't answer, although Carol was right. Graham and the captain had powerful friends who'd saved his butt.

Carol continued his monologue. "Well, I retired a few years after you. Right after I got an offer I couldn't refuse. You see, I found a better use for my skills than you. Certain people will pay a mint for someone to cut packages off the bottoms of boats before they go through customs."

Malik looked at him and said, "So you've joined the scum of the drug trade? Somehow it fits you."

"Don't knock it, Leek. It's responsible for your lovely accommodations, a house with a large basement and a stage that I've built myself. Although I've rented this place, under a false name of course, I could buy this whole city block if I wanted to. I have more than enough to provide for Dr.

Howell. But enough about me. I can see you're becoming bored," Carol said, then walked the three stairs of the stage. "It's time for our entertainment. One last show together before I get rid of you, cutting Dr. Howell's last tie from her old life before she begins to really live with me."

Carol reached Veronica and removed the tape off her mouth. It looked as if he was trying to be gentle, but Malik knew it must have stung. Veronica kept her face blank; she didn't even flinch. Malik was proud of her.

"I knew you'd be like this," Carol said. "Most women would be screaming and crying. Not you. You sit here shooting daggers at me with your eyes, but I can see the love beneath that look. I just have to teach you how to let it show."

While Carol focused on Veronica, Malik assessed his situation. The ropes were so tight he could barely move his wrists and ankles. His fingers and toes weren't numb, which told him that he hadn't been tied that long. He had to do something quickly, or his limbs wouldn't be able to function even if he managed to escape his bonds. The chair was made of iron, so there was no way to break it. He had only one chance, and he'd need at least a minute to execute his plan. But he had an idea, which was the key. Nervousness and fear were being replaced by the dead calm that always covered him when he knew his life was about to be on the line. It was going to be just like any other mission. He had an enemy. Carol. A target. Veronica. And a plan. Now, all he needed was a chance to execute.

Both of Carol's hands moved along the sides of Veronica's face as he bent from the waist and spoke. "Soon you'll appreciate me, adore me like no other. Like your friend, the waitress, I could see in her eyes that she wanted to be my mate for all time. But as you and I know, it wasn't to be so."

Veronica screamed and kicked. Carol didn't even move when her bare foot connected with his hard shin. Malik's heart dropped.

Laughing, Carol said, "That's right, give me all your strength, hold nothing back from me." Suddenly, Carol's hands left Veronica's face as he clapped. "I'm ready for the show, aren't you, Leek? It's time for you to sing a special song for me, Dr. Howell." He bent so his face was close to Veronica again. "Back in the old days, I was quite impressed with how you moved around stage as you performed. Make sure you dance a lot."

She spat into his face.

Veronica noted that Carol wasn't laughing when his right hand wiped his mouth. He dropped to his haunches, so he was eye level with her. Her heart raced, and she fought the urge to lower her lids when he leaned in close and said, "Don't do that. You and me could have fun for the rest of our lives— kids, a house and the whole nine yards, but my plan can be adjusted."

Veronica looked Carol in the eyes and wondered how could a man that appeared so ordinary be so evil? He was slightly over average height, probably a few inches shorter than Malik with black hair, brown eyes and light brown skin. He might have been the mechanic at the garage, or the plumber down the street. Worse yet, she remembered him. Once he waited for her after a performance. After telling her she was a magnificent singer, he'd left. She remembered the encounter because it was so brief. He'd waited at least an hour and he didn't ask for a date, or discuss the merits of jazz as the other admirers did. He'd said his piece and left. Looks were certainly deceiving, she thought as she watched his hand land on her knee.

"Soon, I'm going to untie you, and you will perform, okay?" Carol asked, still squatting in front of her.

Veronica glanced over her tormentor's shoulder at Malik. His face was tight with anger, yet he smiled and nodded when their eyes connected. The exchange wasn't lost on Carol. "Don't worry, he'll be watching, too," he commented. "Just in case you've forgotten how you used to move, I have this." Carol stood, grabbed a heavier, bulkier remote and soon a big screen came down the wall behind Veronica. "Technology is amazing, Leek. I can control the whole house from this thing." Carol hefted the control, which was the size of a large brick and looked about as heavy.

"Tell me, Dr. Howell," Carol asked, "did you know the club owner taped some of your sessions? We had many discussions about you. I had to pay a handsome sum to get him to part with his tapes. His collection was limited, but they've kept me very entertained the last few years. The one I'm playing is particularly good, I think." A life-size image of Veronica in a long, slinky purple dress, singing on stage began to play. The music was loud and her voice was fuzzy until Carol muted the volume.

Veronica looked at Malik, and he stared at her with such intensity that she knew he was trying to communicate something. She stared back, tilting her head ever so slightly.

Carol walked to Veronica's chair and stood over her like a dark cloud before saying, "I'm going to untie you now, honey. Please cooperate. I want to cherish you, not hurt you." When the ropes lay on the ground, Carol stood, motioning for Veronica to stand, as well. She did so.

"Now the robe," he said. She glared defiantly. Veronica was scared. Fear wrenched every muscle in her body, but she was angry, too. A part of her insisted that she'd rather be gone than a mate to this nut. She glanced at Malik and something in his eyes jolted her. He'd said nothing, hadn't moved a muscle, yet Veronica got it. He wanted her to comply.

Fingers and thumb gripped her chin, forcing her head back to Carol's dark, brown eyes. "I said take the robe off."

Veronica pushed it off her shoulders, revealing a formfitting, black silk dress that ended midthigh. Although she was still unsure why, if Malik wanted her to comply, she'd do it.

"I rather you be a nightclub entertainer, than a doctor," Carol said, studying her as if she was a complex map. "It's amazing how little your shape has changed. I would have been severely disappointed if you were heavy. I don't like your hair, though. It's too short. So I took the liberty of buying you a nice, black wig." Carol retrieved a bag from the back of the stage. "Please put it on."

Veronica stared mutely, not taking the bag from his hand. Malik was in her line of vision, and he nodded, obviously wanting her to comply. Lifting her chin, Veronica took the long, silky hairpiece and adjusted it to her head.

"And these." Carol handed her black strappy, high heels, long dark gloves, and a microphone. Without emotion, Veronica held the microphone under her arm and put the items on.

Carol grabbed the big remote and soon the music to "You Give Me Fever," by Ella Fitzgerald filled the air.

"Come on, Dr. Howell," Carol yelled, "my ears can't wait to hear your sensual voice."

The excited man ran to Malik and whispered, "Now, isn't this more like it?" Then he hopped back to Veronica and grabbed the chair she'd vacated. He took it with him off stage and positioned it at an angle, so he could see both his victims.

Stoically, Veronica stood there in high heels with the ends of the fake hair gracing her bottom. Her eyes shifted to Malik, and she sensed him willing her to sing.

"Dr. Howell!" Veronica jumped a little and looked at Carol. "Eyes on me." The man roared above the music pouring from hidden speakers. Veronica turned on the microphone and began singing while slowly moving around.

Despite the cold voice, Shadow was antsy with anticipation. He'd waited a long time for this private show, and he was going to enjoy it. Having Malik to gloat over was such sweet icing on the cake. He shivered in his seat. Then he settled down, gazed into Dr. Howell's eyes, and she just glared right back. Her glare reminded him of how his grandmother would look right before she'd be mean to him. That old lady had a stare and a firm hand. But she didn't have a strong heart, though. Carol found that out at seventeen when he dodged her strike and she fell. One hand clutched her chest and the other reached out to him. He didn't move and five minutes later she'd passed away.

Carol peered at Dr. Howell's chest as she began moving to the music, and he wondered how sturdy her heart was. He didn't know, but he planned to have fun finding out. He would wait until she got used to him first. He wanted Dr. Howell's feelings for him to have a chance to surface, so he would try to be patient with her. He had no doubts that he was up to the task because the navy had sure showed him he had endurance.

He'd joined as soon as he turned eighteen and discovered not only could he take a lot of crap, he had a high tolerance for pain and an abundance of staying power. He persevered and let his commanders shape him into a strong and powerful man. A power he enjoyed using, but not just on anyone; a person had to be unique to receive real attention from him. Dr. Howell was very special, well worth the time he'd invested. He was going to enjoy the payoff that should last the rest of his life, he thought as he shifted his chair a bit toward Dr. Howell. He could still see Malik out of the corner of his eye. Besides, if the navy taught him anything, it was how to tie a good knot. He was confident, that short of gnawing off a limb, Malik couldn't get out of his bonds.

Still unsure of Malik's thoughts, Veronica sang while focusing on Carol and watching Malik out of the corner of her eye. Malik stared at Carol with such steely calm that it occurred to her that he could be waiting for a chance to do something. Hope and determination surged through her body. Veronica's movements became silkier as she focused on making her voice warm and slightly husky. Holding the microphone with her right hand, she raised her left above her head and moved from side to side. If Malik needed a distraction, she could certainly provide that.

Inspired, she pulled off one of the gloves and tossed it at Carol. He caught it and rubbed it into his stomach. Veronica's eyes would have rolled if the situation weren't so serious. She noticed Carol completely faced her, and Malik was stirring. His chair had shifted sideways, allowing her to see his shoulder jerk and his face tense in pain or concentration. Veronica wasn't sure which he was feeling, but it lit off a lightbulb in her head. She remembered Malik's comment that he was double-jointed when she playfully threatened to tie him up.

She sang passionately as she glided around the platform. Carol's head nodded as he watched her. Back bent, leaning forward, Veronica let the fake hair the creep loved hang in her face. Then she belted out a note and stood straight again.

"Ah yesss," Carol shouted above the music and her singing, "I love it!"

Veronica knew she had Carol's undivided attention because he ogled her with half-closed eyes. His focus was way below her face, so she looked beyond him to Malik. She knew the casual observer would have thought his shoulder was broken. He held it at a weird angle, creating slack in the rope, Veronica assumed. Next, he tugged sharply and his right arm slipped out. Her eyes returned to Carol seconds before his head lifted to her face. Veronica belted out a note and continued to gyrate wildly. Despite her efforts, Carol suddenly turned to Malik who was bent over unleashing the ropes at his feet.

Quick as a snake, Shadow darted up, on the move. His chair toppled in the process, and the noise alerted Malik who raised his hands to ward off Carol's tackle. They both went down over the chair, Carol on top of Malik. Veronica reacted instantly by whipping off her shoes and jumping from the stage. Brandishing a spiked, high heel, she struck out at Carol and hit him in his shoulder. Carol bellowed, released his hold on Malik and jerked backward with enough force to fling Veronica into the nearby wall. Veronica dropped the shoe in her hand, and she slumped down the wall dazed, but conscious.

"No!" both men roared like thunder.

Malik stood free from the ropes and the chair. His right hand was pressed against his side where he feared his collision with Carol and the chair had resulted in a broken rib. He'd seen Veronica slide down and he didn't believe it was possible for him to feel more rage, yet he did. Instead of distracting him, it narrowed his vision into a channel that zeroed in on Carol.

The man leaned as if he was going to check on Veronica, then he attacked. Malik was ready because he was seeing everything in slow motion, the type of perception that only came with combat experience. He dodged the strike, fought the horrible pain in his side, and picked up the iron chair that had held him prisoner moments ago. As Carol spun for another attack, Malik swung the chair as hard as his injured body would allow. The effort and the impact of the chair hitting Carol's face made bright colors burst into Malik's world right before blinding pain assailed his brain. The chair slipped from his fingers and he whispered, "Veronica," hoping the name would have enough power to keep him from blacking out.

Malik didn't know how long he stood there fighting to stay conscious. When he was pretty sure he wasn't going to faint, he looked down to see Carol's limp body at his feet. Malik nudged him with his foot. The man didn't move. Malik looked at the chair lying near Carol and doubted he had the strength to lift it if Carol did try to get up. Malik nudged him with his foot again. Carol remained still, so dropping to his knees, Malik stuck a hand under Carol's battered face. He felt the faint heat of his breath. "Carol, why don't you die?" he hissed. Then, he pinched Carol's shoulder. There was no effect, so he knew the man was really knocked out.

Malik stood and then looked from what he'd done to Veronica. She was wide-eyed, sitting against the wall trembling slightly. Malik felt shame, tremendous humiliation. Although he was happy Carol was out, he hated that she'd seen the fighting, something normal people weren't supposed to see except on a movie screen. It probably reminded her of her brother, and he feared that now he repulsed her.

Standing there, pain racked his body. The fact that Carol needed to be completely subdued kept him moving. He gathered the rope that had recently confined him and used it to tie up Carol. He glanced around the room, seeing furniture he hadn't noticed before lined up against the wall. A phone sat on the coffee table. He hobbled to it and dialed 911, yelling into the receiver over the loud music. He had no idea where he was, so the operator told him to stay on line until she could trace the call.

He was tired, groggy and hurting. All he wanted to do was sit down. However, Veronica's condition had him placing the receiver on the couch. He could faintly hear the operator yelling for him as he ignored her and kept moving. Veronica was shivering. Taking care of her seemed to be the most important thing in the world, so he grabbed her robe off the stage floor and gently covered her. Then he saw the remote, which he picked up and he proceeded to fumble with the buttons until the speakers were silent.

When he looked at Veronica, she flinched.

Malik's suspicions were confirmed. He closed his eyes against the pain to his heart that was much worse than the pain to his body. He remembered her question that first night when he'd answered her call, *"I bet you were a nice little boy. How does a kid grow up into a ... killer?"* True, he didn't kill Carol, but she'd still seen an example of what he could do. Ashamed and exhausted, he sat at an angle, trying to shield her from the evidence of his brutality.

Veronica's awareness came in degrees as the shock subsided. Right after Carol's body met the chair, she closed her eyes tight. Images of Mitchell being attacked flashed behind her lids and made her eyes reopen just as quickly. She was determined to keep her lids up. It seemed more important than anything and the focus took all of her effort. But then the music stopped and her eyes closed in reflex. She saw nothing. She opened them as Malik sat down. His attitude confused her. Why wasn't he crushing her to his chest? She noticed his shallow breathing and how stiffly he held himself. It registered he was in pain.

"Malik?" she said.

He jerked and looked at her with such sadness. She tilted sideways so she could see Carol and said, "Is he dead?"

"No, but he should be out for a while," Malik answered.

Leaning forward, she ran the back of her fingers down his face. He turned into the touch and kissed her palm whispering, "I'm sorry. I'm so sorry you had to see…that," he said.

She experienced a revelation. For some strange reason, he thought she resented what he'd done. "Come to me, Malik," she commanded. He stilled and his head rose. Their eyes met and she said, "Nothing you're capable of scares me. I love you."

"I love you too, babe," Malik said. Then, grimacing in pain, he leaned forward until his head rested against her lap and stomach. Her hands stroked, her words soothed him until Malik lifted up and kissed her softly, reverently.

Veronica held his face between her hands and said, "It's weird how I can feel so happy after enduring hours of fear and anguish. Like the sun appearing after a rainstorm."

Malik nodded, kissed one of the palms at his cheek and sat up as straight as he could.

"You know what this means, don't you?" she asked with a wide grin spreading over her face.

Mischievousness bubbled from her and he must have noticed because he replied, "That you want to sex me, even though we both probably have injuries."

"No, silly. I don't have to pay your ridiculous fee!"

Malik laughed, then the robe was crushed between them

as they engaged in a long, deep kiss full of future promise. They were still kissing when the police stormed down the stairs a few minutes later.

Their ordeal made the news, and Veronica's parents were in Seattle the next day. After a thorough exam, Veronica was released from the hospital with a very mild concussion while Malik had to wait two more days before he was allowed to leave. Veronica barely left his side, and Malik cherished the fact that this strong woman was his. Soon he would have some understanding of where her strength came from, because unbeknownst to him, he was about to meet her mother.

Malik was recuperating at home and Veronica had been gone for about an hour when she called, explaining that her parents wanted to meet him.

A short time later, the three of them descended upon his house with all the warmth of a block of ice in Siberia. Veronica and her father were very reserved, letting her mother run the show. In appearance, Malik noted that Mrs. Howell was an older version of Veronica, a very handsome, but cold-eyed, woman. She thanked him for all he'd done for her daughter, and then she ordered him to sit because she realized his broken ribs had to be still sore. Next thing he knew, she was taking herself on a tour of his space! When she returned to the living room, she complimented him on having a dust-free, nicely decorated house!

Then, she thrust her chin forward and said, "Veronica claims she loves you."

Malik responded passionately, "I sure hope so because I'm crazy about her."

"Mother—" Veronica's voice was a shield "—Malik is still recovering. We can discuss this later."

Cold eyes clashed with hot eyes, then Mrs. Howell's pointy chin lowered slightly. "Very well," she said, turning back to Malik. "I insist that you come to Boston with Veronica for Christmas."

Malik smiled before saying, "Yes, ma'am. How about Thanksgiving?" He glanced at Veronica, and she shook her head. He looked at Mrs. Howell and realized she'd seen the exchange. Then, his eyes began playing tricks on him because it seemed as if moisture was glimmering in the black depths of Mrs. Howell's eyes.

As if to cover her reaction, Mrs. Howell started chatting, occasionally pulling Veronica and her husband into the conversation. Little was really said, and he noticed that Veronica listened even less. Every so often, Mrs. Howell glared at him, and Malik understood he was being evaluated. Kind of like an eagle sizing up its prey. He kept waiting for her to swoop in for the verbal kill, yet she never did. He wondered if Veronica's earlier warning was the reason.

As they walked to the door, Veronica hung back and said, "You still interested now that you know where I come from?"

He grabbed her and kissed her deeply. He didn't plan his reaction, but he for sure didn't regret it!

"Wow," she whispered, clinging to him.

"Set the date," he said in a voice meant for her ears alone.

"February 14," she uttered, "Valentine's Day."

Malik nodded. "Very appropriate. I'll be there with bells and whistles."

Then he looked at her parents. Her father focused on something above their heads. He seemed indifferent, and Malik supposed that was acceptance of sorts. As expected, her mother's eyes were like an onyx iceberg, but he was positive he could see the tears this time. He couldn't tell if she was sad, frightened or angry. Whatever she was feeling, she suffered in silence.

A few days later, they were alone in his house. The Howells had returned to Boston the previous day and Veronica had spent the night. Malik woke up early in the morning and knew he was nuzzled into the place he wanted to be most. Savoring the moment, he breathed deeply, ignored the ache in his side, and cherished the faint smell of perfume mixed with warm skin. He kept his lids lowered and rubbed his nose and cheeks into the valley he knew so well. Simultaneously, he heard and felt Veronica's gentle moan. Reaching with his tongue, he licked the flesh he knew was there, and the moan grew louder. Opening his eyes, he turned to give attention to the globes that had been pressed against his cheeks.

"Malik, if you don't stop, we'll never leave this bed," Veronica whispered.

"That's not such a bad thing," he said with his mouth almost full.

"We've been here since I arrived yesterday. It seems so decadent." The way she clutched his head to her breast contradicted what she was saying.

"I can't help it." Emptying his mouth, he looked up with eyes full of love.

"Neither can I, baby, neither can I," Veronica answered before leading his lips to where they had been.

Sometime later, Veronica moaned and stretched. "Goodness, Malik, you're good for me. It erases all the bad feelings of our ordeal and having to deal with my parents."

Malik rubbed Veronica's hair and said, "Have you ever considered that you intimidate your mother?"

She stared at him in disbelief. Next, she waved her hand dismissively and said, "She's a control freak. The minute I started thinking for myself, I became the enemy."

Yeah, sugar, that's my point! He kept his thoughts to himself because she was looking at him with such concern. "What?" he finally asked.

She sighed and admitted, "I hate how easily you can read me." After a brief pause, she said, "Malik, were you being serious when you said 'set the date'?"

"Of course I was, sugar." He kissed her nose.

She reached up and kissed his lips, then said, "Well, I'm happy you want to marry me, but I have to tell you, that wasn't much of a proposal."

He laughed and replied, "We aren't even married and you're already complaining."

He meant it as a joke, so he was surprised when she took a deep breath and said, "Not complaining, just unsure."

His mouth covered hers in a deep, hot kiss. When he withdrew his lips, his hands still cupped her face. "I have a bad habit, Veronica. I assume my actions are enough without all the words. I love you. The funny thing is I'm the security expert, the person who brings comfort to an unstable situation. You have turned the tables on me, made me realize how lonely, cold and empty my life is. I don't want to be alone anymore. I want to create a real home, and the only person I can see myself doing that with is you. You make me a better man and I cherish you for it. Please do me the honor of being my wife.

Veronica took a shuddering breath, and Malik could see the vulnerability in her eyes as she spoke. "Before we met,

I tended to equate caring with controlling. I don't feel that way with you. In fact, I like having someone worry about me a little and wanting me a lot." She paused to join her lips with his again. Then she looked at him with confidence. "The answer is yes, yes, yes. I adore you and I'd love to be your wife." Veronica didn't complain when Malik keep her in the bed a little while longer.

Epilogue

"Malik, I was so grouchy at the clinic Alice forced me to buy the plane ticket and practically kicked me out of the office on Friday," Veronica said to his profile as they drove in the rental car three months later.

Malik chuckled. "I'll have to thank her. You know, my heart stopped when I saw you sitting in the hotel lobby last night, sugar. I didn't know if you were real, or if my aching mind had conjured you up."

"Good. A small part of me feared that you'd be upset. I know you wanted to spend time in Houston alone with your mother," she answered.

"I did. I was here two days before you came, more than enough time to deal with the lingering stuff. I was ready to see you, and I wanted you to see my mother's grave site."

Veronica rubbed his leg. "Well, the way you rushed me to

the room and made passionate love to me certainly did make me feel welcome."

Keeping his eyes on the road, Malik grabbed the hand at his thigh and kissed the palm.

"I hated going home knowing you were out of town," Veronica admitted.

"Really?" Malik looked at her briefly. "In all the excitement of your arrival, I forgot to tell you that my house sold. You're stuck with me, or I'm homeless."

"Oh, Malik, that's wonderful and stop teasing. You know I'm absolutely thrilled that you want to make my house our home."

"Wherever I am with you is home to me, baby," Malik said. Veronica squeezed with the hand he still held. "Also, I forgot to mention, I'm starting a new job a week after we get back."

"Oh." Veronica's heart sank. She hated that his job put him in dangerous situations. They had talked about it several times over the last three months, and she knew it was something that she was going to have to adjust to. It did help knowing that he was cautious and extremely good at what he did.

She looked at him and his eyes were bright with mischief. "What?" she demanded.

"Smile, sugar. I decided to take a six-month position with the police academy. I'm going to help train the divers and new recruits for the harbor patrol. It'll be completely safe and I should have pretty normal hours."

A large grin spread across her face.

"Don't get too excited," he warned. "This position is temporary and I will return to my usual line of work."

"I know, but I'll take what I can get," she said. Then she unbuckled her seat belt and leaned across to tease his cheek and earlobe with her lips.

He stopped at a red light and turned to kiss her fully. Afterward, he said, "Behave Veronica or we'll never reach the cemetery."

She scooted back to her side. Malik grabbed and held her hand as they lapsed into a comfortable silence until he asked what was happening with Carol. Veronica explained that he was claiming insanity and the doctors for the prosecution and defense were evaluating him. Malik grumbled and said that he hoped the legal system would do its job. Veronica hoped so, too, because she feared if it didn't, Malik would take matters into his own hands. It wasn't something she liked to think about.

They arrived at the cemetery and Veronica lifted her face to the hot wind as they left the car. Malik commented, "I think we'll have a rain shower in an hour or so. Look at those clouds looming."

"Good." Veronica pulled at her sticky white blouse and smoothed out her tan shorts. "Maybe then it'll cool off."

"It has been pretty warm for late fall, early winter. But what's up? I thought you loved the heat."

"I did until I came to Houston," Veronica admitted. "How can you stand the humidity?"

"I grew up in the Texas sun, sugar." Malik's blue T-shirt stretched across his muscles as he put an arm around her and leaned down to peck her lips. Veronica's arm naturally curled along the waistband of his jean shorts. Then he began leading her to his mother's grave, talking as they walked. "That first trip was tough. Not only because I hadn't been here in over twenty years, but also because of the condition of her grave. None of the burial sites in her area had flowers or head-stones, just flat, plain markers sinking into the ground, drowning in neglect. I had to search through leaves and sticks for about an hour before I found her."

Veronica listened as they walked. She knew her comments weren't required, just a sympathetic ear was all he needed. Soon Malik said while pointing, "There it is."

"Oh, it's beautiful," Veronica responded as they approached the large headstone.

"It is?" He squeezed her hand before letting go to run his fingers along the top of the granite structure that came to his waist. "This is my first time seeing it, as well. They must have put it up this morning." Kneeling, he reached out and traced the bronze-colored roses surrounding the outside of the gray headstone. Veronica leaned against his back and placed her cheek against his. He turned and she met his lips, realizing she'd never get tired of being with this man, pressed up against him.

Arms around his neck, Veronica read the inscription:

Beloved Mother of Malik Cutler
SHEILA ROSE
Born October 20, 1953
Died December 2, 1976

"You know, you were right," Malik said.

Veronica lifted from his back and he stood, facing her prior to taking her in his arms.

"I was right, huh? That doesn't surprise me, but what are you talking about?" she asked.

He chuckled, and his lips graced her forehead before he answered, "When you said coffins, funerals and monuments are for the living, that they do nothing for the person who's gone. I know that's true, but it certainly makes one feel better. I was depressed before, even though I told my momma I understood and knew she loved me. I hated having her grave be one of the forgotten many. She may have been misguided, but she was important. This—" he tapped the headstone "—is an expression to myself and the rest of the world that my mom mattered."

Smiling down at her, he said, "I feel good. I'm at peace with my mother, and I'm holding the woman who touched my heart the first time I saw her. I love you, now and forever." A tear rolled down Veronica's cheek as he cemented his words with a long, deep kiss.

* * * * *